DAVID LODGE

The Picturegoers

VINTAGE

1 3 5 7 9 10 8 6 4 2

Vintage
20 Vauxhall Bridge Road,
London SW1V 2SA

Vintage is part of the Penguin Random House group of companies
whose addresses can be found at global.penguinrandomhouse.com.

Penguin
Random House
UK

Copyright © David Lodge 1960

This edition published in Vintage in 2016
First published in MacGibbon & Kee 1960
Published with an introduction in Penguin Books 1993

www.vintage-books.co.uk

A CIP catalogue record for this book
is available from the British Library

ISBN 9781784702694

Printed and bound by Clays Ltd, St Ives plc

Penguin Random House is committed to a sustainable future
for our business, our readers and our planet. This book is
made from Forest Stewardship Council® certified paper

FOR MY PARENTS

PART ONE

THE ceiling of Mr Maurice Berkley's office next to the projection room was cracked and peeling. Every square inch of the Palladium cinema, Brickley, except the foyer, desperately required redecoration; but Mr Berkley remarked this particular area of decay because he was staring at the ceiling from his couch, where he was wont to relax for half an hour before changing into his dinner-suit. Why he persisted in the empty ritual of changing his clothes at a quarter past six every evening, he found difficult to explain. It certainly didn't impress the customers, as they sloped furtively across the foyer, out of the anonymity of the pavements, into the anonymity of the auditorium. Nevertheless he swung his feet to the floor and reached out for his dinner-suit. As he slicked down his scanty hair, and tugged his bow-tie deftly into shape, he decided that he changed clothes for his own sake. Like the dress uniform of some historic regiment buried in the khaki uniformity of a modern army, it was a defiant, hopeless gesture to a drab, uninterested world. Hopeless, because nothing could recall the days of glory, when the Palladium had been the Brickley Empire—the grandest music-hall south of the River, and first stop on the suburban circuit for the big names of the West End. All that remained of that era were the faded, curling photographs of once-famous artistes, who grinned vacantly from the walls above their scribbled messages of inadequate goodwill: 'To Maurice, with love, from an old trouper'... 'All the best in life— Maudie Jameson'... 'To Maurice, with many happy memories, and best wishes for the future—Joe Blakey'....

9

Was this, then, the future to which they had consigned him?

He skirted the desk on which lay the still unbalanced ice-cream accounts, and softly closed the door on the accusing columns of figures.

From the head of the circle staircase he looked down at the bare, cheerless expanse of the foyer. In the old days it would have been a bright, babbling crush of people, and he himself would have been threading the crowd, greeting an old friend, politely refusing a request for complimentary tickets, directing the Press to their seats. . . . Sighing, Mr Berkley began to descend the stairs. Saddened, he had watched music-hall die of TV, entertainment tax and the contempt of the young; shamefaced, he had witnessed the failure of sleazy nude shows, with titles of laboured suggestiveness, to win back the customers; stunned, he had stood by while his theatre was knocked down to a cinema-owner. He had been faced with two depressing alternatives: the undignified status of *cinema*-manager; or unemployment. Being a realistic man, Mr Berkley had chosen the former. But the salt had gone out of his life.

Now he stood uneasily beside the box-office, trying to catch the eyes of his customers, if only to smile at them. But they avoided his glance, as if he were some kind of policeman. Morosely they queued for their tickets, joylessly they took them to the ticket-girl, and swiftly they were swallowed up by the booming darkness beyond the swing-doors. Against their cheap frocks and sports coats, his dinner-suit conveyed an impression of unnecessary and eccentric self-display. He exchanged a few words with the girl in the box-office (but what did she know of boxes?).

'How's business Miss Gray?'

'Oh, just about as usual Mr Berkley.'

Which meant just about as bad as usual. Not only had Mr Berkley endured the indignity of managing a picture-palace instead of a theatre: there was the further humiliation that the Palladium had never been a success as a cinema. The conversion had been effected at the very moment when cinema receipts had begun to slump after the post-war boom. The new owner had made a bad speculation, and tended to channel his irritation on to Mr Berkley. If the owner decided to cut his losses and sell out, where would Mr Berkley be? The news that the Rialto in Bayditch was to be converted into a warehouse, lay heavy, an undigested lump of worry, in Mr Berkley's memory. Well, let it lie there. He positively would *not* be a warehouse manager.

He eyed with distaste the interior of the foyer, where ill-advised attempts had been made to impose a veneer of 'contemporary' on the rich, old, Edwardian décor which, even at its shabbiest, imparted a feeling of comfort and opulence, a sense of insulation from the everyday world, which Mr Berkley always insisted was an essential part of the experience of going to a theatre. But then he was no longer manager of a *theatre*.

Restlessly he paced over to Bill, the aged commissionaire, like himself a veteran of an earlier and better era.

'Not like the old days, is it Mr Berkley sir?' said Bill, greeting his employer's obsession fondly, as if it were a cat. The man's sycophancy nettled Mr Berkley unreasonably, and he turned away with a muttered 'No'. He retraced his steps to his office, steeling himself to grapple with the ice-cream accounts. As he mounted the stairs he intoned to himself a cinema-manager's catechism:

Q. What does the margin of profit or loss depend on?
A. Ice-cream.
Q. What therefore, does my livelihood depend on?
A. Ice-cream.
Q. What therefore, is the source of all happiness?
A. Ice-cream. . . .

When the Palladium was made into a warehouse, he

prophesied bitterly, it would probably be used to store ice-cream.

★ ★ ★

Mr Mallory always liked to drop from the bus while it was still moving. He did so now, with practised aplomb, and sauntered after it as it braked to a halt. On the running-board his wife lurched as the movement was snatched from under her feet, and catapulted crossly on to the pavement.

'Oh no, don't help anyone,' she remarked, as he hurried forward, too late. He swallowed the apology that had risen to his lips.

'Come on, the programme will have started,' he merely said.

Not that he was anxious to get to the cinema. He hated hurrying his leisure. The week's work was behind him; idleness lay ahead—if he didn't lift his eyes too high. Tomorrow was Sunday. There was one precept of Christianity he would always conscientiously observe: keeping the Sabbath holy by abstaining from servile work. In that particular respect at least he had always been, unconsciously, a Christian; so he had realized when Father Kipling had explained to him the doctrine of Baptism of Desire. Perversely, this was the one commandment his wife, who had been largely responsible for his conversion, insisted on breaking regularly.

To his mind, even a mere bus-ride to a cinema, on a Saturday evening, should be free from the hustle and bustle of everyday travel. On Monday morning, of course, he would be gripped again by the same frenzy as possessed everyone on the Southern railway in the rush-hour. He would claw and push and run with the herd. But a journey to a pleasant, idle destination should be undertaken without this vulgar fuss and hurry, with leisured ease, oblivious to the crude demands of time, the ultimate entertainment

12

being postponed and savoured in anticipation. It was bound to be a disappointment anyway.

If he were alone, for two pins he would not go to the cinema at all, but just stand at this busy junction, observing the passing show, sharing the relief of a city relaxing its strained, tired nerves at the end of a working week. One of the chief occupations of his youth had been to stand at a street-corner with some pals, just looking and talking . . . he brushed aside the recollection, which honesty forced upon him, that as a young man he had lacked the means to do anything else. Now he could do something else, now he had money in his pocket, the democratic entertainment of street-corner lounging seemed like an unattainable luxury. There was something at once soothing and invigorating in the atmosphere of Saturday night, which he wanted time to absorb. The traffic was moving more quietly now, with more grace and control than during the day; gear changes were sweeter, acceleration less fierce. And the people seemed to take the evening like a reviving drink; one could sense a week-end cheerfulness in the air. From a radio shop late to close, a negro's voice carried to the street:

> *Everybody loves Saturday niiight,*
> *Everybody loves Saturday niiight,*
> *Everybody,*
>   *Everybody,*
>   *Everybody,*
>   *Everybody,*
> *Everybody loves Saturday night.*

There was always a certain amount of truth in these popular songs.

He paused to buy an evening paper from the nimble-fingered newsvendor, who drew it with a flourish, like a sword, from the sheaf under his arm. Mr Mallory scanned the football results which occupied most of the front page, and noted philosophically that he had failed to win a pools dividend. A waste of time and money, Bett called it, but she didn't understand that he cheerfully paid out 3s. 6d. a week, not with any real expectation of receiving £75,000 in return, but simply to add a little interest and excitement to life.

He raised his eyes from the paper and took in the scene with a benevolent regard. He felt no contempt for the flashily dressed youths who sauntered by, nudging and butting each other; and only gratitude for the pretty, gaily-dressed young girls, eddying past in giggling, self-conscious groups. He could pick out in the throng a few late shop-girls prinking home in high heels, their neat little bottoms tightly sheathed in narrow skirts, expensive hair-do's bobbing; once home—homes so much more soiled than their clothes—the sheath would be exchanged for something wide and rustling; a comb through the glossy perm, a flower at the throat, a squirt of deodorant, a fresh layer of powder, a quick renovation of faded lipstick—and they would be ready, smiling, and indefatigable for the palais or whatever else. Who could blame them if they didn't get up and go to church next morning? Only people who had enough time on their hands to compose letters to the Catholic papers about 'pagan' England.

'Well then, come on, if you're going to,' said his wife.

Really Tom was getting so strange these days, this irritating, absent-minded sort of smile on his face, as if he could only concentrate on the thing before his eyes and was rather pleased with it—a habit which somehow seemed to put all the responsibility and worry on her shoulders. She supposed she couldn't blame him for staring after young girls, there was no harm in it she knew, and she should be past the age of jealousy. She had put on so much weight in the last few years it was too late to do anything about it now. 'What do you expect after eight children?' she had blurted out one day when Tom was teasing her, and then wished she hadn't. She disliked showing Tom her real feelings. It placed her at a disadvantage. But she didn't give herself away so obviously as he did, staring after those bold girls, with more money than sense, tight skirts that were almost indecent, well the way they walked anyhow. She recalled, but without affection, the days of her own youth, of her wretched financial dependence on her parents, and the Irish village where to walk through the streets on a summer's day with bare forearms was the act of an abandoned hussy.

She slipped a hand under her coat, and felt the small lump under her left breast. Impatiently she pulled it out again. It was becoming a nervous habit. Yet she couldn't suppress the absurd hope that one day she would put her hand there and the lump would have disappeared. She wouldn't go to a doctor. She had never been to a doctor in her life, except for the babies, and then she had hated the things they did to you. Besides, she knew enough—too much—about lumps from other women. . . .

★ ★ ★

'Take us in, Mister?'

Four grimy, wizened urchins, with an appallingly young infant in tow, involved themselves strategically with Mr Mallory's legs, and peered searchingly up at him. Before he could reply, his wife had taken command of the situation:

'Be off with you, you little spalpeens, and take that child home. He's no age to be on the streets with the likes of you.'

The Irish always came welling up in Bett at times like this. Himself she customarily addressed in the flat, laconic accents of South London.

They passed into the foyer of the Palladium.

'How the mothers can let them, I just don't know,' she continued. Mr Mallory contented himself with a vague murmur of agreement, and joined the brief queue for tickets.

He noted gloomily that prices had gone up again, and

resigned himself to paying extra. Bett got a headache if they sat too near the screen. As they made their way to the swing doors with *Stalls* glimmering over the top, Mr Mallory said: 'I thought Patrick and Patricia were going to this programme.'

'Didn't I tell you at tea, only of course you don't listen. They went together, earlier. I don't want them to be up late.'

'Hmm. I didn't think Patricia would be seen dead with her brother.'

'She wanted to see the film, and I wouldn't let her go on her own,' stated his wife simply. Mr Mallory felt a twinge of sympathy for his daughter.

'And Clare and Mark?'

'I don't know where she's going tonight.'

The girl tore their tickets in half, and they passed through the swing doors and curtains into the hot darkness of the cinema. Once again Mr Mallory thought how easy it would be to buy the cheapest tickets, and show the usherette inside the torn portions of dearer ones which you had saved from a previous occasion. Or did they change the colours every now and then? He would never have the courage to try the experiment anyway. He hung back as he heard his wife wrangling with the usherette.

'Are you sure there are none in the middle? What about those two? Tom!' She wheeled round.

'Anywhere will do, dear,' he said mildly. Someone hissed 'Sssh!' and Mr Mallory manœuvred his protesting wife into the nearest vacant seats.

★ ★ ★

The Palladium. That was it. Mrs Skinner who polished the candlesticks had been quite definite that it was the Palladium.

Father Martin Kipling, parish priest of Our Lady of Perpetual Succour, Brickley, tried to ignore the little flutter of excitement inside him as he paced evenly towards the temple of Mammon towering above the busy pavements. Somehow one couldn't help calling a picture-palace a temple of Mammon even if one was entering it to see an edifying film like *Song of Bernadette*—it tried so hard to look like one. Its ugly, florid architecture was even now bathed in a neon flush of hell-fire. It was not one of those modernistic slabs of ferro-concrete, but apparently a converted theatre, probably Edwardian, and had an air of ill-disguised dilapidation which intensified its baleful aspect. Over the entrance an enormous, crudely coloured representation of what might have tempted St Anthony in his less discriminating moments leered from a couch. Father Kipling lowered his eyes swiftly. Why was she there? She had nothing to do with Bernadette.

It was not surprising that he felt a twinge of guilt as he approached the shrine of materialistic paganism, a fear that his dog-collar might cause scandal to an onlooker unaware of the purity of his purpose. He felt an absurd urge to button-hole the nearest man and explain earnestly: 'You know, I haven't been inside a picture-palace since before I was ordained. Of course I'm allowed to go. Being secular you know. They leave it to my discretion. But I don't think it quite becoming for a. . . . But this time, you see, it's a film I particularly want to see, *Bernadette* you know. All the Catholic newspapers particularly recommended it, I remember. Everyone seems to have seen it, even Canon Birley. So I thought I would take the opportunity. But I wouldn't like anyone to think I made a practice. . . .

With a slight shrug of irritation, he dismissed these nagging anxieties from his mind, and applied himself to mastering the unfamiliar ritual of entering the cinema. *Song of Bernadette*—a poster (albeit a rather small one) caught his eye. Well that was all right. And this *was* the Palladium. The omnibus conductor had very kindly pointed it out to him, and the name was unmistakably emblazoned all over the building's façade. Palladium. Strange that for all its strident modernity the place should bear a classical name. But he was frequently struck by the same phenomemon in the names of various sordid products such as cosmetics and permanent-wave solutions. What impact the manufacturers expected to make on classical dons and theological students, to whom a knowledge of Latin and Greek was now virtually limited, he couldn't imagine. *Palladium*, a defence or protection, from the Greek *Palladion*, the statue of Pallas, on whom the safety of Troy was fabled to depend. How many of the thousands who patronized the place knew the derivation of its name? But perhaps it was not such an inept appellation after all. There was something slightly craven and defensive, something suggestive of a retreat, in the way people were converging on the cinema.

'Take us in, Mister?'

The question startled him.

'I beg your pardon?' he said politely, and peered down through his spectacles at the group of rough dirty children who surrounded him.

'G'orn, Guv, take's in.'

Father Kipling smiled uncertainly, and decided on an I'm-in-the-same-boat-as-you-fellows approach.

'Well, really, you know, I don't think I can afford it.' Things had come to a pretty pass when children begged unashamedly on the streets for money to indulge in luxuries such as the cinema. He began to feel quite indignant.

The ring-leader scrutinized him as if he could scarcely credit the evidence of his ears. He glanced meaningfully at his companions, and began to explain.

'We don't want you to pay for us, Mister. We just want you to take us in.'

'Jus' say we're with yer,' backed up another.

' 'Ere's the money, Guv.' A grimy, shrivelled paw held up some silver coins.

'But why?' asked Father Kipling, bewildered.

18

The leader took a deep breath.

'Well yer see, Mister, it's an "A" and you can't get into an "A". . . .'

Father Kipling listened carefully to the explanation. At the end of it he said:

'Then really, you're not allowed to see this film unless accompanied by a parent or guardian?'

'That's right, Mister.'

'Well then, I'm afraid I can't help you, because I'm certainly not your parent, and I can't honestly say I'm your guardian. Can I now?' He smiled nervously at the chief urchin, who turned away in disgust, and formed up his entourage to petition another cinema-goer. Father Kipling stared after them for a moment, then hurriedly made good his escape.

Inside the foyer he was faced with a difficult decision: the choice of seat. The prices all seemed excessively high, and he was conscious of a certain moral obligation to go in the cheapest. On the other hand, this was a rare, if not unique occasion, and as he had few enough treats, he was perhaps entitled to indulge himself to the extent of a comfortable seat. He couldn't choose the middle price, because there were four. As he hesitated he caught the eye of the commissionaire staring at him, and he hastily purchased a ticket for the second most expensive seat.

For the next few minutes he seemed to be in the grips of a nightmare. When the young woman at the swing door had rudely snatched the ticket from his hand, and just as rudely thrust a severed portion of it back again, he was propelled into a pit of almost total darkness and stifling heat. A torch was shone on his ticket, and a listless voice intoned:

'Over to your left.'

In the far recesses of the place another torch flickered like a distant lighthouse, and he set out towards it. When he couldn't see it he stopped; then it would flicker impatiently again, and he would set off once more. Beneath his feet he crunched what appeared to be seashells; he gasped in an atmosphere reeking of tobacco and human perspiration. Dominating all, the screen boomed and shifted. At last he reached the young woman with the torch. But his ordeal was not over. She indicated a seat in the middle of a full row. The gesture was treacherously familiar. Horror of horrors! He had genuflected! The usherette stared. Blushing furiously he forced his way into the row, stumbled, panicked, threshed, kicked his way to the empty seat, leaving a trail of execration and protest in his wake. He wanted to die, to melt away. Never again would he come to the cinema. Never again.

★ ★ ★

Hands thrust deep into the pockets of his beltless, once-belted, black, sharp-shouldered raincoat, Harry moved alone, on noiseless crêpe-soled shoes, threading his way through the crowd, never breaking his step, twisting his shoulders to avoid the contamination of their brightness, happiness, stupidity. You could read in his face that Harry was different from them; he didn't wear flash clothes and take cheap little tarts to the pictures, not Harry. He wore black, all black, except for the white, soft-collared shirt, and he took his pleasures alone. Any girl could tell at once that she'd get no change out of Harry; she'd tell from the pale, taut face, and the hands thrust deep in the black pockets, that Harry was one who walked alone, one to be feared and respected. He wasn't interested in any of these little tarts dressed up to kill. He preferred to wait until he could have class.

'Take us in, Mister.'

Poker-faced, terrible in his black suit and raincoat, he sliced through them, a big, aloof fish through a shoal of sprats, ignoring their insolence.

'Oooer!' called a mocking voice from behind. 'Oo's 'e think 'e is—Robert Mitchum?'

Fury burned inside him. Ignorant little bastards, didn't know who they were talking to, how near danger was. But his face showed no flush or twitch of anger. He had perfected the disguise of his feelings, preferring to ignore, for the time being, the insults and the indifference of the ignorant sods around him. One day he would show them all. Meanwhile he treasured up the insults and the indifference, feeding his store of hatred, which one day he would dash like vitriol in the face of an appalied world.

Reluctantly he queued for a ticket; resentfully he removed one hand from his pocket and put two coins on the metal ledge.

'Two and nine and ten Woodbines,' he said curtly.

'Didn't nobody teach you to say please?' inquired the girl.

He cauterized her with a savage glare, palmed his cigarettes and twisted aside. Her turn would come too, that poxy blonde, when she lay tied naked to a table, and he slowly swung a red-hot poker in front of her eyes, bulging with terror:

'No don't . . . I'll do anything . . . anything . . . I'll give you a good time . . .'

He cut her short with a cold smile.

'I don't have to ask your permission for that, baby. Besides, I always had a weakness for pokerwork. . . .'

Inside the usherette indicated a seat in the middle of the central block. He ignored her gesture, and with hands still deep in his pockets, slumped into a seat against the cinema's wall.

Doreen, the usherette, shrugged her shoulder-straps, and, erect in her Second Skin corselet, her tummy gently perspiring through the new Miracle Fabric, her breasts held lovingly aloft in the 'A' cups of her Treasure Chest bra, turned the indifference of her smoothly sheathed back

21

upon the indifferent Harry, and walked, as gracefully as was possible against the incline, up the aisle. Queer lot she was getting that evening, what with that fussy woman and the clergyman and now this bloke who preferred to sit right at the side, where everybody on the screen looked long and thin like in the Hall of Mirrors at Southend.

★ ★ ★

With calculated gallantry Mark Underwood assisted Clare Mallory off the bus. He wasn't naturally polite, but the pleasure she derived from such tokens was so ridiculously out of proportion to the effort required that it would have been both churlish and impolitic not to gratify her. As they walked towards the cinema she slipped an arm through his. There were times when he liked this demure gesture a lot, but this evening he found it difficult to suppress the desire to shake off her hand. He fumbled for his handkerchief, making this the pretext for disengaging his arm. Clare waited patiently until he had finished, then put her arm through his again. He didn't want to be touched. But he didn't want her not to be there. He wanted to worry her, to inflict his depression on her.

Masochistically he probled for the root of his discontent. Oh yes. The story. Of course he should never have sent it to those people. 'We sell your story and keep 15 per cent of the payment. If we don't think it will sell, we will tell you why and suggest how you can improve it.' It had been the last sentence that had really hooked him. The polite inscrutability of rejection slips was driving him mad; perhaps the London Institution of Fiction would explain the mystery. But the pseudo-academic name should have warned him that behind its façade was just another quack peddling literary cure-all pills.

Dear Mr Underwood,
    My Chief Reader was so impressed by your story A BIT

MUCH, that he passed it to me for my special attention—something which, I am sure you will appreciate, I am not able to give to every work which passes through this organization. I enjoyed reading it, for it shows unmistakable talent, but I do not think you are quite ready to publish yet, though you are very near it. To be quite candid, your story lacks dynamism of characterization, slickness in dialogue, and a scientifically constructed plot.

What I would recommend is that you enrol in one of our Advanced Students' Correspondence Courses, which I myself specially designed for promising young writers like yourself. If you prefer, you can submit your story for a Detailed Criticism for one guinea, or a Complete Scientific Analysis and Rewrite for three guineas. In any case, I have enclosed a copy of the illustrated booklet *Fiction: a Science not an Art* which gives details of all the courses and professional advice open to you. I hope to hear from you soon.

Wishing you a steady flow of editors' cheques, I am,
Yours sincerely,
SIMON ST PAUL
Principal L.I.F.

The recollection of the neatly-typed words on the too-opulent note-paper made him want to spew. When he got home he would pencil 'BALLS' in crude, heavy characters across the letter and post it back. Or else annotate that bloody booklet with deflating quotations from Virginia Woolf and Henry James. On the whole he rather thought he would do the former: it would require less effort, and the immediate impact would be greater, especially if Simon's sycophantic secretary opened the letter. (He was bound to have a sycophantic secretary; she was probably his mistress too.)

Still, he could not help feeling that the only adequate retort would be to get the story published, and there seemed no chance of that. His mood had not been improved by reading in that evening's paper a review of a play by some seventeen-year-old barrow-boy, which had been successfully presented at a West End theatre the night before, and which as far as he could judge, had said most of the things he himself had been pondering for the last two years.

'Never mind!' he exclaimed abruptly. 'To the pictures! To the pictures! To the warm embrace of Mother Cinema. Where peanut shells are spread before your feet, and the ice-cream cometh!'

This sort of deranged poetic declamation never failed to amuse Clare.

'Well, at least you've said something,' she remarked, 'even if I didn't understand a word of it.'

She smiled, but the smile hid a certain anxiety. She was a little tired of falling back on the amused, uncomprehending, common-sense, womanly response to his behaviour. Sometimes she knew he was not talking pure nonsense, and wished she could appreciate the jokes and allusions. In fact it was a mystery how he could tolerate anyone so hopelessly uninformed as herself. 'You must educate me,' she had said to him once. 'I'm not absolutely stupid you know; it's just that you're not encouraged to read very widely in a convent.' But he had just said 'I don't want you educated. I've got educated girls round me all day, and they give me a pain in the ... neck.' 'But *I* want me educated,' she had complained; but he had only laughed and hugged her with his arm. And that had been nice, she remembered bashfully.

Also it had been nice to know that he didn't care for the girls at his college. He seemed strangely reluctant to take her anywhere where they might encounter his college friends, but she had a very clear idea of the girls, with their urchin-cuts and trousers and feline spectacles—all of which features seemed much more likely to appeal to Mark than her own puzzled and timid experiments with her appearance.

24

He returned her smile, thinking how sweet it was, and how its sweetness, its slight suggestion of patient suffering pluckily disguised, might become rather cloying in time, an annoyingly insistent claim upon the emotions, like a dog's eyes. Nevertheless, as he turned to look at her, he felt a wave of affection for the delightful picture she presented: the clumsily applied lipstick of the wrong colour; the superb clarity of complexion (why did so many nuns have faces like polished marble); the too-long skirt; the blouse, bought on a wild impulse, its plunging neckline abbreviated, on a modest afterthought, by a brooch representing Our Lady of Lourdes, with arms extended as if to tug the offending garment together; the short, tent-like coat that made her look pregnant, and in fact disguised a firm, well-fleshed and almost flawless torso. Clare was a treasure, and only he had the map. It pleased him that she should resemble a child who had blundered into a big store and amused herself by 'dressing-up', because it guarded the secret so much the more effectively.

'You look very fetching this evening,' he said.

'Do you really think so, or are you only saying that?'

'No, honestly.'

'Well, that's nice then, I never know whether you regard me as a girl or as a huge joke.'

He chuckled, rocking somewhat from the accuracy of her stroke.

'Won't we be late?' Clare asked.

'The later we are the better. The second feature's only some second-rate crime film.'

They passed a shop which called itself *Modern Menswear*.

'Do they?' inquired Mark. 'So much?'

'Do who what?'

He pointed.

'Do modern men swear?' It seemed awfully feeble. Clare laughed merrily, shaking her head.

'You are a fool, Mark.'

In the window of the shop the suits stood stoically, crowded shoulder to shoulder like men in a rush-hour tube. Gaudy shirts thrust out their chests, and detruncated trousers crossed their elegant legs. A multitude of banners and posters exclaimed hysterically 'Giant Sale!' 'Total Clearance!' 'Premisses [*sic*] to be Demolished' 'Unrepeatable Offers' 'Buy! Buy! Buy!' Though the shop was closed, and he knew that there would be nothing he would want to buy anyway, Mark stopped and ran a critical eye over the merchandise.

'Not a bad tie, that, for the price,' he remarked, indicating a black silk tie with a discreet lightning pattern. 'Club tie for the Schoole of Night.'

'I'll buy it for you,' said Clare.

'Don't be ridiculous,' he said, moving on to the next shop. It sold lingerie.

'Tell me,' he said, pointing to a suspender belt. 'Tell me, do you wear that over or under your pants?'

Clare felt her stomach knot, and blood rush to her face so violently she could scarcely see.

'I think you're . . . not very nice,' she said, and began to walk on.

Without hurrying obviously, he managed to catch her up.

'I need the information, you see, for a story I'm writing,' he explained casually.

'Then it must be a vulgar story.'

Mark was about to object that it depended on what you meant by vulgar, when he reflected that the statement was probably valid whatever you meant by it, so he merely replied, 'Very possibly.'

As they walked on in silence it occurred to him that there was room for a London Institute of Pornography, of which he might be the prosperous Principal.

Dear Author,

I have read your novel *Undress Rehearsal* with interest and appreciation; but to be quite candid, your understanding of the technicalities of feminine underwear is woefully inadequate, and your seduction/page ratio is well below the required average. May I recommend that you take our correspondence course 'The Mechanics of Masturbatory Literature' which I myself designed for ambitious pornographers like yourself?

'It's under,' said Clare suddenly. She blushed deeply. He smiled.

'Thank you Clare. I just wanted to know.' He chalked up another minor tactical success in the siege of her innocence. It was just as well, he reflected, that Clare did not know how he had first found the answer to his question.

Clare was glad she had managed to say it, and hadn't let him be cross with her. Nevertheless he was a bit queer, or 'rude' as they used to say as children. She supposed it was because he was a writer and had to know things. It was nice anyway to think that she could help him with the writing.

'Take us in, Mister?'

Mark looked down at the group of urchins skipping backwards before him.

'Do you solemnly promise to sit in the corner of the cinema farthest from us when we get inside?'

'Yer, we always do, Mister. Trust us,' said the leader, winking cheekily at Clare.

'Where's your money?'

'But, Mark, you're not going to take them in?' said Clare.

'Why not?' he said, taking the warm silver coins and counting them. 'You'll have to go in the two-and-nines,' he added.

'But suppose their parents are looking for them?'

'My dear girl, this is how their parents get rid of them.

And don't tell me the film's unsuitable. Most of these kids have home-lives that would give the censor fits.'

The kids were looking crestfallen, and the infant, sensing the general depression, began to whine.

'Woi we got to go in the two-an'-nines, Mister? We ain't got the money.'

'Well, I can hardly say I'm looking after you if you go in different seats from me, can I? And I personally intend to go in the two-and-nines. However, I suppose I can scrape together the extra. Come on.'

And in they went, with Mark putting on a little act for the benefit of the commissionaire, calling out, 'Come along, Jimmy, don't leave Bobby behind, Joe,' and Clare's heart thumping, but filled with a sudden surge of affection for Mark.

* * *

From his seat on the top deck of a traffic-locked bus, Damien O'Brien watched the charade with tight-lipped disapproval. That fellow Underwood was doing his best to degrade Clare, and she was almost co-operating. He could not understand how a girl who had once intended to be a nun could keep company with a person so obviously worldly and unprincipled.

A man, breathing heavily, slumped down beside him. Damien glanced at the frayed, greasy cuffs of the man's raincoat, and wrinkled his nostrils as the pungent odour of beer reached him. He wriggled into the corner of his seat as the bus lurched forward and removed from his vision the scandalous advertisement of some half-naked film actress, spread across the entrance to the cinema. It was time some organization of Catholic action organized a protest against such advertisements. He might bring it up at that evening's meeting. . . . The thought recalled him to the beads he was fingering in his pocket. He passed on to the Third Joyful

Mystery of the rosary: the Birth of Our Lord. The image of the crib in the seminary chapel at Christmas flashed upon his mind. What a moving and eternally significant group! Our Lady gazing tenderly at the Child, while St Joseph stood, proud and watchful, at the door of the stable. The Holy Family. God had decided that he, Damien, should not become a priest. The vow of chastity was no longer an obligation, and although he had toyed with the idea of a private vow of celibacy, he had rejected it as being liable to cause misunderstanding. No, it was the ideal of the Holy Family that allured him, the ideal which no priest could realize. And Clare Mallory was the obvious, providential partner for such a work. The moment he had heard that she had left a convent after being a novice for two years had been like a moment of prophetic revelation. She was his cousin, it was true, but twice removed. What could be more fitting than that they should join forces, and overcome their spiritual setbacks by realizing an ideal comparable to a successful religious vocation? Her great kindness in finding him more suitable accommodation than he had first obtained on crossing to England, had encouraged his hopes, which he had only very discreetly hinted at, knowing from personal experience how sensitively one required to be treated on returning to the world from the cloistered calm of the seminary. And then Underwood had arrived on the scene, like the Serpent into the Garden, deceiving everyone with his so-called charm, and insinuating his disturbing influence between Clare and himself.

Underwood hadn't, of course, appreciated the delicacy of Clare's situation, which somehow gave him the advantage, as she never took offence at anything he did or said. Underwood had been with the Mallorys barely a week when he asked Clare if she would like to go to the pictures with him —in front of the whole family too—just as he himself had decided the moment was propitious to suggest to Clare that she might join the Committee of the Apostleship of Prayer (of which he was secretary) as an Ordinary Member. No one but himself seemed to appreciate the indecorum of Underwood's invitation—that a girl not four months out of the convent should go gallivanting off to a picture-palace with a virtual stranger. In fact, when he mentioned his concern privately to his aunt Elizabeth she had laughed, and said:

'Ah you're a queer gloomy sort of fellow, Damien. Sure it will do the girl a world of good to see a little life now she's left the convent for good. I wonder you haven't asked her yourself before now.'

It wasn't, of course, that Clare preferred Underwood to himself: he wouldn't do her the injustice of supposing that. No, it was this accursed urge she had to 'convert' him, an urge which Underwood encouraged for his own purposes, keeping up a pretence of interest, and even consenting to go to Mass again. It was useless to point out to Clare that the fellow, even though he did seem to have been baptized a Catholic, was a confirmed sceptic; in fact, she had turned on him quite sharply when he had expressed this opinion. Her retort still stung: 'You seem to think that Mark is incapable of faith just because he's cleverer than you or me. I don't think that's very charitable, Damien.'

Clever. That was the trouble with Underwood, he was too damned clever—or at least he made Clare think he was, and she grovelled before his almighty brain, which after all didn't amount to more than a cynical wit and a few quotations. And in any case she had been going out with him more and more frequently lately, to theatres and cinemas, which couldn't be attributed entirely to disinterested motives. Yes, the more he thought about it, the more convinced he was that he would be doing her a favour to point out the dangers of her behaviour, the danger of her motives being misinterpreted, and of these wordly amusements actually gaining a hold on her. And perhaps he might convey some hint of the pain it was causing to himself.

The bus stopped with a jolt, and clutching the Minute Book of the Apostleship of Prayer, Damien hurriedly alighted from the bus and made his way to the church of Our Lady of Perpetual Succour.

★ ★ ★

Picking absently at a pimple on her chin, Patricia Mallory sat waiting for the gangster film to end so that she could see the first half-hour of the main film. She hated going in halfway through a picture. But Mummy would insist that she went to bed early because she was 'swotting'—(how naïve and superstitious it was, her reverence for study—but useful sometimes)—and also insisted that she didn't go alone to the pictures, which meant taking Patrick.

'Patrick, don't fidget,' she hissed.

He ignored her rebuke. In fact he had only spoken to her once that evening, to ask her for the money for an ice-cream, which she had had the satisfaction of refusing. After all, she didn't get much more pocket-money than he did, considering all the extras she had to buy—stockings and lipstick and aspirins and so forth—while he lived as economically as a young animal. Boys had all the best of it really, no headaches and suchlike, not expected to do much around the house, no wonder Patrick did well at school, whereas they somehow expected her to do everything, to study *and* help with the housework. And when that day before the exams it had been just too much to bear, and she had shouted that she must have some time when she did nothing, not study or housework, but just nothing, and cried and made a scene, they had all looked very surprised and shocked and hadn't understood at all. But Mark had understood, though he had only been with them a short time, and must have been terribly embarrassed by the scene, he wasn't used to the family, with people always bursting into tears, other people didn't live like that, with emotions going off like mines under

31

your feet, the trouble was there were too many of them living at too close quarters. . . . And she had dashed upstairs and slammed her door and locked it, with her mother's annoyed worried voice coming up the stairs with, she could just imagine, the corners of her mouth drawn in, how old that made her look, 'Well, she can stay there as long as she likes, the silly great baby. Perhaps she'll appreciate how well she's treated when she's hungry.' But Mark had understood, for she had met him when she unlocked her door and crept out to the george, and he had grinned at her, and invited her into his room and given her some chocolate and a book to read, it was called *A Portrait of the Artist as a Young Man*, which she took back to her own room. And she had read it through, soaking up like a dry sponge its sadness and revolt and rebellion and need to be free, and how she wished she could have met Stephen when he was her age, and talked to him and said how she understood. The chocolate too had enabled her to stay upstairs for a reasonable time, to compose herself and gain prestige, so that she had command of the situation when she finally went downstairs, and behaved very calmly and sweetly, and sat with her knees together and her skirt smoothed demurely over them, saying thank you and making conversation, while all the rest were confused and embarrassed and didn't know where to look. Really that day had been a turning-point, for she had built her examination answer round the book Mark had leant her, and Miss Brooks had been so impressed with it she had shown it to Mother Superior, who made a tremendous fuss because one of her pupils had been reading James Joyce; and that had rather made her reputation among the girls, and placed her almost on a par with Lucy Travers who had nearly been expelled for coming to school on her boy friend's motor-bike.

In fact that book had made her decide to be a writer, and she found that unlike all her previous determinations—nun (shapeless clothes, straight hair, quiet voice, kindly to juniors), Olympic athlete (too few clothes, short hair, hearty voice, encouraging to juniors), and ballet dancer (flared skirt and flat shoes, severe scraped-back hair, no voice, oblivious of juniors), this new enthusiasm, which under ridicule had swiftly shed its trappings (dark clothes, unkempt hair, resonant voice, baffling to juniors), still retained its hold on her imagination.

She suddenly saw the silhouettes of Mark and Clare against the screen, as they sat down a few rows in front. She also became vexedly aware that she had drawn blood from a pimple on her chin. She was glad that she and Patrick would be going home before Mark and Clare, so that they wouldn't meet.

She wondered if Clare minded Mark helping her with her work. He *did* help her an awful lot. And if it wasn't for her friendship with Mark, how would she keep her sanity and self-respect under the absurdly puritanical discipline imposed on her by her mother, which made it almost impossible for her to make friends with anyone her own age— not that there was anyone worth knowing in Brickley anyway.

'Patrick, do stop fidgeting.'

★ ★ ★

Father Kipling gradually emerged from his confusion and embarrassment, and began to assemble the data of his situation as a first step towards restoring his shattered self-possession. He risked a glance to his left, but the stout lady on whose corns he had been accused of stepping with such brutal violence, had apparently forgotten the injury and was gazing fixedly at the screen while her hand moved rhythmically from a noisy paper-bag in her lap to an equally noisy mouth. Emboldened, he looked around him, and found that everybody seemed to have forgotten the disturbance, which had apparently been nothing more than a temporary interruption of their trance-like communion with the screen. Relieved, he turned his own attention to it.

After several minutes of close application, visual and auditory, he was still defeated as to the form and purpose of the performance. It was not *Bernadette*: that much was obvious, and disturbing. He turned to his left, changed his mind, and turned to his right, where an odoriferous young woman sat fondling her hair.

'Excuse me,' he said, 'but could you possibly tell me if there is another film being shown this evening. You see I was under the impression. . . .' But he was already wilting under her insulted, contemptuous gaze.

'Shouldn't be surprised,' she drawled coldly, and turned to mutter something to her companion, who leaned forward to examine him. Father Kipling pressed back against his seat, and resolved to wait and see.

In the warm darkness Len felt for Bridget's warm, moist hand, and warmly she squeezed his rough, strong fingers in return. They had been in the cinema about ten minutes now, and already the warmth was making Bridget pleasantly drowsy. Gradually the ache drained out of her legs into her feet, and, as she eased off her shoes, was absorbed by the carpet. With the ache vanished the strain and irritation of another day behind the counter of XYZ cafeteria: the burnt toast, the greasy rags, Raymond the Italian washer-up who pinched on sight . . . a good job for him Len didn't know. She rested her head in the crook of Len's neck and shoulder, and he chinned her curls. The pupils of her askew eyes kept sliding to the bottom corners of their sockets from weight and weariness; after a time she happily allowed them to stay there, and closed her lids on the black and white crooks and detectives punching each other's jaws. Distantly she heard their grunts, the crunch of flesh and bone, the crash of splintered furniture. Len sat very still. Then, as she expected and wanted, he moved his arm up and over and round her shoulders.

If only the stubborn plush barrier of the seat-arm would melt, she would be in absolute bliss. But the seat-arm was the little piece of grit she encountered so often at the happiest times that she had come to think of it as inevitable, and almost necessary. Never had she known a moment of happiness without that little piece of grit pricking her. Whenever she was with Len it was wonderful, but there was always an end to it, a comfortless kiss on the porch with Mrs. Potts probably peering through the curtains at them, she wouldn't have men in the house at any price. Mostly the kiss was at the bottom of High Hill where Len caught his last bus, because usually he didn't have time to see her home, and though he would have walked home she wouldn't let him, and anyway there was his mother. . . . It would be the same this evening and every evening until he went into the army, which would be even worse—they didn't dare talk about it, but it was hanging over them all the time. In the end, when Len had finished his apprenticeship and his national service, they would be married, and how wonderful that would be, no more good nights then, and no more cafeteria for her, but there would be babies and Len's moods and night-shifts and illnesses, always something. Perhaps if it wasn't for the something, life. . . . But Bridget's dim speculations petered out as she surrendered drowsily to the luxury of Len's strong arms around her shoulders.

★ ★ ★

Doreen for a moment turned a straight back on the incoming customers, and, with feet together, watched the only bit of the film she could still enjoy at the end of a week's repetition, where the gangster's moll insulted the vicar who was cleaning up the racket, wearing the most heavenly black nylon négligée, almost see-through, but just saved by frothy lace all down the front, and black lace undies dark underneath, no wonder she was mad that he wouldn't make love to her.

As he eased his shoulders through the door, the minister turned and slid his eyes up and down the négligée.

'Why don't you take some of that paint off your face? It may be quite pretty underneath.'

'Get out!'

Father Kipling goggled at the scene. This bovine person in the flashily-cut suit was apparently intended to be a clergyman, though his parish seemed to consist exclusively of night-clubs, and his ministry of punching jaws. He received the advances of this disgracefully undressed Jezebel with disquieting composure. Really, it wasn't surprising that the Protestant churches were in decline if this was the state of affairs.

'Bet she takes off her make-up,' said a woman in front of him.

Sure enough, the actress sat down before her dressing-table and wiped experimentally at her face.

'How remarkably acute,' thought Father Kipling.

'Told you,' said the woman, nudging her husband triumphantly.

'All right, all right, I heard,' he said.

'Mum, I want to go 'ome,' whined a child who was sitting with them.

'Ssh!'

'Mum, can I 'ave a lolly?'

'Give 'im sixpence, Fred.'

''E's 'ad two already.'

'Well you know we won't get a moment's peace without.'

★ ★ ★

'Damn,' said Mark, as they seated themselves. 'There are your parents just over there. Patrick and Patricia are here too, aren't they? Soon have the whole bloody family.'

'Mark,' she reproved sadly.

'Sorry.'

He had agreed that she could rebuke him for bad language, 'as long as I'm not expected to reform'. The force of this condition was only too apparent to her, and yet this was the dream she cherished—to reform, or rather, to convert Mark. It would not be easy. He was so bitter and cynical sometimes, and so flippant. 'A confirmed sceptic' was Damien's verdict; but she couldn't agree. After all, Mark had been a Catholic once. And already she had persuaded him to go to Mass again, to give the Faith a fair chance. Yet, she had to admit that there was a hard core of reserve and secrecy in him which she despaired of ever penetrating. Perhaps this was her fault.

Since leaving the convent she had suffered from a kind of spiritual numbness which, she knew, was a common malady of religious, and probably ex-religious too. She was just going through the motions of piety at the moment. But she longed to be able to communicate to Mark some of the enthusiasm she had commanded in previous years. At school, for instance, when she had been captain of St Agatha's House, ninety per cent of her girls had been daily communicants. Mark had teased her about this achievement, maintaining that it reduced Holy Communion to the level of a hockey tournament; and she was obliged to question the value of that kind of religious zeal since it had recoiled so disastrously on her in the case of Hilda. Nevertheless, she knew that she had once possessed a gift for generating religious feeling in others; but it had been a gift which had derived directly from her own piety. Mark's religious life was of far greater interest and importance to her than her own at the moment, but she longed to be a participant in, not merely a spectator of, his rediscovery of the Catholic faith. She was racked by a sense of impotence, like standing on the sidelines with a pulled muscle when your team was on the verge of winning the match.

'I wish you wouldn't swear so much, Mark. Especially about Mummy and Daddy.'

'Sorry, Clare. You know how much I like your mother and father,' replied Mark in a low voice. 'It's just that you're so shy and withdrawn with me when they're around, I was afraid that you wouldn't let me do this.'

He put his arm round her shoulder. Inevitably she blushed.

'I don't mind. While there are no lights,' she whispered.

He turned his head to look at her. How did she manage to make it sound as daring and exciting as a midnight swim in the nude? With Clare he was reliving all the breathless excitement and sense of discovery that accompanied adolescent love, without its pain and misunderstandings. He delighted in the frugality of her kisses, looked forward like a young kid to the one, chaste good-night embrace—chaste, but perhaps a little warmer each time, each time a little more reluctantly broken. It was fascinating to watch Clare, like another Chloe, fumbling innocently towards real passion. For the time being he was content to play the part of an only slightly more knowing Daphnis. It was typical of the whole family, he decided, this refreshing delight in ordinary experiences which most people were either too sophisticated or too bourgeois to appreciate. It had laid its spell upon him as soon as he had spent a day at 89 Maple Road, and had kept him there, a willing prisoner, ever since. He would not quickly forget the impact of that first afternoon.

Back from a month's hitch-hiking and youth-hostelling on the Continent that summer, he had gone up to London four weeks before the term started, ostensibly to lay the foundations of his final year's study, but in fact to avoid a prolonged stay with his parents at Blatcham.

He had never felt any affection for Blatcham, a dull, featureless town set in the no-man's-land between London and 'the country', belonging to neither, but affecting a combination of both. In practice, the men of the town exhausted themselves in the diurnal pilgrimage to the City and back, leaving their womenfolk to wave vacantly after their receding figures each morning, before they returned to the dusting of clean furniture, the knitting of Fair Isle jumpers, and the bored manipulation of television knobs.

Nevertheless, after the dubious comradeship of barrack-room life, even Blatcham and his parents' solid, comfortable villa seemed to represent civilized living; and for most of his first year at college he had lived with his father and mother (who hadn't seen much of him during his National Service), travelling up with his father each day. But the constraint of their carefully insulated lives gradually became intolerable. Their almost congenital blindness to the claims of any life different from their own, aroused in him alternating anger and pity, emotions to which they were equally impervious. In his note-book was his bitter and unfilial appraisal of the situation in his second term:

My father suffers from chronic catarrh, though he cannot be persuaded to admit the fact, and generally abstains from the use of a handkerchief. Sometimes it seems to me that the very arteries of his brain are clogged with snot, so difficult is it to penetrate there with any new idea. He sniffs unceasingly, drawing up into his head quantities of mucous that must curdle and thicken into a morass which stifles the faintest stirrings of intellectual curiosity. I would like to admire and love my father, but the mere sight of his scanty hair combed painfully across the bald, bumpy scalp, the furrowed lumpish face, the sagging chicken-neck, the dark striped suit tight under the armpits, all buttons fastened, shiny over the haunches, swollen with too much sitting, as he carefully licks an envelope before sealing it with unnecessary pressure, affixing the stamp at exact right-angles to the corner—all this is enough to fill me with a desperate irritation which I have to struggle hard to suppress. It seems incredible that a person whose vision of life is a mere chink in the wall of his self-satisfaction should, by mere plodding, have secured such a comfortable salary; though it is fortunate, as it relieves me of the responsibility of planning a career with the possibility of having to support my parents in their old age.

My mother is well-intentioned but stupid, her ambitions embarrassingly petty: security, a nice house, a car. Had she been thwarted of these, some sympathetic quality, some pathos, or hint of suburban tragedy, might have made her more endearing; but having achieved them all before she was thirty, she could conceive of nothing beyond their meaningless multiplication: another insurance policy, new loose covers, a bigger car.

The war left us untouched: my father was exempted from military service because of some trivial medical defect, and took the opportunity to feather his nest in the Civil Service. The greatest hardship we endured was the sheltering of an evacuee family, whose lives we made so unhappy that they left us voluntarily after three weeks. We have no relatives or friends whose deaths caused us genuine pain. We have had no spectacular good fortune. There has been a paralysing absence of deep joy or sorrow from our bleak triangular existence, which, when I have left, will be but apathy's shortest distance between two points. I have woken up to the fact that if I go on any longer endlessly discussing the rise in prices, the gardening programme for the next week-end, the traffic in Blatcham, the traffic in London, the punctuality of the morning and evening trains, and the temerity of our coalman in motoring to Italy for his holidays—imperceptibly the capacity for living, in any significant sense of the word, will slip away from me, and I shall be left mouthing the expected responses at the tea-table.

I must go; but I do not wish to hurt. They are mildly puzzled that I should be willing to suffer the discomforts of living in a bed-sitter in London merely to avoid excessive travelling (my excuse), but they do not suspect anything. Our conversation is a game I deliberately lose again and again to disguise my real feelings. They are satisfied. It relieves me of guilt. I will leave them slumped before the TV, and quietly open the door and slip out into life.

He had over-written the situation, but he had no regrets about his decision. In his second year at college he shared a flat with two fellow-students, and lived a free, unreflective, experimental and, on the whole, happy life, which he characterized as 'the welfare Bohemia'. The drink was beer, the books were Penguins, the entertainment continental films, and the girls suburbanites disguising their respectability with tight trousers and unkempt hair. It was a game, but rather pathetic effort. One should live either like Oxford before the war, or like Paris after it, he decided—either have too much money or none at all. The compromise afforded by a benevolent State was feeble. That, at least was how he felt now. At the time he had thought the life gay and enviable enough.

But for his final year at college he had felt the need of some change of existence and environment. For one thing, the amount of work to be done for Finals was oppressive, and the distractions of shared accommodation and the time-absorbing chores of keeping house, however haphazardly, were unthinkable. Digs were indicated. But the task of finding comfortable digs was formidable, as he learned to his cost in a week's weary trekking across London.

But when he alighted at Brickley station one afternoon, with a crumpled *Accommodation Advertiser* in his hand, he had a presentiment that this time he might be luckier. The place was so ugly that it could not possibly be either fashionable or fashionably unfashionable: the sort of place no one lives in from choice—only if one were cast up there by birth or chance. Nevertheless its ugliness held him with an obscure fascination that was to grow more and more insistent, until it entirely occupied the vacant space in his mind that should have held an affection for home. In future years, he felt sure, when he experienced a pang of home-sickness, it would not be for the neat, clean villas and smug, dull shop-fronts of Blatcham, but for the grimy, arid streets of Brickley; for the tall, decaying Victorian houses, from each of whose windows sagged the washing of a different family; for the long, maddening rows of squat, identical nineteenth-century workers' homes with big new cars parked outside in incongruous opulence; for the worn, soft pave-ments; and for the honourable scars of the blitz, of the suffering he knew only by repute, the patches of new bricks, slates, paving-stones, the pre-fabs sprouted like mushrooms from the dung of destruction, new raw blocks of flats, and even the occasional neglected bomb-site, its stark out-lines softened by the work of weather and vegetation, a playground for children, and for him a kind of shrine too.

But of course the main reason why Brickley would always retain its hold on his emotions and imagination was the Mallory family, to whom he had been led by that terse advertisement in the *Advertiser*: 'Board and lodging for business gentleman or student £2 5s. per week.' 89 Maple Road was a tall, deep, narrow house with a basement. The Mallorys occupied only the ground and first floors, but he never became really acquainted with the other occupants of the house. They were the dull bread that sandwiched the rich and abundant humanity of the Mallorys; they crept apologetically in and out of the house, plainly overawed by the family's vitality. Once Patricia and himself had surprised a thin, etiolated little man softly ascending the stairs from the basement—to judge from the towel in his hand *en route* for the bathroom.

'Oh, here's Mr Parsons,' Pat had exclaimed, in a tone of such greedy enjoyment, that the poor little man had shot one startled glance at them both and scuttled down into his dim abode again, muttering that he had forgotten something.

There had been the same zestful enjoyment of people in Mrs Mallory's smile of inquiry as she opened the door to him that hot summer afternoon, her hair turbaned and her hands gauntleted with flour.

'The room? Ah, of course, and me forgetting all about it. My, but you're sharp. I only put it in the paper the day before yesterday. You must excuse the condition I'm in, but I'm baking this afternoon.'

She pushed back with the back of her wrist a wisp of auburn hair which had escaped the turban, and led him into the kitchen. The architecture of the house was quite extraordinary, and to get to any room one had to pass through dark, perverse little passages with unaccountable ascents and descents of steps. As he stumbled over the first hurdle Mrs Mallory apologized:

'Oh, I'm sorry, I should have warned you about that step. This is a terrible house till you get used to it. And then it's worse. Are y' all right now?'

'Oh yes, quite all right,' he replied, deciding that the slight accent in her speech was Irish.

'You know, that step'll be the death of me one of these days, the times I've tripped on it. Sometimes I feel like kicking it, I'm so vexed. But then I offer it up to Our Blessed Lord, who fell three times, and hurt himself a good deal more, I don't doubt.'

Irish and Catholic, he decided, with a certain uneasiness. He eschewed Catholics on the whole. They resurrected the odd, remote period of his Catholic early childhood, and he had no wish to roll back the stone from *that* tomb. His mother had been a Catholic, and had married his father in a Catholic church. He dimly remembered kneeling to say the *Hail Mary* with her, in his pyjamas. Then he had been sent to a convent school for his earliest schooling. Neither of his parents had gone to Mass however—a cause, he seemed to remember, of considerable pain to him, not so much spiritually as socially. When, after they had moved to Blatcham, he was sent to the County school, he had himself given up going to Mass without reproach. Doctrines of mortal sin and hell-fire had caused him some moments' anxiety; but the threat of immediate punishment by human authority was more compulsive, and as the two were confused in his mind, the absence of the latter led him to forget the former. When he attained the age of philosophical curiosity he remembered these doctrines only to dismiss them, with a passing irritation that they had ever influenced him. In fact he deeply resented this tenuous claim Catholicism had upon him—the undeniable fact that he *had* been a Catholic, a fact from which his Catholic acquaintance derived an exasperating satisfaction. 'Oh, you'll come back in the end,' they would say confidently at the end of every inconclusive argument. God, in their view, seemed to be a sort of supernatural Mountie who always got His man. The whole thing was a further source of unfilial resentment: it was the final indignity that his parents had imposed upon him—that they, utterly soulless as they were, should have taken it upon themselves to saddle him with a religion.

The kitchen into which he was ushered confirmed his suspicions about Mrs Mallory's religious background: the evidence of the plastic holy water stoup askew on the wall, the withered holy Palm, stuck behind a picture of the Sacred Heart which resembled an illustration in a medical text-book, and the statue of St Patrick enthroned upon the dresser, was conclusive. Not that these constituted the only decoration. 89 Maple Road was like the dwelling-place of some inadequately evangelized savage tribe, where the icons of Christianity jostled incongruously the symbols of obscure pagan cults. One day, to satisfy his curiosity, Mark counted fifty-five articles adorning the walls of the house. These included, besides a fair proportion of devotional objects: faded photographs of people whose names were forgotten, out-of-date calendars, pictures torn from magazines, fretwork cut-outs of atrocious design, plaster plaques, souvenirs of obscure seaside resorts, and in a dark corner of the hall— the item Mark treasured most of all—a small wooden panel, on which was painted a dog's pathetic face, inscribed 'Please don't forget my walk', and furnished with a hook from which depended an ancient, broken dog's lead: the memorial of a mongrel run over by a lorry six years before. All the articles shared the neglected appearance of this last item: each enshrined a sentimental memory which no one bothered to recall, but which no one could make the effort to erase. The pagan gods were no longer invoked; but a proposal to remove them, Mark quickly discovered, carried with it a suggestion of sacrilege.

As Mark received his first impression of the kitchen, Mrs Mallory chattered on about the vacant room.

'We've never had anyone before—we never had the space for one thing, with a family of eight children. But now they're growing up and leaving home. James—that's my eldest—was ordained at Corpus Christi, and he's gone abroad to the African missions. And Robert's doing his National Service—he's in Germany. So the boys' room was being wasted, and with four children still at school we can do with a little extra, so we thought we'd have a lodger.' She used the last word—anathema in Blatcham—without hesitation or self-consciousness. While she spoke she washed her hands, took off her apron, and freed her hair from its turban. The bulkiness of her body was a monument to the labour of frequent child-bearing, but the richness and abundance of her auburn hair surprised him as it came toppling down. It was a young girl's hair.

With what seemed miraculous speed she had produced a hot, tangy cup of tea, and he was being pressed to a slab of home-made fruit cake. It was all so different from the treatment offered to him that week by shrivelled, embittered landladies, in dressing-gowns and carpet-slippers, who suspiciously permitted him a brief glance at 'the room' before enumerating the rules of the household, and who affected to be insulted when he declined their accommodation—it was all so different that he listened in passive contentment to Mrs Mallory's chatter about her son James, whose severe portrait held pride of place among the religious and secular bric-à-brac on the mantelpiece. Then he suddenly realized that she had casually asked him:

'You are a Catholic, aren't you, Mr Underwood?'

'No, Mrs Mallory. What made you think I was?'

She looked confused.

'But I thought—the advertisement. . . .'

He glanced down at the newspaper where the Mallorys' advertisement was ticked off, and immediately saw that printed beneath the address, so that he had thought it had belonged to the next advertisement, was the postscript: 'Good Catholic family—co-religionist preferred.'

'I'm sorry,' he said. 'I didn't see the co-religionist bit.'

She giggled.

'That was Patrick's idea. I think he was afraid we'd all lose our faith if we allowed a heretic into the house. Seriously, though, Mr Underwood, it's not that we have anything against non-Catholics, in fact I've far more against some Catholics I could name—no, it's just that it could be uncomfortable and awkward for a non-Catholic living with us—no meat on Fridays, everybody rushing about like mad things on Sunday mornings, and so on. . . . I remember my aunt Jemima, she was a Baptist or one of those queer religions—I don't know why my uncle Michael ever married her, but marry her he did, and brought her back to Ireland to stay with us, and I don't know what she grumbled about most, the religion or the lack of plumbing.'

46

He was glad of this turn in the conversation, for the religious content of her previous remarks now appeared in a less propagandist light. But, as he discovered later, none of the family flaunted their religion in the eyes of strangers. Until he became really intimate with them the Mallorys retained a pleasing modesty before him where their religion was concerned. Their communal prayers were conducted without fuss, and his own abstention was taken for granted, even by the young ones. Not that they didn't care. One night he had overheard one of the twins at her prayers say: '. . . and please let Mark be a Catholic like us.' He had been moved. It was difficult to react in any other way to a kid saying her prayers.

Almost with an effort he had guided the conversation back to the room, and Mrs Mallory led him to it. It was not bad, not at all bad, plain and bright. The inevitable religious and sentimental rubbish on the walls could soon be replaced by his Paul Klee prints. There was a writing-table and a good arm-chair.

'I'll take it, Mrs Mallory,' he said.

He wasn't ushered to the street door after he had fixed up the details. Somehow he found himself back in the kitchen again, accepting a second cup of tea. He must have sat in that worn and battered kitchen for hours, but only towards the end of the evening did his buttocks begin to ache from the hard contours of the Windsor chair, so engrossed was he in his experience of a strangely novel way of life: novel to him, yet having an indefinably natural quality. It was the kind of life one could live for years, he thought, without becoming bored or dulled by routine. There were many things about the family which antagonized him at first. Occasionally amusement would turn into irritation at the fifty-five ugly ornaments that littered the walls, the clutter and confusion of the scullery, the essential utensils that were always missing, the incorrigible accumulation of useless junk in corners, cupboards, everywhere, the blind indifference to the latest books, plays, news (Mr Mallory was the only member of the family who read a newspaper from one year's end to the other). But gradually their charm and good nature wore down his resistance. He recognized ruefully bourgeois upbringing or superficial sophistication behind his own criticism. He never got round to substituting his Klees for the photographs of Rugger teams and First Communicants in his room. He began by patronizing the Mallorys; he ended by admiring them.

On that first evening, however, such considered judgements were out of the question, and he was content to sit back and observe the tide of humanity that seeped in and finally flooded the small room as the alarum clock on the mantelpiece ticked tinnily on into the evening. One after another the members of the family were greeted, introduced, put in their place, fed. Monica and Lucy, twin girls of twelve, with short spiky plaits, battered at the door, toiled wearily into the kitchen, and allowed their satchels to slump on to the lino.

'Pick them up,' ordered Mrs Mallory from the scullery, 'and take them into the hall.'

Subdued by Mark's presence, they obeyed her. But shyness soon thawed, and they began to blurt out incomprehensible accounts of an insane French mistress. Mrs Mallory snorted incredulity.

'But she *did*, Mummy!'

'It was *awful*!'

Patricia padded into the room, smiled wanly, reached for the aspirins on the mantelpiece, and squátted by the stove, which was not alight. Mrs Mallory expatiated on her absent children, James the priest, the eldest daughter Christine, a nurse, Robert the next eldest son, a National Serviceman in the artillery, who was due to go to a teacher's training college when he was released. Gradually Mark was piecing the family together. Patrick blundered in, dumped his ravaged attaché case on the floor, ignored his mother's rebuke, eyed

Mark suspiciously, and applied himself to tea. Mr Mallory, moving, despite his evident exhaustion, with the grace that characterized all his actions, stole almost unnoticed into the room, and threaded his way across it towards a high-backed leather arm-chair in the far corner, with the air of a ship-wrecked man who has gambled his last shred of energy on a desperate attempt to reach a raft. Having achieved his refuge, Mr Mallory sighed happily, and, taking a cup of tea from his wife, consented to give audience.

'Tom. This is Mark Underwood. He came about the room.'

'How d'you do, Mark,' said Mr Mallory, nodding pleasantly over his tea-cup.

'I'd like to take it, Mr Mallory, if that's all right by you,' said Mark.

'Certainly. If my wife's agreeable.'

'Grand. Then that's settled,' pronounced Mrs Mallory.

'And how are you two?' inquired Mr Mallory, tugging the plaits of his twin daughters, who squatted beneath his knees.

'Owwweeer!' screamed Monica.

'Eeeeeowwww!' shrieked Lucy.

'Stop that racket at once you little divils,' said their mother.

'It's all right, Mummy,' said Patricia sardonically. 'They read nothing but comics, and now they even talk like comics.'

'Thinks: Patricia is a rat,' said Lucy *sotto voce*.

'All girls are soppy. One makes allowances,' stated Patrick pontifically from the table. 'But you two are the silliest, daftest pair of idiots. . . .' His eloquence dried up, and he bit disgustedly into a slice of bread and jam before continuing. 'I was on their bus the other day, and the way they were fooling around I was ashamed to recognize them.'

'Thinks: Patrick is a rotten sneak,' said Monica.

'What's this about the bus?' demanded Mr Mallory, pulling on Monica's plait.

'Ouch! Well. . . . Gulp! Did you have a nice day at the office, Daddy?'

There was a burst of laughter, in which Mark joined, at this transparent evasion.

And then Clare had come in. She stood at the door for a moment, hesitating until a place was cleared for her, and slowly unbuttoning the navy-blue schoolgirl's raincoat she wore. Her auburn hair, a vivid fragment of her mother's, was scraped back cruelly into a pony's tail; Mark almost felt the strain along her brow. She was dressed and she moved as if impatient of her own beauty. He perceived that hers was a more than ordinary shyness, that she was unused to society; and the way everyone's face lit up at her entry suggested that she was a special favourite, or had recently returned to the family after a long absence.

'I'm sorry I'm late. I've been helping Miss Skinner with the syllabus. You wouldn't think infants would need a syllabus, would you?'

She was introduced to him. The appearance of a personable girl of a suitable age naturally provoked a reflex of ordinary curiosity; but he soon perceived that this was something new, rare and challenging.

After tea, which he was willingly persuaded to share, Mrs Mallory explained that it was the family practice to recite the rosary together. Would he mind . . . ? He begged them to proceed as if he were not there.

They all got down upon their knees, and drew out their beads. Mr Mallory recited the first half of each prayer, and the others repeated it in unison. The experience was uncanny and disturbing. He felt quite alone. Among those kneeling figures his sitting posture seemed awkward and unnatural. Gradually the youngest children began to fidget, and he felt less of an intruder on a perfect act of worship. Indeed the Rosary had always been a monotonous devotion; it was not surprising the children were distracted. Ten *Hail Mary's* to one *Our Father* and one *Glory Be*. In the cosmic league table of his infantile mind this had seemed to settle pretty conclusively the precedence of Our Lady over the Trinity, with God the Father runner-up as he had a whole prayer to himself, and a mention in the *Glory Be*. Perhaps it wasn't so inaccurate an assessment of the Catholic Faith either.

He took advantage of his position to study the girl Clare. She presented a very charming picture—and picture was the word. In contrast to the awkwardness of her entry, there was now a conscious grace in her posture, as if it were part of her prayer. Her body was quite erect, yet without strain, her eyes closed, her hands carefully joined, finger to finger, through which her beads were passed steadily, by some undetectable knack. Altogether she seemed a person used to praying. Her face was as smooth and clean as sand left by the receding tide, a face in which devout concentration had appeared without a trace of self-righteousness. Nevertheless, the warm, full lines of the body, suggested rather than revealed by her unflattering dress, the shapely bosom, full hips and long legs, seemed intended for something better than praying, traditionally the plain girl's substitute for sex.

As the clearing of the tea-things, and the washing-up were being organized by Mrs Mallory, with the reluctant help of the twins, and the other children became absorbed in homework, Mark had an opportunity for a word with Clare.

'You pray a lot, don't you?' he asked.

She blushed, and answered, 'I did once.' Then she blushed more deeply still, and added : 'Well not so much really. Not compared to some people. Why do you ask?'

'You do it very gracefully,' he replied, smiling.

'Do you think that's very important?'

'I suppose it isn't—if you believe in prayer.'

'Don't you then?'

'Unfortunately—no.'

'How funny.'

51

He regretted having turned the conversation on to religion, as it seemed to have come to a full stop. But after a short pause Clare volunteered:

'I was a novice for two years. Perhaps that has something . . .'

'A novice?' he inquired blankly.

'In a convent you know. Before becoming a nun.'

'Oh. And you became one?'

She laughed.

'Of course I didn't. I'm here.'

'Oh I see. Yes, that explains about the praying, doesn't it.' They seemed to be getting on famously.

'Didn't you find it difficult to settle down to ordinary life again?' he inquired.

'Yes, I do,' she answered. He noted the tense. 'Would you like another cup of tea?'

'No, thanks.' Checking the question that rose to his lips as to her motives for leaving the convent, he said:

'I suppose you've gathered that I'm coming to live here?'

'That will be nice.' She blushed violently. 'For you I mean. This is a very nice house.'

'I'm sure I shall be very happy here,' he replied.

The only shadow cast across that first, pleasant evening was a rather grotesque and ominous one—the dog-like facial silhouette of Damien O'Brien, with the sloping lines of his forehead, nose and jaw almost parallel. One could forgive his ugliness—though it was difficult not to be disgusted by the small pale eyes, the rough, scurfy skin, the yellow crowded teeth—if he hadn't been so insufferably oblivious of it himself. His arrival interrupted Mark's tête-à-tête with Clare, and as Mark took his limp, clammy hand, he looked into eyes full of hostility and suspicion. At that moment he was, paradoxically, more certain of Damien's rivalry than of his own attraction to Clare.

'This is Mark . . . ?' Clare began.

'Underwood,' supplied Mark.

'Mark Underwood. He's a student at the London University, and he's coming to live with us. This is Damien O'Brien, Mark, a cousin of ours over from Ireland.'

'I am pleased to make your acquaintance,' said Damien stiffly. There was very little brogue in his voice, and he seemed to have carefully sifted his diction of Irish idiom. His speech was characterized by a queer old-fashioned formality. 'I studied for three years at Maynooth,' he volunteered.

'Maynooth is the largest seminary in Ireland,' explained Clare.

'In the world, Clare,' Damien corrected. Another disappointed religious? The coincidence was odd.

'I called to thank you again for finding me such grand digs,' said Damien to Clare.

'You make too much of it, Damien, really you do,' she demurred.

'Indeed I don't,' replied Damien.

'Indeed he doesn't,' agreed Mrs Mallory, who breezed into the room at that moment, having overheard the conversation from the scullery. 'You see,' she explained to Mark, 'when Damien here got flung out of the seminary by the good fathers . . .'

'Mummy!' exclaimed Clare, laughing.

'Ah go on with you, Damien knows it's only my fun. Well, when he left the seminary so, he comes to London, like they all do, hoping to find the streets paved with gold . . .'

'I did not hope for any such thing, Aunt Elizabeth. But Ireland has no work for her educated sons.' (So we're educated, are we? said Mark to himself.)

'. . . Hoping, as I said, to find the streets paved with gold,' continued Mrs Mallory blithely, 'he found himself something terrible in the way of a room, and th' old woman who kept it swindled him entirely. And when Clare here saw the pitiable state he was in, she hooshed him out of it and put him in some clean, decent lodgings with Mrs Higgins next door here, who's a decent sort of woman, for all her faults.'

'And very grateful I am too,' said Damien, staring at Clare. But she had not looked in his direction. . . .

Mark turned to look at her now. The film was entering a rather brutal phase, and she was pressed back against her seat, her lips slightly parted with revulsion. Yet the screen compelled her attention. Any dramatic or cinematic performance, however crudely executed, seemed to draw from her the same rapt, child-like attention. To her, as to a child, what she saw on the screen was real. However unpleasant or improbable the action, its visible enactment by recognizable human beings urged the truth of what was being presented, and she seemed oblivious of the artificiality of the whole affair, of the cameras and mikes and props just out of sight. Sometimes he envied the primitive intensity of her dramatic experience.

★ ★ ★

The little girl walked into a church and knelt with face upturned to the altar. A shaft of light slanted down upon her face.

Praying for big tits, thought Harry. He stirred restlessly. Too much religion about this picture.

Gradually however, crime asserted itself. A smile slowly appeared in Harry's face, and spread like a crack running through dry earth. This was the gear. The gang running the racket had slugged the soft vicar bloke and tied him up, and now they had got the tart who was trying to go straight because of the vicar, and they were torturing her to tell them the combination. Serve her right, the poxy little traitor. A squat, hairy man, known as 'Brute', sucked deeply at his cigarette, and threatened her face with the glowing end. The economy and effectiveness of this torture appealed to

Harry, Unfortunately the tart broke down without being touched, and began to whimper the numbers. The whine of police cars interrupted the scene, and Harry witnessed regretfully the capture of the crooks—not effected without some vicious exchanges of fire however. At least two of the police were killed, and the leader of the crooks, who swore he wouldn't be taken alive. Not a bad film in the end. Not bad at all. Harry winced as the lights went up.

The audience stirred uneasily in the sudden light, yawning, blinking, looking up and around for something to fix their gaze on. The abrupt abstraction of their entertainment left them for a moment baffled and resentful, though impotent. Then to their evident relief, a record boomed out. *'Love is a many-splendoured thing,'* sang a vowel-murdering voice to the accompaniment of a quasi-heavenly choir.

> *It's the April Rose*
> *That only grows*
> *In the early spring.*

People whistled it, hummed it, tapped their feet to it. Shades of Francis Thompson, thought Mark:

> *The angels keep their ancient places;—*
> *Turn but a stone and start a wing!*
> *'Tis ye, 'tis your estranged faces,*
> *That miss the many-splendoured thing.*

Bridget's heart swelled with the soaring and swooping notes of the melody. It was so beautiful. She closed her eyes and let herself float on its cadences, as if she was being rocked by the motion of the sea. She longed with love for Len. 'Isn't it lovely Len?' she murmured.

Len was a bit puzzled by the 'many-splendoured thing'. He

wasn't quite sure what it was. But he liked the song on the whole. The tune had a sort of lilt to it, and the words were simple, apart from that first line.

The golden crown
That makes a man a king.

He would have died before saying it, but he did feel like a king when he was out with Bridget, so pretty and smiling and adoring.

They were playing Laurie Lansdowne's record of *Love Is A Many-Splendoured Thing* again. Doreen listened through to the end, singing the words lightly under her breath. She never got tired of hearing it. There was that parcel from his Fan Club to be opened when she got home.

'Let me out Len,' whispered Bridget, as the record ended. 'I must see a friend.'
   'Right,' he replied gruffly, and stood up to let her pass. 'Like an ice-cream?'
   'Mm. Lovely.'
   'What kind?'
   She hesitated.
   'What's flavour of the month?'
   'Banana, I think.'
   'Banana, then.'
   On the screen the management appealed to patrons not to leave their seats. The sales attendants would visit all parts of the cinema. Nevertheless two queues were already forming in front of the two ice-cream girls down at the front. If he didn't go now they might run out of banana. Though someone might pinch their seats if he left them. After some moments' deliberation, Len laid his coat across the seats and, glancing warily over his shoulder from time to time, walked rapidly down the aisle to join the queue. As a precaution he

carried Bridget's handbag with him, though he felt rather a fool with it. He held it by one corner, so that no one would think it belonged to him. Still, anyone might think he was paying for the ice-creams with Bridget's money. Altogether he was glad to be back safely in his place, balancing a banana ice on each knee, waiting for Bridget to come back before he started. Meanwhile he gazed stolidly at the advertisements for local shops, cafés, hairdressing *salons*, that were whisked on and off the screen.

In the passage Bridget collided with a black-suited youth, who swore rudely, and swung into the Gents without apologizing.

'*Well!*' muttered Bridget to herself, rubbing her arm. 'The nerve. Lucky for him Len didn't see.'

Squatting gingerly on the cold seat she dwelt with pleasure on the protection Len's hard muscles afforded, the lovely helpless feeling when he took you in his arms.

Harry pissed savagely into the wall behind her back. Seeing a block of camphor in the channel by his feet he directed his urine at it like a hose, but succeeded only in spattering his suède shoes. He buttoned his flies slowly, studying the pencilled drawings on the peeling distemper, and the words he didn't have to spell out laboriously to understand. Yes, that was what he'd like to do to that curly-haired little tart. It was what she needed. It was what they all needed. Take the cockiness out of them. Tarts. Harry combed his long, oiled hair with care, and adjusted his mouth in the mirror to a thin-lipped, contemptuous smile.

★　★　★

'*Coming next week!*' Into the passive audience a portentous voice pumped monotonous imperatives and superlatives: '*You will thrill as never before . . . you will laugh as never before . . . you will cry as never before.'* Rapidly the trailer ran through the gamut of cinematic experience: ADVENTURE: horse-riders galloped pointlessly through a copse. PASSION: a girl sagged back in a man's arms as he kissed her wetly. SUSPENSE: tense, unintelligible scraps of dialogue were exchanged. AGONY: a woman awaited the result of an operation on her lover. LAUGHTER: the comic relief fell backwards into a pool. *Coming next week.* Could it not be averted? No, it was coming, coming next week.

Mark glanced at the people around him. Now and again, the brightness of the screen illuminated their torpid countenances: torpid, yet with a vague, undefined yearning in them. Like fish in a glass tank, their stupid, gaping faces were pressed to the window on a world they could never hope to achieve, where giant brown men stalked among big-breasted women, and where all events kindly conspired to throw the one into the arms of the other. The hysterical affirmations of the trailer's commentary rolled easily off each person's saturated consciousness; yet perhaps only the assurance of this window on the ideal world, on the superlife, made the waking nightmare of their daily lives tolerable. It was in a way a substitute for religion—and indeed a fabulously furnished pent-house, and the favours of awesomely shaped women, offered a more satisfactory conception of paradise than the sexless and colourless Christian promise—the questionable rapture of being one among billions of court-flatterers.

On the other hand, there were religious people among the audience. Mr and Mrs Mallory for instance. What was the cinema to them? Perhaps just an opportunity to let someone else take over the burden of living for a few hours. But life didn't appear to oppress them. He gave it up.

But himself and Clare—why were they here? When they might be doing something significant. He tried to think of something 'significant' they might conceivably do together.

58

Art? His mind seemed to have temporarily borrowed the technique of the trailer. He saw himself scribbling furiously in the early hours of the morning. Pouring out his inspiration white-hot. But Clare, what was she doing? Brewing the black coffee? Typing the MSS.? Filing the rejection slips? He dismissed the image impatiently.

Significant. Something significant. Making love? In some wild, extreme and instinctive way that would express their contempt for the pantomime endearments of eunuchs and whores offered for their diversion on the screen? He saw himself and Clare spread a mattress on the floor before a roaring fire in a darkened room, and the flickering red light on their naked bodies as he exultantly deflowered her. The image provoked a sharp abdominal reaction, and he was jerked back into reality. The young virgin at his side would not see such an exercise as significant—merely as sinful.

Then, something significant *she* did. He could not think of anything. Except perhaps praying. That was something she did remarkably well, it seemed. But himself? He had gone so far as to attend Mass again after so many years, and, with the help of a book on the subject, found it quite interesting, considered as a liturgical drama. (In fact he had once been able to correct Damien on some obscure historical point concerning the Kiss of Peace, which had been worth the total effort.) He had, in a way, come to respect religion—but to commit himself to the extent of personal prayer? No. 'What is prayer?' he had asked Clare. 'The lifting up of the mind and heart to God,' she had replied. He remembered that much from the catechism. Lift oneself up to someone who wasn't there, in case He was? He would rather look a knave than a fool on the other side of death, rather depart into everlasting fire (where, according to Shaw, the company was so amusing) than redden under the mocking laughter of Chaos and Old Night, those two cosmic wide-boys to whom religion was a huge practical joke for tricking a man out of his fair share of lust and selfishness. 'You really fell for all that stuff about heaven and hell . . . ? Well, there's one born every day. . . .'

Perhaps that was why he and Clare were sitting here, because they could agree on no common activity. It seemed an awful waste. And it raised again the puzzling question of why Clare should be necessary to his contentment. His arm was beginning to ache, and he withdrew it from her shoulders.

Why had he taken his arm away? Had she not done something she should have done? Had she rebuffed him by some unconscious lapse in the strange new etiquette of . . . She was always at a loss to define her relationship with Mark in words that would not either overstate or understate the reality. Love? The mere word made her blush—(this hateful blushing!)—despite her ignorance of what it might mean. Friendship? Even she knew it was more than that, or entirely different. Affection? She was not his aunt. With a certain guilty and timid pleasure she was forced back on 'love'. But what was it? Fragments of fifth-form Tennyson and Bridges tangled absurdly in her mind with 'The Purposes of Christian Marriage' expounded by a blue-faced priest at a recent mission sermon in Brickley. Neither seemed remotely connected with what she was experiencing at present—the strange traffic of hours of worry and misery for an occasional moment's happiness, the need to be with him all the time, and the need to disguise that need, the constant embarrassment of not knowing whether she was being too forward or too cold, whether she was welcoming occasions of sin, or, as Mark had hinted more than once, dragging the convent watchfulness into ordinary life, where it strangled innocent pleasure.

She still remembered vividly that when she was in her last year at the convent as a pupil, she and another girl who intended to take the veil had been skilfully abstracted from a particular R.I. lesson given by Sister Anthony, a grimly efficient nun who was generally given the unpleasant jobs, like dealing with the occasional boarder who smelled. She had been immensely curious as to the content of that lesson, but too proud to ask. It never failed to arouse giggles when mentioned, and the sophisticated Christina Lloyd had referred to it as 'How *not* to make friends and influence people'. She was convinced that the solutions to all her doubts and difficulties lay in the lesson which had been denied to her. Her exclusion still rankled: why shouldn't a novice know about such things?

She had read books of course: pamphlets snatched hurriedly from a rack in some dim corner of a church, with titles like *Growing Up*, and *Holy Purity*, but they were all equally unhelpful. 'A good Catholic boy or girl should not indulge in passionate kissing' they said. But what *was* passionate kissing? She wanted to know if Mark should put his arms right round her, if their bodies should touch, and for precisely how long they should kiss. Not that she thought of such things when he kissed her good night, but afterwards she was always troubled by scruples of conscience. She couldn't bring herself to ask a priest in confession. That was bad. But she was too shy. Or was it that she was afraid the priest would say she had been doing wrong, that she must retrace her steps, deny Mark the intimacy she had so far allowed him—which, she was only too well aware, would be to deny herself. Perhaps, having known him for such a short time, she should never have allowed him to kiss her at all. She just didn't know. After all, she had known him for such a short time.

She remembered the first evening so clearly, when she had returned home, fagged from working late at the school, to find Mark seated among the family like some lean, brown prophet from out of the desert. Was she foolish and vain in thinking that his dark eyes had flickered with a special interest when she was introduced to him, and that every time she looked at him that evening she looked straight into their thoughtful depths? Fortunately the blushes that followed inevitably on these glances were unnoticed in the babble and hilarity of the family circle. And how irritating Damien had been that evening. He had never stopped harping on that wretched room she had found for him. Why was it that whenever you did someone a good turn, they entwined you with their tentacles, and most unfairly made their debt a kind of claim on your attention and friendship? It always seemed to have been her eagerness to do good that led her into trouble. That, after all, had been the cause of her leaving the convent under a cloud. She had only tried to be kind to Hilda Syms. . . .

The painful memory scuttled towards her like a spider out of a dark corner. She squashed it with a slight shudder, and concentrated deliberately on the screen, which was showing the credit titles of the main film of the evening.

★ ★ ★

Father Kipling was beginning to worry. He had been in the cinema for over an hour now, and still *Song of Bernadette* had made no appearance. As the lights dimmed his hopes rose again. But no. *While The Cat's Away* was announced as being considered more suitable for adult audiences. Perhaps it was another short film however. The curtains on the stage drew back to reveal a wide, slightly concave screen on which, heralded by a frightful squeal from some invisible jazz-band, appeared the mysterious words 'AMBER LUSH'. Not till they were followed by 'And LEN GESTE' in *While The Cat's Away* did he suspect that Amber Lush might be someone's name. 'I baptize thee Amber Lush.' Frightful thought!

There followed in rapid succession a series of strange, uncouth names—Mo Schnieder, Xerses Smith, Fritz Pitz,

Lulu Angel—connected with equally bizzare functions: continuity, lyrics, additional dialogue. Finally it was announced that Color was by Technicolor, whoever, or whatever, that might be. He had always thought colour was by Almighty God.

The first scene represented a luxurious room overlooking —was it not Brooklyn Bridge? He seemed to recollect having seen it before in a geographical periodical. One could not but be impressed by the magnificence of the scene, the wonderful panorama of the river. The room itself, though ugly and strident in appearance, was richly furnished with deep-piled carpets, broad, low sofas like beds, and gadgets with unimaginable functions cunningly disposed around its broad area. In the far corner, beside a kind of highly polished bar littered with bottles, a man sat slumped in an arm-chair, clinking lumps of ice in a large glass of some pale yellow liquid. He was in his shirt-sleeves, with the collar undone and the tie loosened in a rather slovenly manner. He seemed to be of an artificially preserved middle age, and wore an expression of comical gloom.

'This,' said a choric voice, '*is a portrait of a man whose wife has gone home to Mother.*'

An appreciative chuckle rippled through the audience. They evidently perceived some joke unrecognized by himself.

'*It all started over such a little thing,*' continued the voice. '*Just because he didn't like his wife's new hat. After all, it wasn't such an awful hat. Or was it?*'

The scene melted into a picture of a really execrable hat— a kind of inverted lampshade decorated with seaweed. This time Father Kipling laughed with the rest of the audience. Very cleverly the picture was lowered to take in the wearer's face—an angry, rather hard-faced woman. She was having a furious argument with the man seen earlier, now dressed in a light-coloured suit. Suddenly it flashed upon Father Kipling that this was happening in the past. He felt quite pleased with his perspicacity, and wondered if everyone else around him had understood.

'If that's all you think of me,' said the woman, 'I might as well go home to Mother.'

'Well, why don't you. Try yelling at her for a change,' replied her husband crossly. A smile lit up his face. 'That I would like to see.'

'All right then, if that's how you want it. And I'm taking the children and Betsy Ann with me.'

'Take anything you like. Take the icebox, take the television, take . . . take the bed!'

With fascination and amusement Father Kipling followed the rapid preparations for departure. A cheerful-looking negro servant (evidently Betsy Ann) said to her mistress: 'Sure Massa Kennedy will starve without us ma'am; why, he can't look after hisself no more than a baby.'

'Exactly,' replied Mrs Kennedy. 'That's why I expect to have a long-distance call to Mother's tomorrow morning. Perhaps this will teach him to appreciate his wife.'

Now the film was faded back to the future—or was it the present? Goodness, he was getting quite confused. Anyway the man, now back in shirt-sleeves, slapped his thigh and stated emphatically:

'No woman's gonna get the better of me.'

He consulted a telephone directory, gargantuan like everything else in the room, and lifting the receiver snapped, 'Get me the Ajax Home Help Service. Zero Two Double-Four Six.'

'Enter Amber,' prophesied Mark silently. Sure enough, it was the world-famed yellow hair, pouting underlip and undulating body, coaxed into a dress three sizes too small, that stepped from the elevator and advanced hippily towards the door of Len Geste's apartment. The latter's astonishment on opening the door and identifying the vision as his 'home help' contrived to be funny despite its predictability. And this, he knew, would be true of the whole film, the course of which he could anticipate in every detail. Yet it would all be so professionally done, it would all cater so efficiently for the lowest and laziest responses, that he would enjoy it as uncritically as any of those around him, who knew of nothing better.

He censored the undergraduate arrogance of this last thought as soon as it formed. He was no longer sure that there *was* anything better to know. His mind shrank nowadays from exposure to those gloomy, clumsily executed foreign film 'classics', those pathetically dedicated productions of esoteric poetic dramas on which his fellow-students expended their enthusiasm and energy. He was getting to the stage where the unambiguous sexual appeal of an Amber Lush seemed more honest and significant than the pretentious obscurities of the cultural establishment.

In the Mallorys he felt he had rediscovered the people. The phrase smacked somewhat of 'Thirties affectation, but there was no other way of stating the fact. And it was a fact. But the popular art he looked for to accompany this rediscovery was sadly lacking. What he was witnessing was a fair sample of popular entertainment, and it was quite artificial and valueless: a circus cynically provided for the bread-filled masses by big business. Surely there must be an alternative? Something solid, earthy. . . . But what could be more solid, more earthy than that? he reflected, as Amber, lifting a leg to examine a stocking, tensed her skirt over one of her famed buttocks.

What a delightful girl, thought Mr Mallory, slumped comfortably in his seat, with his legs in the aisle. Voluptuous, yes; like ripe fruit waiting to be plucked and squeezed—but *waiting*, innocent. Yes, innocent. Never mind if she had been married three times, to him she was still innocent. He would think no evil of that round, babyish face, haloed with a poignant silliness. Lord, but these girls were bad for a man. They were beautiful, much too beautiful. They made him unhappy, discontented. Look at those magnificent breasts, how they jutted out as if eager to escape the constriction of clothing, and how they swept in sharply to a firm, flat diaphragm, how the curve of her rump bit deeply into her thigh as she lifted a leg . . . how could a man see all this, and then go home and caress sincerely the undramatic slopes of his good wife? It would be like the South Downs after the Pyrénées.

Through a haze of growing drowsiness, Mrs Mallory disapproved of these exaggerated figures you saw everywhere nowadays on the films and in the papers. It wasn't good for the children, especially Patrick and Patricia, growing up. Perhaps she shouldn't have let them go and see it, but what could you do, there would have been a terrible row with Patricia that would have done more harm than good. What a beautiful room though, no cleaning to speak of, everything smooth and fitted, not that she liked the style much, didn't have much time for this contemporary, though Patricia was always on at her to paint the walls in the living room different colours, wasn't homely enough for her taste. The film was a lot of rubbish as usual, a waste of money, but Tom would insist on going every Saturday night, he was such a fanatic for a fixed routine, and if once she let him go on his own, well, there was no knowing where it would end. Though she was so tired after that shopping, and having to wait twenty minutes for a bus and then stand, wished she had given that conductor a piece of her mind, that she could have done with an early night. What Mass tomorrow? Better go to eight as usual to have breakfast ready for the others back from nine, must remember to set alarm clock or is it. . . . With the index finger of her right hand just touching the small lump on her left breast, Mrs Mallory dozed.

Father Kipling was shocked to find himself studying closely

the very striking golden-haired young woman as she lifted her leg. Really, this was too bad. This Jezebel was of a most disquieting physique, and she was exploiting its disturbing properties by every gesture and art of dress. He was saddened by the presence of so many young people in the cinema, even some of his own parishioners—had he not seen two of the Mallory children when the lights were on? Surely this was to expose them to the influence of Satan, always tireless in leading young souls into sins of the flesh. And when was *Bernadette* going to appear? Reluctantly he resolved to interrogate the stout woman on his left.

'Excuse me, madam . . .' he began in a whisper; but stopped, as she continued to gaze raptly at the screen, guffawing from time to time. He touched her arm, and she started indignantly.

'Excusememadam,' he gabbled, 'but could you tell me if *Song of Bernadette* is being shown tonight?'

'Not as far as I know, mate,' she answered cheerfully, 'Amber Lush film tonight i'n it?'

The woman with the whining child in front of him turned in her seat, and said:

'*Song of Bernadette's* on tomorrow, Sunday.'

There were several irritated 'Shh's' around them.

'Thank you, madam,' hissed Father Kipling, sinking back into his seat.

So that was it. How very trying. After all the expense, inconvenience, embarrassment, to have missed the film he had expressly come to see. How had he contrived to muddle the dates? He felt the incongruity, nay more, the unseemliness of his situation, more keenly than ever, now his one pretext for being in the cinema was removed. There was no reason why he should continue any longer to witness this unsavoury performance. Now, for instance, she seemed about to undress—well really! Good gracious, she *was* undressing! But this was disgraceful. Why one could almost see her. . . . He could swear he could see her. . . .

Behind his spectacles, Father Kipling strained his eyes to see if he could see her. . . .

With envy and with cold lust Harry watched the antics of Amber Lush. He slipped from his pocket a slim flick-knife. Amber unzipped the front of her dress and stepped out of it. Harry applied his thumb to a stud, and a blade shot out of the handle. Amber moved behind a screen, and began tossing her underclothes over the top. A brassière flew out of the door, and landed on the head of Len Geste, sitting in the next room. Harry cackled. A pair of rank, sweaty tit-holders on his head. Slipping the point of his knife under the upholstery, Harry made a long slit in the seat between his legs. Amber now emerged from behind the screen in a carelessly tied négligée. As she bent forward to pick up a slipper she paused, and the cameras lingered on her drooping breasts. Harry swallowed, and his spit was like bile in his throat. He wanted a tart like that and a car like that and a swank apartment like that, Christ, how he wanted them. He pushed his hand through the slit and grabbed a handful of Amber's sorbo tits. Savagely he tore out a great lump and kneaded it between his fingers.

Clare frowned. Surely all this was rather unnecessary? It was certainly embarrassing. Not for the first time she felt glad of the protective darkness of the cinema. Surely this woman was not considered beautiful? Her figure was too . . . well, big. She had always been embarrassed by her own tendency to plumpness, and had welcomed the enveloping folds of the nun's habit. Even now, when she was free to try and make herself attractive, she counted her full bust and rather prominent seat embarrassments rather than assets. Yet this woman, in whom the same features appeared, grossly exaggerated, seemed deliberately to draw attention to them, and, to judge by the vulgar whistles from one section of the audience, was considered attractive. What did Mark think?

Amber's vital statistics were 38–22–38, and Mark thought of the contemporary cult of the bust, and what it might signify. Of course the female breast was 'vital' in a more than journalistic sense—it was the fountain of nourishment, of life itself. Blessed are the paps that gave thee suck. But child-bearing was not in favour nowadays. Amber herself had enjoyed three totally contraceptive marriages. Was the attraction sheerly erotic? Yet the dimensions of some of these film-stars might seriously incommode the performance of the sexual act. Mere size was not sufficient. It had to be combined with a small waist measurement, and balanced by a hip measurement, as near as possible, equal to the bust measurement. In the difference between the identical first and third vital statistics and the second, there resided a mystical erotic tension. In classical times the tension was aesthetic. According to the Greek sculptors, ideally the distance between the nipples, between the lower breast and the navel, and between the navel and the division of the legs, should be exactly the same. But today the Venus de Milo wouldn't make the front page of *Reveille* if she was dressed up in a bikini. The bust survives the city. Would Amber's pneumatic charms, protruding from some faded and flickering revival in A.D. 2000, survive Holly-wood?

★ ★ ★

'Come on Patrick. This is where we came in.'

Patricia tugged at her brother's sleeve. Receiving no response, she pinched his arm.

'Ouch! Brute.'

'Are you coming?'

'No.'

'I'll tell Mummy.'

'Tell her.'

'Why won't you come and do as you're told?'

'I want to see the film.'

'You've seen it once.'

'So what?'

'Mummy said we were to be in by nine.'

'She did not, she said half past nine and it's only ten to nine now.'

'Well I'm going.'

'All right.'

Really he was the most exasperating boy. Well, she had a headache, and had to wash her hair—why should she wait until he was sated, which wouldn't be till the National Anthem was played if she knew Patrick. The discovery that he could see a film as many times as he liked for the same price as one time had rather turned his head, and he sat doggedly through the most boring films until he was forcibly removed from the cinema. Well she wasn't going to get worked up about it. Let him stay. She would be blamed for it, naturally, but never mind.

'For the last time, Patrick, are you coming?'

No answer. As soon as she left her seat and turned her back on the screen, she regretted her move. Depression and worry seeped under the exit door, and trickled down the aisle to meet her. Once she had pushed through the swing doors she was swamped. Immediately, the awful flat feeling you always got after the cinema enveloped her. Suddenly you became aware of what a false, worthless film it had been, and that the same old life was at home waiting to be lived.

★　★　★

'Kiss me, Len,' whispered Bridget. Obediently he bent his head and kissed her lightly.

'What's the matter, Len?' she asked, dissatisfied. He couldn't deceive her. A kiss was as precise as any instrument he used on the bench at work. He fended her off mechanically.

'Nothing, dear. Why?'

Bridget was silent. She let her head fall back on his shoulder, and squeezed his hand tightly. This he recognized as no loving pressure, but a desperate clutch at departing happiness. His own happiness had slipped away when he first glanced at the illuminated clock on the cinema wall, which had the letters THE PALLADIUM arranged in a circle instead of numbers. It had been half past D then; now it was M to I.

He was worried about seeing her home, about *not* being able to see her home. Every time they went out he worried about not being able to see her home, and every time it spoiled his evening almost before he had begun to enjoy it. He would have cheerfully walked home for Bridget's sake, but if he was late in, Ma was bound to have an attack, just out of spite. Still, the fact remained that he *could* see her home, and hang the consequences. Perhaps that was what nagged at him. If it had been utterly out of the question, he would feel easier in mind. As it was, he had to make the same difficult decision again and again. Bridget hated it as much as he did—more, probably, as she had to walk home through the dark streets, and she got frightened easily— but somehow she seemed to be able not to think about it, until the actual moment of separation arrived, and then she was nearly in tears. That made him feel terrible. It wasn't fair really—he felt that she should be like him, and let the misery of parting into her mind by degrees, so that it wasn't so crushing when the moment came. As it was, she wanted to be happy when he was miserable, and then she broke down just when he had steeled himself to withstand the separation.

But there was one appalling separation yawning up before

71

them, which even he could not bring himself to consider calmly: National Service. Instead of getting better, things were going to get worse. When, O when, were they going to get married? He couldn't save, let alone support a wife on his apprentice's wages. Army pay was even less. They were both determined to start off properly—no furnished bed-sitting room for them, and turned out as soon as a baby arrived. Bridget wanted a family, and so did he. Neither, money apart, did he want to get married while he was in the army. It didn't need much imagination to realize what it must be like to live from one leave to the next. If it was agony saying good night to Bridget now, when he could see her the next day, what would it be like to say good-bye and not see each other for a week, a month, a *year*? There was Bill Baker, who used to work at the next bench: went into the army, got married on his embarkation leave. Now he wrote to the boys in the workshop about the brothels in Hong Kong ('It's one bloody great brothel', he had said in his last letter), while his wife was, by all accounts, the easiest pick-up any night of the week at the Bayditch Palais.

Bridget would never become an easy pick-up. But you could understand a bloke who went to a brothel when he was 10,000 miles away from his wife. He couldn't swear that he wouldn't himself, though he had never had a girl in his life. And if you didn't blame the bloke, could you blame the girl? It wasn't their fault. It was those who sent him away. What right had they? What *right*?

Len fretted under an impotent sense of injustice. The mood passed rapidly, leaving him tired and miserable. He knew he didn't really care about anyone else. He didn't care if Bill Baker caught the pox and his wife ended up under the Bayditch railway bridge with the lowest women in the neighbourhood. They could all go to hell if only he could stay with Bridget.

Sometimes he wished they hadn't met so young. If some-

72

how he were offered a miracle by which his memory of Bridget could be wiped out, and he would meet her and fall in love with her again in five years' time, he would have accepted it.

★ ★ ★

The tide was on the turn now. Slowly the customers were beginning to ebb away. For Doreen the evening's work was almost over. Her feet throbbed, and the backs of her knees ached, but, mindful of the magazine article 'Graceful You', which she had read that morning, she stood erect, a foot from the back wall of the cinema, her weight evenly distributed between her feet. By the central exit, the other girls slumped and sagged against the wall, whispering. Occasionally a coarse laugh rose above the whispers, a laugh she was intended to hear. Because of that day off she had had last week. Now they sneered every time Mr Berkley spoke to her. Well let them, the cats. Just jealous they were, mostly married they were, and knew they didn't stand a chance. Not that Mr Berkley had done anything or said. . . . But he was nice. A bit old. But very nice.

People were going now, the rows were thinning out, and the laughter was patchy. Every now and then there was a muffled clatter of seats tipping up, half a row would heave to their feet, clasping coats to their laps, and allow a few people to stumble into the aisle. Leaning against the slope these would toil slowly towards the exit, pausing at intervals to look over their shoulders, in case they were missing anything; and when they got to the back of the cinema, they would linger over putting on their coats, stealing glances at the screen. Silly fools. Why didn't they stay in their seats?

What a gorgeous apartment it was in the picture. Just Amber's luck to stumble on a job like that. Think of having that bathroom all to yourself, hot water galore and a thing

73

for showers if you wanted one. Everything warm and clean and white.

★ ★ ★

Patrick was bored with the film. He waited impatiently for the really funny bits to come round again. There weren't nearly enough. The grown-ups seemed to find it funny, but he couldn't see the point of the jokes.

The person next to him stood up and pushed out. A man moved up from a few seats away, and sat down next to him. Pity Patricia had gone off in a huff so early; he could probably have been persuaded to leave *now*. Couldn't go yet, of course, after that row.

Suddenly he felt a hand on his leg, and the unexpected contact sent fear pulsing through his body. It was as if frightened messengers were running helplessly between his leg and his brain—'It's someone touching me!'—'Someone touching me?'—'Yes, it's someone touching me.' It was the man who had moved up and sat next to him. His heart pounded. He must be a pickpocket. What should he do? Shout for help? Either he would be murdered immediately, or the man would protest that he had done nothing. He *hadn't* done anything—perhaps he didn't know that his hand was there. He tried to imagine how silly it would be if the man didn't know his hand was there. But he knew the ·man did know. He didn't dare turn his head to look. It became terribly important that he should disguise his own knowledge. He laughed emptily at a joke in the picture. The man beside him laughed too, and that frightened him more than anything. He didn't move—just kept his hand there. O God, please help. This was to punish him for being naughty to Patricia. Please, God, and I'll do anything You like.

With a tremendous effort Patrick stood up and fled from the cinema.

★ ★ ★

'You look tired, Miss Higgins.'

'Saturday night's always a bit of a rush, Mr Berkley,' replied Doreen, trying to ignore the ill-concealed interest of the exit-cluster.

'Well, you can have a good lie-in tomorrow morning,' he answered. 'You might as well go now.'

'Thank you, sir, but it's my turn to see the customers out tonight.' There was no point in aggravating the other girls.

'Never you mind; I'll see to that, Miss Higgins. You run along home.'

Doreen left. There was no point in aggravating Mr Berkley, either.

Mr Berkley glowed with the appreciation of his own magnanimity. Miss Higgins deserved a little kindness. She took her job with exemplary seriousness. Trim little figure too. . . .

Mr Berkley moved on to the group of usherettes by the main exit. They became sullenly silent at his approach.

'Mrs Bertram, I have asked you before not to wear that jersey under your tunic.'

'I can't 'elp it, it's me chest.'

'I don't see how it can be necessary in a warm place like this. I must insist that you wear a blouse like the other ladies. Now will you all please draw back the curtains in front of the exits.'

He passed on. Muffled insults thudded into his back. He leaned over the back row of the stalls, and gloomily watched the closing scenes of the film. Beneath him interlocked couples writhed in their awkward embraces. Why on earth did they bother to come to the cinema? The seats were ill-adapted to love-making. Perhaps they had nowhere else to go. The cinema was a kind of low-voltage brothel for half its customers, and an ice-cream parlour with entertainment for the other half.

The film faded out on a scene of universal and improbable felicity. As soon as it became evident that this was the end, there was the usual frenzied stampede to avoid the Queen. Three minutes after the lights came on, there were only a few stragglers by the doors, and the inevitable woman, who had lost her scarf, poking about under her seat.

Mark and Clare shuffled out with the yawning, patient crowd, urged on like cattle by attendants anxious to get home. Suddenly Mark found himself suffocated by an enormous depression, which closed over him like tons of cotton wool. Grimly he resisted the urge to fight his way out, to scream and thresh and tear his way into the open air. It wasn't just claustrophobia, though no doubt that had something to do with it. It was difficult to describe or diagnose these fits, to which he was periodically subject. Holding out Clare's coat for her to slip on, nudged and bumped by the struggling crowd, he wanted to put up his face and howl. He felt he was a prisoner inside his own body, which was compelled to act exactly like the rest of the crowd, to go through the same motions as these dumb, patient beasts, holding out a coat, queuing for a bus, boarding it, twisting in his seat to capture the change from his trouser pocket, asking for two fares to Ringwood Road. The fact that he would have to say 'Two to Ringwood Road, please', or, rather, the foreknowledge that he would have to say it, seemed suddenly intolerable.

'How 'bout walking?' he said to Clare, as they pushed mercifully out on to the cold pavement.

'It's rather a long way, isn't it, Mark?'

'Look at queue,' he articulated with difficulty, nodding in the direction of the bus stop. The words were like felt in his mouth.

'All right then. If you want to.'

He set off with a long fast pace, hands clenched in the pockets of his duffle-coat. Clare hurried along beside, and a little behind him. Sometimes he would pause and wait impatiently for her to catch up. They walked in silence, threading the dull, chill streets. Wisps of fog clutched at her throat and made her cough. She was cold in her short jacket and thin blouse. She was puzzled and unhappy and a little frightened.

As they left the main road and began to climb up High Hill, Mark's steps became slower and more plodding. At the top of the hill, he sank down on a wooden seat of neglected appearance, inscribed 'Traveller's Rest'.

'Sit down,' he said.

Clare hesitated, looking at the wet, dirty surface of the seat with disfavour, conscious of the oddity of sitting in the damp, cold darkness at the side of a London street. Mark stared bleakly before him. Then he looked up at her, and something like human recognition flickered in his eyes.

'Sorry,' he said, smiling wearily. 'Here, sit down.'

He spread his handkerchief on the bench, and she sat down.

'Sorry to be like this,' he apologized, taking out a cigarette. She didn't like it if he smoked when they were alone. Somehow it meant that he didn't want to be touched, or to touch her. It kept her at bay. She sat uncomfortably erect on the seat, holding her back away from the wet grimy wood.

The seat was placed at a cross-roads that scored High Hill like a hot cross bun. From it you looked directly down the hill to the London plain. It was one of the highest of the first hills that ringed London, and on a fine day you could see the whole city, right to Highgate in the north, spread out before you in a smoking, shimmering expanse of buildings, punctuated here and there by the splayed fingers of river-side cranes, and great buildings like St Paul's and their own cathedral. She knew the landmarks well: when the younger children were babies she had often pushed the pram up to the top of the hill and—the memory came back to her suddenly—she had often sat looking out from this same seat. At night it was a glittering mass of lights, as if some great hand had flung down a fistful of stars. Tonight, however, the panorama was veiled by fog, hanging densely over the river, and slowly creeping through the low-lying streets. But Clare did not miss the view. The mournful lowing of the fog-horns, and the muffled, lonely rattle of a suburban train, which were the only sounds that carried to her ears, seemed sufficiently appropriate to her mood.

'Then why . . .' She stopped.

'Why what?'

'Why be like this, Mark?'

'I don't know. I just get these moods. I feel so fed up at the moment.'

'Have you had another story sent back.'

'You've guessed it.'

'I'm sorry, Mark. It's a shame. I think your stories are awfully good. I know . . .'

'For God's sake don't.'

There was a silence, and then he must have heard her catch her breath.

'Oh Christ. I'm sorry, Clare. Look, I didn't mean to be rough. Here, borrow my handkerchief. Oh blast, you're sitting on it.' He put an arm round her and she smiled feebly.

'It's all right. I'm silly.'

'No you're not. But look, it's like this: I think my stories are good, and you think my stories are good. And all my friends think my stories are good. Now that's fine, but it's all completely beside the point. Because someone in an office miles away, who doesn't know me from Adam, whose only interest in my stories is to decide whether people will read them, he doesn't think my stories are good Now he may be soulless and mercenary and semi-illiterate, but I've got to admit that he is the least biased of all of us; and that's what stings. I suppose I can't face facts. I've got all the ambition, but no talent.'

There was another long pause, as Clare searched desperately for some comforting word that would bear exposure to his present mood.

'Mark . . . if only you had faith . . .' she murmured.

'What kind of faith?'

'Oh, any kind. Faith in yourself. Faith in God.'

'I don't inspire faith in myself. And God can't help me, I'm afraid. My problems aren't religious. I'll try and explain. Look: out there is London; beyond is the world. I can't see it because of the fog. But even if the fog cleared, I wouldn't know what it all meant. Looking out over a city gives me a sort of sick feeling—a sense of the appalling multiplicity of life. I get a sort of dizziness—that helpless feeling you get when you read that a star is ninety million light years from the earth. I think of sewage pulsing through thousands of miles of pipes, of trains crammed with humanity hurtling through the tube, of the people who never stop walking past you on the pavements—such infinite variations of appearance, none of them alike, each with his own obsession, his own disappointment, his own set of values, his own magazine under his arm catering for his own hobby—railway engines or beekeeping. One feels that one wants to gather them all in like a harvest; or stop one, understand him, absorb his identity, and then pass on to the next one— but there's no time, there are too many, and you're swamped.'

He paused for a moment, thinking. Clare sat very still.

'What gets me is that so much of life passes you by, without so much as touching you, and it's beyond recall. Art? It's like being asked to conserve a waterfall in a thimble.

'Listen. As I talk to you now, a conductor is punching a ticket on a 53 bus in the Old Kent Road; down there in Bermondsey a drunken docker is getting into bed with his daughter; in Buenos Aires a beggar spits; in Pittsburgh someone puts a nickel in a juke-box; in a Chinese village they are crucifying a priest to the door of his own church; in a Paris cellar they are staring at a naked dancer; in a Birmingham hospital an old man dies on the operating table; in Germany a soldier shivers on guard; somewhere a boy wets his bed, a woman screams in childbirth, an athlete tears a muscle, a man pencils an obscene drawing on a wall, a poet finds his word; in the Grande Chartreuse a monk prays; in Delhi a legless man drags his torso along the gutter; in Baghdad an Arab scratches his stomach. And so on. And none of us knows or cares about the other. To each, all that matters is his own existence. The world is held in a state of hideous indifference and selfishness—if it weren't I suppose we'd all go mad. But as a writer I feel painfully conscious of this infinite pullulating activity, I feel I must try and fix this multiplicity. If life was like a film which you could stop or slow down at will, you might be able to study it, to find a pattern, a meaning. But you can't. Even as I described them, each little precious atom of individual experience had perished irretrievably, become something else. And there were countless millions of other moments of experience that I didn't have time to mention.'

He stopped suddenly, and looked at her. He laughed.

'D'you think I'm mad?'

'No, Mark.'

'Let's go home.'

'Yes.'

★ ★ ★

Reluctantly they dawdled towards the hated corner where they had to say good night. Len took his arm away to look at his watch. Three minutes left.

80

'D'you have to look again, Len?'

'I'm sorry,' he said, cross and unhappy. He thrust his hands into his coat pockets.

'Len, don't.'

'Don't what?'

She stopped, and looked up at him in dumb misery. Her face was blue under the street-lamps.

'Oh, Len, why does every evening have to end like this?'

'Is it my fault?'

'Of course it isn't. It's no one's fault. But . . . well, what's the use of getting worked up about it?'

'I'm not worked up about it. You're the one who gets worked up.'

'That's because you're . . . like this.'

He knew that she was trying to be good, and brave, and that he was hurting her, but somehow he couldn't help it. Because he wanted to go home with her and stay with her and sleep with her in his arms. And nothing else would do.

'I don't like letting you go home on your own. It worries me. It's not safe around here.'

'I know it's because of me, Len,' she said softly. 'But just be nice to me before you have to go.'

'There's my bus,' he said, looking over her shoulder.

He took her abruptly into his arms, and pressed a kiss on her lips. There was no pleasure in it.

'Good night, Bridget. I love you.'

'I love you too, Len,' she whispered. But he had broken away, and was pounding after the bus. She watched his broad, heavy form thud on to the running-board and climb the stairs. He didn't look back. She watched the bus till it turned the corner.

Across the street she caught sight of someone watching her from a shop doorway. Turning on her heel she began to walk smartly up the hill towards home. As she left the main road, the lights became more feeble and more widely spaced.

She hurried across the great oceans of gloom and rejoiced each time she reached an island of light. Round the throat of each lamp-post there was a scarf of fog. Out of the dank, uncared-for gardens the great gaunt houses towered above her. Why were there always so few lighted windows in this street? A negro suddenly padded out from an alleyway, and she gasped with fright. But he passed on. Not fair really, the way you naturally expected a black man was up to no good. But she couldn't help it. She couldn't like them. She hurried on; the steel tips of her high heels clipped the paving-stones with a lonely sound.

Someone kicked a pebble behind her, and she glanced nervously over her shoulder. A youth. Was he following her? Of course not. Why should he? Yet he looked like the one who had watched her at the street-corner. Couldn't you stop for two seconds on a public street without being thought one of those?

She turned sharply into the dark chasm of Dean Street, glancing casually over her shoulder again. Yes, it was him, and he was crossing the road to follow her. She accelerated her pace almost to a run, and tripped on a projecting paving-stone. Almost crying with vexation and fear, she recovered herself and hobbled on. If only she'd worn flatties that evening. Thank goodness it wasn't far now.

Emerging from the long, blank walls of Dean Street, she took the short cut across the bomb-site as the lesser of two evils, scrunched across the freshly-laid gravel of Barn Street, and almost fell up the steps of number 46. She lost several seconds fumbling for her key in her handbag, then remembered that it was in her overcoat pocket. She let herself in. Before turning on the light in her room she tiptoed to the window and peeped out. A white-faced youth in a dark raincoat slouched past without giving the house a glance. Most likely she had frightened herself for nothing. Nevertheless she was glad to be inside. As she turned back into the room, it seemed a bit spooky, with the dark outlines of the old-fashioned furniture, and the heavy plaster relief on the ceiling which always looked about to fall, faintly illuminated by the glow from the street-lamps outside. She switched on the light and drew the curtains. Then she lit the gas-ring and prepared a cup of cocoa. She began to hum 'Love is a many-splendoured thing', softly, so as not to disturb Old Mother Potts. She sipped her cocoa slowly, giving the hot-water bottle time to warm the bed and toast her pyjamas. She knelt and said her usual prayers: three *Hail Mary's,* an *Our Father,* an *Act of Contrition.* She couldn't go to sleep without having said them; it was the only thing the nuns at the home had taught her which had really stuck. Good job Sister Grizelda didn't know she didn't go to Mass any more. Even at this distance, the thought of her wrath was scaring.

Bridget pulled back the bedclothes, and sat down on the warm place made by the hot-water bottle, which she guided carefully down into the cold depths of the bed with her feet. She turned off the light, and snuggled down, tugging the blankets over her head.

She drowsily reconsidered the film. Pity that Len Geste had been married; Amber had been much nicer than his wife, and it would have been nice if they could have got married. She began to reconstruct the film to her own pleasure, substituting Len for Len Geste—funny they had the same names—and herself for Amber. Of course there wasn't much story if Len wasn't married, but the story didn't matter much anyway. The scenes she lingered over were the kisses, the nice things Len said to her, the wonderful clothes she had, the super flat they had, the kitchen with the gadgets for all kinds of things, and the big low sofas with Len, Oh I'm crazy about you. Oh, darling. . . .

And Bridget slept.

★ ★ ★

Harry prowled on through the dark, deserted streets, hands

plunged into the black depths of his raincoat, his crêpe soles sliding occasionally on the damp film of mud that coated the pavement. So the little curly-haired tart had slipped him. Bet she thought she was mighty smart. Well she would find out just how smart one day. It was healthier to let some people have their own way. Himself, for instance. He got . . . annoyed when people crossed him. Especially tarts. He wasn't used to being crossed by tarts. He didn't like it.

A giggle from a doorway startled him, but it was only somebody touching up his piece. Dirty bastard. Harry spat. A cat slunk from his approach. Harry prowled on.

At the Triangle he stopped at the coffee stall for a cup of the hot, bitter brew, and a pork pie. He ate and drank dourly on the rim of the bright circle of light, warmth and chatter that radiated from the stall, challenging with his stony glare the noisy joviality of the other customers.

'It's bein' so cheerful as keep's me goin',' said one of them. 'Like our little ray of sunshine here,' he added, indicating Harry. Smarting under their silly bloody laughter, he gulped down his coffee and stalked away. He turned down the cobbled hill that led to his house. On the river the ships were moaning about the fog. Turning into his house he fouled his shoes in some dog's filth, and swore. He slipped the key noiselessly into the lock, and eased the door open. The smell of stale fat lay heavy on the air. The hall light wasn't working, and he felt his way silently up the stairs. A voice sounded thickly from his mother's room. He didn't recognize it. The door suddenly burst open, and a fat man in long yellow underpants lurched against the banister.

'Where do I piss?' he demanded.

Harry pointed along the landing. His lips curled in disgust, he entered his own room and switched on the light. The raw bulb cast a harsh light on its dirt and disorder. Harry carefully draped his suit on a hanger, kicked off his shoes, and threw himself down on the lumpy, unmade bed.

He found a half-smoked Woodbine on the floor, and lit it, letting the smoke drift slowly past his eyes. Christ, what a life.

Somehow he must get to the States. That was the place for a guy who wanted to make the big time. Plenty of money, cars, suits, shirts. A dame like Amber Lush. She had class all right. He would have class, all class. An apartment like the one in the film, with a bar and refrigerator. A big black Cadillac, and a bright yellow convertible for taking his dame down to the beach. Tough, unsmiling men under him, obeying his every command, ruthlessly eliminating the opposition.

Suddenly pain seared his lips. With an oath he tore the cigarette stub from his mouth and flung it to the floor. He peeled off his damp, sour-smelling socks, and took off his shirt. Shivering, he switched off the light at the door, and felt his way back to the bed. Getting in, he pulled the blankets around him, and, straddling the naked thighs of Amber Lush, grunted with pleasure.

★ ★ ★

Mr Mallory tugged at his tie until it came apart, and pulled off his jersey in the way that was bad for it. He tossed them over the back of a chair. He was glad that they had stopped in at the Bricklayers Arms for a drink. Extravagant really, drinking spirits, but so what? If it made you feel cheerful, it was worth it. Even Bett was quite good-tempered now. Made her look younger. Pretended she didn't like gin, had to be coaxed to take it like medicine—but it took some of the starch out of her—eased the strings of her corsets, so to speak. Those corsets, underwear pink, now rested, exhausted, on a chair. His wife, in night-dress and dressing-gown, sat before the dressing-table, brushing her hair. He had wrenched one shoe off without undoing the laces, and stood now in a stork-like posture, arrested half-way through the removal of the other shoe by the beauty of his wife's hair. Tell her.

'That's a fine head of hair you've got still, Bett,' he said. She began to brush it with special care.

'It's an experience the younger generation miss you know, seeing a woman let down her hair. Why, when I married you it gave me more of a thrill the first time you let down your hair than the first time you let down your drawers.'

'Tom!' rebuked his wife. But there was no edge to her voice. She didn't even reprove him when he let his trousers slide to the floor, and stepped happily out of them without bothering to hang them up. With a faint surprise he felt a stirring in his loins. What was it—the drink, or Amber Lush? Moving over to the dressing-table he put his arms round his wife's ample body. She stopped brushing with mock annoyance. He grinned at their reflection in the mirror.

'You ought to be in films yourself you know.'

'Oh yes?' she inquired ironically. 'On the wide screen?'

'No, honestly. I mean this fashion for buxom film-stars, with plenty of curves. Now that *is* a bust.'

'Don't be vulgar, Tom,' said his wife happily.

'Hallo, what's this lump?'

'Oh nothing.'

'You sure?'

'Yes, it's been there for years. It's nothing.'

Mr Mallory's ardour wavered for a moment. He wobbled like a tight-rope walker who feels his confidence vanishing: the gravitational forces of worry began to assert themselves.

'You ought to go to the doctor's,' he said uncertainly.

'Don't talk to me of doctors. It's nothing I tell you. Does it show?'

Mr Mallory lunged forward on the tight-rope.

'You needn't worry,' he said, pinching her affectionately on the rump where it overlapped the dainty dressing-table seat. 'You're still a fine figure of a woman. That Amber Lush is a bag of bones beside you.'

'Now stop it, Tom.'

'And maybe I could teach that Len Geste a thing or two.'
He hoisted her up from the seat, laughing and protesting in
his arms.

'Come on, let's try one of those open-mouth kisses, all spit
and breath.'

After a few seconds his wife came spluttering to the
surface.

'Oh, Tom, you are a fool, really. At our age.'

Deftly he reached out and turned off the light.

'It's a very nice age,' he said.

Fifteen minutes later she said:

'Tom, are all the children in?'

'What children. We haven't got any children. We were
only married this afternoon, remember?'

She giggled.

'You are a fool, Tom.'

★ ★ ★

It had been a particularly trying evening for Damien.
Attendance at the meeting had been poor. Even the parish
priest had been absent, and the curate didn't command the
same prestige and authority. Then on his return there had
been that regrettable scene with Mrs Higgins when he
complained of the way her daughter strewed her underclothes all over the bathroom to dry. He had had difficulty
in making Mrs Higgins understand that it wasn't the inconvenience he objected to, but the immodesty. Why, at home
his mother and sisters would not think of even washing such
garments in his presence. Then the young baggage herself
had come in, and appeared highly amused by the whole
affair. He had stalked angrily out of the room, leaving
mother and daughter giggling impertinently. He flushed at
the memory. Really he was most uneasy in this house. He
deeply regretted that he had not insisted on taking the
room next door which Underwood now occupied; but Mrs

Mallory had said that she didn't want to take him away from Mrs Higgins, who was a widow, and hard-up. But his aunt was too soft-hearted. Mrs Higgins wasn't hard-up. At least, she quite spoiled that daughter of hers, who must spend large sums of money on clothing and similar luxuries. Really it had been a most trying evening. And now this disturbance.

Crossing himself slowly and precisely, Damien rose from his knees, and closed the breviary with an irritable snap. He liked to read the Office every day, though it was difficult to find the necessary time and peace in the hurly-burly of modern secularized society. But it was completely impossible tonight, with the murmur of Clare's and Underwood's voices floating up from the street. He padded to the window, and squinted down at the steps next door. Chalky-blue in the street-lamp's light, they stared blankly back at him. Clare and Underwood must be inside the porch. Why? Why were they there, talking? It was most inconsiderate of them. Surely they must realize that his window was just above them, and that some people might be trying to make their devotions? Clare, too, ought to have more care for her good name. Why, they might be a couple in the shadows behind a dance-hall. He strained his ears to catch the conversation below, but without success. Perhaps if he eased the window open a little. . . .

'We ought to go in now,' Clare whispered to Mark.

'Cold?'

'No, but it's late. And suppose someone in the house should hear us.'

'You're shivering. I shouldn't have made you walk home. You haven't enough clothes on.'

'No, I'm all right, honestly,' she replied, but allowed him to put his arms round her.

'Better?'

'Mmm. But really we ought to go in. Mummy will worry.'

She struggled feebly against the temptation to surrender to the peace and happiness of the moment—a kind of harmony of mutual exhaustion that, she felt, must exist between two people who have shared some trial or adventure, and reached a special understanding in the course of it. Love—if this was love—dealt out its rewards in an eccentric way. The moments of joy and understanding never came when you wanted them—at a home-coming or for a special occasion—but on a damp, dirty seat on top of a hill, or with a good-night embrace in a cold, draughty porch.

Mark put his hands under her coat, and gently massaged her back with his broad, flat palms, smoothing away her cold, her stiffness and her reserve. His fingers manipulated her spine, making her squirm pleasantly, and push her body against his with involuntary force. She closed her eyes. Now his fingers were playing over every bone and muscle in her back as if they were the strings of an instrument, and in his sensitive hands her body suddenly became extraordinarily responsive. And all the time he was kissing her, nibbling kisses around her throat and under her chin, and she wanted to exhale everything from within her, to flatten herself against him, but all that came out was a kind of moan with his name mixed up in it. And his other hand crept slowly up her side, and she shuddered as his hand crept slowly up and closed over her breast and a window squeaked loudly overhead and she had said 'No, Mark!' and had broken from him and was fumbling with the latch, and was inside and upstairs before she began to blush.

'No, Mark!' He was quite sure he had heard her say that. Locking the tail of his night-shirt between his ankles to prevent it riding up, Damien got carefully into bed. What had Underwood been up to? Some familiarity no doubt. Well, that would show her what sort of a fellow he was. She would see that he had been right after all: Underwood was no good. You could tell it as soon as you set eyes on him.

That sly grin, all those immoral books in his room. That kind only wanted one thing from an innocent young girl. Well he wouldn't be allowed to ruin a good Catholic girl like Clare—he himself would see to that. She had been foolish, and a little ungrateful, but he would not desert her. Soon she would be rudely disillusioned about Underwood, and when she was weeping with shame and anger he would come to her and comfort her. 'No, no!' she would say. 'Please go away. I feel so ashamed. You are too good to me. I have not been kind to you in the past. Why should you be kind to me now?'

'I am prepared to forget all that, my dear Clare,' he would reply, 'if you would consider favourably the idea of our marriage.'

'You . . . marry me?' she would exclaim, dry-eyed with surprise. 'But why? How long . . . ? I am not worthy.' This last said with a pretty droop of the head.

His imagination sped on to the wedding night, and to an idea which had been pleasantly preoccupying him of late. Clare, exquisitely beautiful, began shyly to divest herself. She smiled gratefully as he left the room in deference to her modesty. When he returned she was attired in a soft white night-dress, her long auburn locks resting lightly on her shoulders. Decked to please him, she came to him, gave herself passionately to his embrace. But he steadied her, calmed her.

'Clare, most married people spend the night of their wedding indulging in the pleasures of the flesh, thoughtless of God. I suggest, my dear, that being two people specially dedicated to God, we spend this night instead in watching and prayer.'

Surprise, admiration, and joy flooded across her face in quick succession.

'Damien, you are so strong. And I am so weak.'

He caught himself falling asleep. He rattled off a quick *Act of Contrition*, and thumbed hurriedly through his mental picture book of the Four Last Things: Death, Judgement, Hell and Heaven. His soul tidied for the night, he composed himself for sleep.

★ ★ ★

In the privacy of her pink bedroom at the top of the house, Doreen gleefully unpacked the new panties. She had received them that morning from the Laurie Landsdowne Fan Club. That was a marvellous record of his, *Love Is A Many-Splendoured Thing*, they never got tired of it at the Palladium. The panties had Laurie's own finger-prints on them. She giggled, wondering what the lodger would think of them when he saw them in the bathroom. He was a queer one and no mistake. Gave her the creeps. Ooh, she couldn't stand him. No sense of humour. And so ugly. Seemed to be frightened of girls.

Boldly undressing beneath the leers of her photographic gallery of film-stars, she slipped on the pants and opened the wardrobe. In the long mirror a perfectly normal image confronted her. She turned and peered over her shoulder. Like the finger-bones of some amorous skeleton Laurie Landsdowne's printed hands gently clasped each swelling buttock. Stretching her own hands over the imprints, Doreen began absently to manipulate her bottom, as she hummed:

> *Love is a many-splendoured thing,*
> *It's the April rose*
> *That only grows*
> *In the early spring. . . .*

Suddenly she felt the weariness attack her legs again. Slipping on her black see-through nightie and white bed-socks, she got between the warm bed-clothes and switched off the light above her bed. Stretching luxuriously, she placed the hot-water bottle under the joints of her knees, and felt the tiredness blissfully released from them. Soon she was dropping off to sleep, dreaming of pantie-raids in an American girls' college—she had read about them in the newspaper. Grinning, muscular, alphabet-chested college boys invaded the shrieking delighted dormitory gathering handfuls of frillies. Then, oddly, Mr Berkley threw his leg over the sill, and advanced towards her with a roguish gleam in his eye. Tantalizing him with a wave of her bra, she challenged him to the chase. . . .

★ ★ ★

Mark pushed open the door of his room, switched on the light, and stepped wearily inside. He threw himself down on the bed. So Clare was still a respectable girl. You could always tell a respectable girl. Their bodies could be mapped out like the butcher's charts showing the different cuts of meat. You could only touch certain parts before marriage. Touch one of the forbidden areas—breast, rump or loin—and you encountered resistance. Still, he couldn't grumble. He'd had quite a good feel around. She was yielding slowly. Take your time.

It was the little speech on top of the hill that had got her defences down. To be fair, it hadn't been at all a bad piece of rhetoric. It was worth noting down while he could still remember it:

He swung his legs off the bed, and turned towards the desk. His note-book lay open. He read the last entry:

'If you remove the "s" from *nostalgia* you get *notalgia* which means "back-ache".'

Now that was extremely interesting. But it was so *lonely*. His writing resembled rockets going off singly at long intervals. This note-book habit was terribly dangerous, unless one was quite prolific of fresh and startling ideas. Otherwise one came to regard the little stockpile of metaphors and apothegms as the essential foundation of one's work, to be eked out with parsimonious care. He would probably write a completely worthless short-story just to enshrine that one flash of word-play, which itself seemed feebler the longer he looked at it. He decided not to enter the hill-speech in his note-book.

He lit a cigarette and fell back on to the bed. Funny how reassuring was the action of lighting a cigarette. There was nothing to it, yet in the moment of static concentration, hunched over the flame, and the triumphant flick of the head as the first smoke came, one experienced a fleeting sense of identity: one was a man lighting a cigarette. Perhaps it was because a cigarette cost tuppence, and therefore to light up was an act of calculated extravagance. Anyway, it gave one a sense of being, for once, decisive and positive: it was a defiance of circumstances, a reckless devil-may-care defiance of circumstances.

Were other people like this, he wondered—always observing themselves, trying to surprise themselves in a spontaneous emotion? It was the penalty of being (or trying to be) a writer. To create characters you took a rib of your own personality, and shaped a character round it with the dust of experience. But it was a painful, debilitating process. Usually the characters were still-born, and the old Adam got weaker and weaker, less and less sure of his own identity.

Through the thin wall to his left the over-worked lavatory clanked and gurgled after someone—who was it?—sounded like Patrick's heavy tread—had used it. Gradually the frenzied gurgling was hushed to a faint dripping. He waited to see how long it would take to be quite quiet. It was one of those times when there seemed to be nothing else to do but measure something quite meaningless, like the number of red motor cars on the road, or the time a cloud took to cross the moon. Now all was still.

But someone else was coming. The lavatory-seat was never cold in this house. Even so, it was late for all this activity. It must be Clare—yes, those were her floppy slippers. The seat squeaked, and he heard the rustle of her skirts. Carefully, as if it were a Boy Scout's game, he visualized the movement accompanying each sound. In America you could buy a record of a girl undressing: a good sideline for the London Institute of Pornography.

It was a good job girls like Clare had to relieve themselves: it made them face the facts of human nature. Otherwise they were prone to think themselves bloody little angels. But perhaps even the angels had to pass their nectar. The toilet roll rattled as two sheets were torn off. There was a silence, then a hiss, then a deep, resonant battering of water by water. It was strangely musical. But someone had said that before. Joyce in *Ulysses*, of course. But that was a chamber pot. Yes there was that marvellous bit as it filled up: 'Diddle iddle addle addle oodle oodle hiss.' The acoustics were different: this was a single deep note, like a bass. It would be fun to write an ode: *On Hearing His Beloved's Urination*:

> *O gushing stream*
> *You bring sweet music to my troubled ear;*
> *And as I lie upon my restless couch,*
> *I fit a picture to each sound I hear.*

Clare was sustaining the deep note very well. It was a kind of robustness attractive in a woman. Like Yeats's great-bladdered Emer. Apparently there was a kind of competition among the Celtic goddesses to see who could make the deepest hole in the snow with her urine. You could imagine them squatting in a row, with the steam rising all round. They should make it an event in the Olympic games —Winter Sports.

It was strange really, this attachment to the cloacal in writers and intellectuals. There was Yeats and Joyce and Smollett and Swift and Rabelais and himself. Well he was attached to the cloacal all right, but was he a writer

94

or an intellectual? Why not simply admit that he liked smut—made respectable by the presence of literature, of course.

The steady flow trickled into silence. Again the rustle of skirts, the jerk on the chain, again the ponderous deluge. Clare flopped out in her loose slippers.

D. H. Lawrence had written somewhere that the writer who confused the excremental flow with the sexual flow was the real pornographer. But Lawrence was fundamentally effeminate. He couldn't face the fact that the excremental flow led you to the channel of life. It was the irony of the thing that appealed to the healthy masculine mind:

> *'Love has pitched his mansion in*
> *The place of excrement.'*

Take the little wedge of flesh itself, 'those mysteriouse parts' as Spenser called them. He was as bad as Lawrence. The latrine wall's four-letter word was much more satis-factory. Clare's——

He sat up, suddenly and unexpectedly revolted. He was getting bored with his mind. It was like being trapped in a *cinéma bleu*, seeing the same film over and over again. He was nauseated, and felt a desperate need to cleanse himself in some way.

Awkwardly he dropped to his knees. He didn't want to pray to anyone, but just to humiliate himself in his own eyes, to make expiation. He said a *Hail Mary*, then started the *Our Father*, and got stuck at Thy will be done. Give us this day our daily bread. No, there was something in between. Never mind. And forgive us our trespasses as we forgive them that trespass against us. He rummaged in the toy-cup-board of his childish memory for old scraps and fragments of prayers. Hail holy Queen, Mother of Mercy Hail our Life our Sweetness and our Hope. O clement O loving O sweet Virgin Mary. O Sacred Heart of Jesus have mercy on us, O Sacred Heart of Jesus have mercy on us.

Help me to do the things I should,
To be to others kind and good;
In my work and in my play,
To grow more loving every day.

He realized that he had been reciting this infantile jingle over and over again. Wearily he got to his feet and undressed. Slipping on a dressing-gown he went out to the lavatory. It was occupied.

★　★　★

Patricia was wide awake as soon as the door squeaked and Clare tiptoed in. She took off her coat, put on her slippers and flip-flopped out to the george. By arrangement the curtains were drawn so that Clare could go to bed by the light of the street-lamps without disturbing Patricia. When she returned, Patricia yielded to the temptation of observing her unnoticed. The planned modesty of undressing, the careful folding, putting on hangers and stowing away of clothes, bespoke the convent, and carried a mute condemnation of her own explosive methods of undressing. The dressing-table mirror reflected the dim, blue rectangle of the window, and Clare was silhouetted against it. Really, she had the most marvellous figure. If only she wore a decent bra. Goodness knows where she found the things she wore. In fact, with a little application, Clare could be a real beauty. She could tell her what to do, but she was a little shy of her. She didn't quite know how Clare would take it—it would be a bit cheeky. Still, it wasn't surprising that Mark was keen on her. How keen she was on Mark you couldn't tell. She was so innocent that you couldn't apply the usual tests. You'd think that sharing the same room these last months Clare would have blurted it all out, but she was strangely reticent about things that were really important, such as Mark, or the reason she had left the convent. So were most of the family really, they had formed deep friendships outside, but they never really let themselves go in the family circle. Mummy, for instance, was full of love really, but she seemed to distrust it, and when anyone tried to make a fuss of her, even Daddy, she said they were being soft. Only Mark seemed to be able to compliment her, but he did it in a half-joking way. That last book he had loaned her was rather weird. Mother Superior would have kittens if she caught her reading it. But that was what she liked about Mark, he treated her like an adult. *She* knew what was right and what was wrong, what would do her harm, and what wouldn't. After all, you had to gain experience somehow, and a Catholic couldn't get practical experience. It had to be books. Sunday tomorrow. There, Clare was getting down on her knees, as if to underline her own lack of real piety. She usually said her prayers in bed. And Clare said such terribly long prayers. The whole rosary at *least*. Perhaps she'd better say some more. Hail Mary full of grace. . . .

Hail Mary full of grace. . . . Clare stopped. It was no use repeating the words of the prayer faster and faster, like a skipping rhyme, when her mind was feverishly occupied with other things. Was it wrong of Mark to put his hand there? Was it wrong of her to like it? *Had* she liked it before she broke away? Had she broken away because it was wrong, or because of the noise of the window? Should she be angry with him? Or couldn't he be expected to know better—was it really her fault that it had happened? These questions pulsed in her head and made it ache. Should she go to Communion tomorrow? Well, it couldn't be a mortal sin, because there hadn't been full knowledge or full consent.

She hadn't considered the possibility of being in a state of mortal sin since that Christmas when she was eight and Boxing Day was a Sunday and she had pretended to be ill because she didn't want to go to church two days running.

All that week she had gone about in fear and trembling in case she would die before she could go to confession on the Saturday. It was significant that now she felt no such guilty panic—just a tired academic curiosity. This was due partly to her spiritual lassitude, partly to Mark's influence. He had the same effect on her as certain books he lent her. He said she should learn to accept the presence of immorality in life and literature without condoning it. But it was a trick she found difficult to learn. Often the casual disregard in such books of every moral principle she had been taught to observe and respect, threw her into a whirl of doubt and uncertainty, and she had been shocked lately to find herself wondering whether the Catholic moral code wasn't just a tedious and complicated game with which theologians amused themselves at the expense of ordinary people's happiness.

Rule-of-thumb moral theology would indicate that she should give up Mark's company. But Mark wasn't just a disturbing influence; he was an unhappy boy without a Faith. To give him up now would be cowardly—there was an element of risk in everything worth the attempt. Of course she would only be a medium for God's grace, but unworthy as she was, she might represent Mark's last chance of salvation. For he *did* seem to like her, to find some relief in talking to her. And already she had persuaded him to go to Mass again. Tomorrow he would be kneeling beside her at Mass. It was quite an achievement, considering how short a time he had been with them. But there was a long way to go yet. God must do something to help. Please God, You must do something to help. When the priest elevates the Host at Mass, You could appear to Mark. You've done it before. Sister Veronica had told them of many such miracles. And Mark was worth a miracle. At least, to her he was.

The clock in the Anglican church-tower at the top of the hill struck three. Only very remotely did Father Kipling's ear record that, as always, the note was flat. He was deaf, and almost blind and dumb too. He lay prostrate before the altar of his church, as he had done on the day of his ordination.

'Lord,' he groaned, 'I am a sinner.'

It was a shattering admission to have to make. Oh, of course, he was a sinner in common with the rest of fallen humanity; but up till now this had been a mere formal admission, his confessions brief, dull accounts of a few trifling venial sins—a moment of irritation with a sleepy acolyte, an uncharitable thought about his housekeeper's cooking. But now he found himself, at an unseemly age, steeped in real sin, yielding willingly to the temptations of impure thought—a sin almost certainly mortal, a sin he had always held in particular abhorrence, and treated with special severity in the confessional. It was horrifying. He felt physically sick as he pictured himself straining forward in his seat to stare at the lewd posturings and licentious antics of that infamous woman, like a spectator at some pagan orgy. Worse still, he was bound to admit that when she had walked into that man's bedroom by mistake, he had actually wished, at heart, that they would consummate their unlawful desires. He had actually been disappointed when he had been reunited with his wife. He had connived at adultery. It amounted to that. He shuddered. And was this the man to care for the spiritual welfare of two thousand souls, to inspire them with zeal for the virtues of holy purity and marital chastity? A man who crumpled at the first brush of temptation?

But how had it escaped his attention that these cinemas were such cesspools? He could not think how his parishioners were able to reconcile the patronage of such corrupt entertainments with attendance at Mass and reception of Holy Communion. They must be warned of the grave dangers to their immortal souls from this source. Perhaps, after all, his misdemeanour would be put to good use by God, working in His mysterious ways.

Wearily he rose to his knees and looked up at the crucifix. He began to recite the fourth Penitential Psalm:

Turn away Thy face from my sins, and blot out my iniquities.

Create a clean heart in me O God, and renew a right spirit within my bowels.

Cast me not away from Thy face, and take not Thy holy spirit from me.

Restore unto me the joy of my salvation, and strengthen me with a perfect spirit.

I will teach the unjust Thy ways; and the wicked shall be converted to Thee. . . .

Father Kipling repeated this last verse to himself as he locked the church doors. The night was cold, and he fumbled in his pockets for his gloves, only to find that he had left one in the cinema. It was not the only thing he had left there.

In the presbytery he sank into his old arm-chair, and dozed uneasily for a few hours before the first Mass.

★ ★ ★

The clanking of over-taxed plumbing woke Mark. Nobody in the house seemed to understand that you had to let the cistern fill before pulling the chain. They just yanked at it again and again with stubborn impatience. He peered at his watch and groaned into the pillow. Ten past eight. Soon Clare would come and make sure he was awake. Why was it that when you woke up the most important thing in life was that you should stay exactly where you were?

There was a tap at the door, and Clare came in with a

smiling morning face and a steaming cup of tea. She was fully dressed, but her scrubbed, shiny face and fluffy, newly brushed hair made her appear ridiculously young and more enchantingly unsophisticated than ever. In the presence of her moist, bud-like freshness he felt old, coarse and soiled. He was made guiltily aware of the rough stubble on his chin, his greasy, unwashed face, the stale taste of last night's tobacco in his mouth, the rumpled bed-clothes sealing the rank air round his body.

'You're like some beautiful but accusing sunbeam shining into a den of vice,' he said.

'I hope this is no den of vice,' she replied, carefully placing a newspaper under the saucer on his bedside table.

'You remind me of duty. You're so disgustingly awake and industrious and clean. Three qualities which I find uncongenial.'

Clare drew back the curtains and opened a window.

'It's a fine day.'

'For heaven's sake, if you must open that window, close the door. There's a howling draught.'

'Well you could do with some fresh air in here,' she said as she returned to the door. 'Don't be long getting up, will you Mark, or we'll be late for Mass.'

'All right. Clare.'

'Yes?' She paused by the door.

'I'm sorry about last night.'

She blushed. 'That's all right' she murmured, as she passed through the door.

'And, Clare.' She pushed her head back round the door. 'Thanks for the tea.'

'That's all right.' She smiled.

Well, that was one good job done. It was always best to get apologies over as soon as possible. Thanking her for the tea had been a happy inspiration too. She had a touching appreciation for such little gestures. In fact, it was so

101

easy to draw appreciation from her that it was like cheating.

He sipped his tea, letting it scald away the bad taste in his mouth. He was almost certainly the only person—except Patrick (who had served at some appallingly early Mass) and perhaps Mr Mallory—who was drinking tea at that moment. All the rest would be heroically fasting for Holy Communion. Heroically? Or perversely? The Pope had recently issued an edict allowing the Faithful to drink non-alcoholic beverages up to one hour before Communion. But Mrs Mallory and her children had declined to take advantage of the new regulation, almost as though they suspected it of being a trap, a little too easy. They preferred to win salvation the hard way. It was the same with the evening masses which were now becoming common. Mrs Mallory stubbornly refused to attend them, although, as a hard-worked housewife, she was precisely the sort of person they were designed to help. She insisted that she felt 'wrong' all through Sunday if she didn't hear Mass in the morning. There was something at once admirable and irritating about this family's ability to bring the body into subjection. It wasn't that they didn't like tea. They did. And it wasn't that they liked getting up. They didn't. But somehow they managed to get up and not to drink tea.

The house resounded now with their energy: the bustle was like an accusation. He threw back the bed-clothes; found it, as he expected, cold; and pulled them over him again. There was a rap on the door.

'Mark!' Clare reminded him.

'Oh, all right. I'm getting up,' he grumbled, throwing back the blankets a second time. Scratching his head, he peered into the mirror, and scraped the sleep from his eyes with a finger-nail. Pulling on his dressing-gown he staggered, weak-legged, out to the bathroom.

* * *

Well, here he was on his knees again. He felt rather sheepish and embarrassed remembering his collapse of the night before. The explanation was perfectly obvious of course: the libido, deprived of sexual fulfilment, conspired with the ego and the super-ego for religious fulfilment. In the abasement before the supernatural it found a substitute for the abandonment of the sexual act. Prayer was spiritual orgasm. If he could have copulated with Clare, or merely stroked her breasts a bit, he would never have toppled to his knees in so abject a manner.

Kneeling in church was a rather strange way of witnessing to one's intellectual independence. But it was essential if he was to regain Clare's confidence. Like a trout, she could be caught by very skilfully and delicately tickling her religious susceptibility; tickling her belly would have to come later. He must beat Damien at his own game. Thackeray had said that every woman was a match-maker at heart; but she was also a missionary at heart. She always wanted to reform her man—it gave her desires a certain respectability. The challenge of his scepticism held a greater attraction for Clare than the holy, still and cold conversation of Damien. All she needed was a little encouragement. That was why he was here.

The church was stuffy: only one tiny window was open. The congregation did not seem to mind. But they were stuffy too, in ugly felt hats and buttoned raincoats, behinds tilted ungracefully on the edges of the benches, mostly staring vacantly ahead, with a few ostentatiously following the service in their missals, making a great show of turning over leaves. Here and there a child fretted, bored and uncomfortable, penned in by dull, sabbatical adulthood. Rows of grey, cross faces. Why were church-goers so unlovable? There was no getting away from it, all the beautiful, witty, intelligent people were sufficient unto themselves. It was only the failures and defectives who slunk into the temples and listened greedily to their promised revenge—they and the

103

prosperous who wished to insure themselves by an hour's boredom and discomfort against a reverse of fortune in the next world.

Yes, that was all very well, but what about the Mallorys? They were beautiful, they had a rich sense of humour, and they were undeniably intelligent. The Mallorys upset all his pet theories. It was damned annoying.

Father Kipling emerged from the sacristy, paced slowly across the altar, genuflected, and mounted the pulpit, pausing on each step like an old man. Clasping the pulpit with two hands, he gravely regarded the congregation as Father Francis finished the Gospel. He continued to gaze at them as they noisily settled themselves, and for several moments after, until there was almost complete silence. Mark sensed that people were curious, and slightly uncomfortable under that unblinking gaze. They were not used to the preacher seeking to make an impression, unless he was some missionary, and it troubled them.

Father Kipling looked tired and strained. When he spoke it was in a dull, lifeless voice.

'Today is the last Sunday after Pentecost. The 6.30 Mass was for Mrs Duffy's intention, the 7.30 for . . .' The notices droned on. 'Your charitable prayers are asked for the following who . . .' Always the same names insinuating themselves on some pretext or other—illness, an anniversary, or at the last resort, death. 'May their souls, and the souls of all the Faithful departed, through the mercy of God, rest in peace. Amen.'

Father Kipling proceeded to read the Epistle, stumbling through the awkward syntax. St Paul: surely, after Henry James, the most unreadable of all the great stylists. As he finished, a few eager souls leapt to their feet to show that they knew the Gospel came next. Sluggishly the rest of the congregation heaved up, listened, at last with some show of comprehension, and subsided again. Father Kipling waited until everyone was still, and then he cleared his throat.

'My dear brethren in Jesus Christ'—the congregation dutifully nodded their heads—'I had intended to talk to you this morning on the subject of Grace—the Grace we derive from the sacraments, particularly Holy Communion. Without this Grace, this supernatural food—our souls will wither and die. Therefore it is most important that every Catholic should understand what supernatural Grace is, and how it is to be obtained.

'However, this topic has had to give place to an even more urgent matter. Before the graces of the sacraments can be obtained, with the exceptions of Baptism and Penance, it is essential that the soul should be free from mortal sin. And a potential source of grievous sin for many people now in this church has come to my notice. I feel, my dear brethren, that it is my duty to warn you.

'Last night I went to a picture-palace. I went in the belief that the well-known religious film *Song Of Bernadette* was being shown, but I was mistaken. My subsequent experience was shocking and painful in the extreme, but instructive. I saw a scandalous presentation that deliberately exploited the basest passions of man, and that viciously attacked the foundations of a Christian society—the family—all in the name of entertainment. I saw a woman employ all the arts of coquetry to degrade the sex which was glorified by the Mother of God. I must conclude that the entertainment was typical, for I was the only member of the audience, as far as I could tell, who was shocked. Everyone around me laughed and smiled as if it was the most natural thing in the world to see the precepts of clean, decent, Christian living travestied upon the screen. I noted angrily that there were children in the audience—many, mercifully, too young to be contaminated, though they should have been in their cots. I noted sadly that there were some of my own parishioners there too.

' 'You have heard me speak unfavourably of the cinema before, my dear brethren. You have heard me urge you to give up patronizing it as a penance for Lent, or in order to contribute more fully to some charity. But whereas in the past I regarded it simply as a profitless, worldly pleasure, I now regard it as a source of serious sin, a dangerously infested swamp in which the unwary soul may easily be swallowed up, and so perish.

'I address myself particularly to parents. Remember, my dear brethren, that the moral welfare of your children is your solemn responsibility. I beg you not to expose them to the temptations of the flesh such as they find flagrantly exhibited and condoned in the picture-palace, at an age when they are most vulnerable to such influences. Remember that when you give them money for the picture-palace, you may be enabling them to purchase the loss of their immortal souls. And remember that you must yourselves set a good example by avoiding these demoralizing entertainments. Do not over-estimate your own strength. The evil effect of these shows is gradual and insidious: it gradually undermines religious principles, renders the conscience slack and tolerant of sin. Behind all is Satan's cunning and directing power. In the Name of Our Lord Jesus Christ' (dazed and punch-drunk, the congregation still remembered to nod) 'I exhort you to avoid these temples of Mammon and Belial.

'It will not be easy: that I know. For many of you it has become a habit. You have seen nothing evil in it. But from the pulpit of your church, I, your priest, beseech you to give up this habit. With God's help nothing is impossible, and He will bless your sacrifice.

'As Saturday evening is apparently the most popular time for people to visit the cinema, I propose to transfer the Thursday Benediction to Saturday. On Saturday evening, my dear brethren, I wish everyone who would normally have gone to the picture-palace, and thus put his soul in deadly danger, to come instead to the church, to give honour and glory to God, and to join with me in saying the Rosary for the conversion of England. Who knows, from this humble beginning in Brickley may spring a full-scale crusade against immoral and worldly entertainments. But at the very least we will have the satisfaction of knowing that we are witnessing to the principles of Catholic Christianity. In the Name of the Father, and of the Son, and of the Holy Ghost, Amen.'

Father Francis rose to begin the Creed in a numbed silence, suddenly punctuated by the sound of a loud handclap. It was not, however, the instinctive applause of some enthusiastic listener, but the noise of the organ getting up steam. At the Offertory more coins than usual were dropped to the floor. Mark wondered if Father Kipling had been in the Palladium the previous evening. The lascivious woman sounded like Amber Lush. It had been an extraordinary sermon—easily the most impressive he had heard Father Kipling deliver—but it had missed the point. The menace of the cinema was not surely that it was lewd and sensual, but that it encouraged people to turn their back on real life. Escapism had always been a fundamental and harmless function of popular art; but the cinema invested such escapism with a new and sinister plausibility, projecting a seductive image of a stream-lined, chromium-plated, hygienically-packed, deep-frozen, King-sized superlife, which could be vicariously and effortlessly enjoyed by slumping into a cinema-seat. Father Kipling was fighting a losing battle. The cinema, or the whole system of processed mass-entertainment for which it stood, had already become an acceptable substitute for religion. What was more alarming was that in time it might become an acceptable substitute for living.

The ancient organ wheezed into life, and the congregation staggered into the opening lines of *Just For Today:*

> *Lord, for tomorrow and its needs,*
> *I do not pray;*
> *Keep me, my God, from stain of sin,*
> *Just for today.*

This, of course, was the most revolutionary doctrine in the Christian code. Be not solicitous. But there wasn't a single person in the church who would apply the words of the hymn to his own careful accumulation of Savings Certificates and Insurance Policies, his persistent intriguing for promotion. When you considered the matter, the so-called Bohemians were the only true Christians. They toiled not, neither did they spin; often they didn't know where the next meal was coming from, or where they would sleep from one day to the other. Yet they were condemned outright by the cautious, prudent, God-fearing church-goers as beyond the pale.

> Let me be slow to do my will,
> Prompt to obey,
> Help me to mortify my flesh,
> Just for today.

Of course you could give the refrain an ironical twist, and interpret it as a careful reservation made by the singer: all right, help me to mortify my flesh—but just for today mind. Tomorrow I'll have one hell of a good time.

> Let me be faithful to Thy grace,
> Just for today.

He felt the same wry amusement as Thomas Hardy must have enjoyed when he heard the anecdote, related in *Under The Greenwood Tree*, about the church where the Ten Commandments were inscribed by some tipsy masons who left out all the 'not's'.

It would be difficult to persuade Clare to go to the cinema now—or any of the Mallorys for that matter. Although going to church was like going to the cinema: you sat in rows, the notices were like trailers, the supporting sermon was changed weekly. And people went because they always went. You paid at the plate instead of at the box-office, and sometimes they played the organ. There was only one big difference: the main feature was always the same.

Yes, that was something you couldn't get away from, and instead of becoming more boring, it became more interesting with each repetition. That was the difference between drama and ritual probably.

'*Dominus vobiscum.*'

'*Et cum spiritu tuo.*'

'*Sursum corda.*'

'*Habemus ad Dominum.*'

'*Gratias agamus Domino Deo nostro.*'

'*Dignum et justum est.*'

'The pressing nature of this dialogue,' he read in his missal, 'shows clearly that we are coming now to the very heart of the Mass.'

'*Sanctus,*
　　　Sanctus,
　　　　　Sanctus.'

The bell rang out three times, and the congregation pitched noisily on to its knees. It fidgeted, sneezed, coughed, whispered. How could they be so inattentive, if they really believed in the stupendous thing they claimed would happen shortly? Perhaps, for them, it was too common an occurrence. Christ risked making himself cheap by mass-production. *Mass*-production. Rather good that. More than ever he was convinced that Catholics did not really believe what they professed to believe. Because, if it was true, that at the Consecration God was really present on the altar, whole and entire, under the appearance of bread and wine, as Clare's dog-eared Catechism stated—then it was quite simply the most important thing in life. If you really believed it you would shiver in dreadful anticipation of this tremendous mystery, you would follow each movement and word of the ritual with breathless attention, and at the climax, at the moment of divine epiphany, the universe would collapse and swirl around you, and you would pitch forward on your face with a low moan. Human nature could not endure such a strain. As to Communion, the cannibalistic fusion with the Godhead, one could conceive of entranced Oriental fanatics performing such a rite, but these drab, smug, self-righteous people who coolly lined up to snap their dentures on the living Christ—could they know what they were supposed to be doing? Yet if you tackled them on the subject, even kids like the twins, they were quite cheerfully positive about it. Yes, of course they believed in the Real Presence. But how could they walk about with such terrible knowledge? Browning, hoary old Protestant that he was, had detected the essential indecency behind the candles, the incense and the flowers:

And see God made and eaten all day long. . . .

That was the bald, terrific idea these people asked you to swallow like a pill. Christine Mallory's fiancé was not a Catholic, and had been taking Instructions. 'He's stuck on Transubstantiation,' Mrs Mallory had said in casual conversation one day. 'A pity if she can't have a nuptial mass.' Speaking for himself, he choked on it.

The bell rang again, and at last there was silence of a sort, interrupted by an occasional baby's whimper. Everyone was bowed and hunched, but there was no feeling of worship or devotion. Now here was the large print in his missal:

WHO THE DAY BEFORE HE SUFFERED TOOK BREAD INTO HIS HOLY AND VENERABLE HANDS, AND WITH HIS EYES LIFTED UP TOWARDS HEAVEN, UNTO THEE, GOD, HIS ALMIGHTY FATHER, GIVING THANKS TO THEE, BLESSED, BROKE AND GAVE TO HIS DISCIPLES, SAYING: TAKE AND EAT YE ALL OF THIS, FOR THIS IS MY BODY.

110

The priest stretched up, lifting the Host on high. Mark stared at it, and belief leapt in his mind like a child in the womb. The pale disc was snatched down by the priest, but Mark continued to stare at the space in the air which it had occupied. The chalice rose in its place, containing the consecrated wine, but he could not recapture the extraordinary awareness that had filled his being for a fleeting second. It was as if for an instant the scales had fallen from his eyes, and he had seen how simple it was really, how it all fitted together. But now he was back on the ground again, a little puzzled and disgruntled, like a man who has been ignominiously picked up by a great bird and dumped back in the same place again.

The bell rang for the sixth time as the priest bowed low. There was an almost audible exhalation from the congregation as the tension was relaxed; people permitted themselves to shift their positions, blow their noses, cough, scold their children. Clare recalled a time when she had resented this relaxation, which seemed to imply that the miracle of the Mass, the miracle of God's love which had made her heart swell with adoration, was not still continuing on the altar. But now, though she strained towards the elevated Host, saying silently, 'My Lord and my God,' her faith was only of the head. In her heart was nothing but a sense of strain and the hollow echo of St Thomas's words. Devotion to the Blessed Sacrament was like love—you couldn't explain it or produce it at will; it was just there, or it wasn't. Sometimes when Mark was rude and indifferent, she just couldn't recognize him as the person who had enkindled such a flame in her, couldn't begin to make contact. Suddenly they would be strangers: speaking different languages, they would just stare blankly at each other. The blank face—the blank, pale disc that hovered like an enigmatic moon over the priest's fingers. In her head she knew that it *was* Mark, that it *was* God, but her heart did not thump with the knowledge. She had not felt that excitement at Mass since leaving the convent. Since then, only Mark had given her the same sensation. It seemed one couldn't have both at once.

She had scruples as to whether she should receive the Blessed Sacrament while she was in such a cold, loveless disposition. But she had asked Father Francis in confession and he had said yes, many people experienced the same spiritual deadness at times, even the saints, and the sacraments were themselves a means of overcoming this. But she knew that when she returned from the Communion rails, God would only be a slightly sour taste on her tongue; and that when she bowed her head and covered her face with her hands, shutting out everything else, she would be in the hollow cavern of her heart again, asking her own echo the way to God.

The thin, pale sunshine gave little warmth, but it was a welcome extension of the autumn, and unusually fine for the last day of October. Outside the church many parishioners lingered, distributing leaflets and gossiping. Mr Mallory, whose stomach was noisily urging its case for a prompt breakfast, collected his offspring and set off home. Every Sunday morning when his wife woke him he soundly (if silently) cursed his adopted religion; but the hell of getting up when all sensible creatures were lost in lovely sleep, was more than compensated for by the feeling of well-being after Mass, which made him beam and glow like an advertisement for salts—'It's Inner Cleanliness that counts!'— and look forward with relish to eggs and bacon with a righteous sense of having earned them, and the lazy hours to follow.

It didn't seem to take Bett the same way though. She always seemed snappy and impatient when she came back from church. Perhaps it was because she went to an early

Mass to have breakfast ready for them when they returned; but she didn't like lying in bed in the mornings anyway, and as he had said many times (admittedly without great enthusiasm) they could quite easily go to Mass together, and wait a little longer for breakfast. No, she liked to hint obliquely that no one's pleasure or comfort was obtainable without some sacrifice on her part. This morning, as always when they had made love the previous night, she had been short and bad-tempered, complaining of a headache. Often in the past he had tried to keep her in bed in the morning, but always she had pushed off his sleep-drugged advances with a brusque reminder that she had work to do, stubbornly shutting her mind to the tenderness of a few hours before. In the cold morning light the lover died, and the housewife was born again. It had taken him a long time to adjust himself to this, but now it no longer irritated him, and he felt only pity for his wife.

He took in the familiar surroundings with a refreshed, amused eye. For most people, he reflected, Sunday should be renamed Carday. Cars had replaced gods. With the same heroic self-denial as early church-goers, the car-owners were out in their numbers, washing-down, polishing, tinkering. In the afternoon they would don chamois gloves and make aimless ritual drives into the Green Belt, in-laws glumly ensconced in the back-seat, stopping at the side of an arterial road to circulate solemnly a vacuum flask. Some youths astride shining motor-cycles had congregated outside a closed motor-cycle shop. Mr Mallory heard the mutter of their liturgy as he passed: '. . . Overhead valves . . . conrod . . . horizontally opposed twin . . . two-fifty two-stroke . . . swinging-arm. . . .' It was like an open-air service.

They met Damien hurrying to the ten o'clock Mass. His raw, ugly face was still bleeding from two shaving cuts.

'Hallo there, Damien,' said Mr Mallory. 'You're slipping. I thought you usually went to the seven-thirty?'

'I overslept, Uncle Thomas,' replied Damien liverishly.

113

'The London streets are so noisy at nights I find it difficult to get to sleep.' He hurried on.

Somehow Mr Mallory couldn't honestly say he felt any affection for Damien. It wasn't simply because he was ugly —he knew men equally ugly and ten times more lovable. But because his personality was objectionable one held him responsible for his ugliness—it became impossible to overlook it. He was cold and dank like the inside of a morgue. He had no sense of humour, and he would keep harping on his seminary training instead of thrusting it into the background and making a fresh start. The fellow carried his failure before him like a monstrance.

His eye fell on Mark, just ahead, clowning to amuse the twins, uninhibited by the glances of passers-by, or by Clare's mild remonstrations. He was really a very likeable lad, though a bit mysterious and withdrawn at the deepest level. However, for someone supposed to be very clever, he seemed to get a great deal of pleasure out of ordinary things. And he had been a healthy influence on Clare when she most needed it—when that creeping Jesus of a Damien had threatened to infect her with the mildew of his own damp piety. His wife had disapproved of this development at first —he suspected that she had paired off Damien and Clare in her mind—but when it transpired that Mark had been baptized a Catholic, and when he started to go to Mass again, she had become favourably disposed to the idea of their going out together. Personally he thought Bett was counting her chickens. Mark showed no signs of being really inspired with religious enthusiasm, or, for that matter, of having matrimonial intentions where Clare was concerned. Bett just didn't realize that keeping company was no longer a walled alley leading to the altar. He only hoped Clare didn't think so.

Mr Berkley blinked resentfully in the morning sunlight. He

hated the morning, hated the light. He was a night-bird. He liked to be in a warm, dimly-lit room, thick with cigarette smoke and vibrant with witty conversation, with the dark outside, protective and all-enveloping. He hurried along the deserted early-morning pavements to the cinema. The exit-doors were open to allow the air to circulate. He passed in.

The familiar waste-land of the empty auditorium engulfed him with its seedy, oppressive presence. Even in its golden age as a theatre, its morning aspect had imparted the same momentary shock of disillusionment—as a tousled, un-powdered woman to her lover of the night before. But the disgusting habits of cinema-goers had intensified the squalor of the scene. He crunched pea-nut shells under his feet and waded ankle-deep in ice-cream cartons, paper bags, cigarette packets, half-eaten apples. The Palladium was a woman growing old, and since all theatres are coquettes, this was a tragedy. The sunlight that inched its way into the stale gloom shed a tactless illumination on the threadbare carpets, the worn seats, the peeling gilt décor. Like an elderly coquette hiding her wrinkles, she didn't allow much sunlight into the auditorium, but it was enough to give the game away. Poor old coquette. Nobody would spend any money on her, beyond a splash of cheap cosmetic on the exterior. After being a highly-prized mistress she was now little better than a common prostitute, and her owners were now interested only in squeezing the last drops of revenue from her tired body.

And there, fittingly ministering to her in her decay, were two old crones, daughters of the game, ex-chorus girls who *hadn't* married earls, Dolly and Gertrude. The two old dears slowly but methodically sifted the rows of their debris, creaking and grunting with every movement as if it would be their last. Mr Berkley walked round the back of the auditorium, and stood in the shadow of some curtains.

'Warm today, Gert.'

'Yerse. Better than that cold though.'

'Gerna rain though. It said so on the wireless.'

'Don't I know it. Alf kep' me awake orl night with 'is roomatism. I didn't get a wink. Shokin' it was.'

Dolly cackled.

''Ere, Gert! Can Alf use one of these?' She held up a contraceptive sheath.

'Oo, Doll! You are rude. You ought to be ashamed of yourself showin' such a thing to me.'

Dolly cackled as she dropped it into her dustpan.

'I don't know what they'll bring to the pictures next,' she wheezed. Her cackle turned into a bronchial cough. Gertrude stopped working, and collapsed ponderously on to a seat.

'Ooh, me feet. . . . Yer know, Doll, when I was about fifty, and goin' through you know what, well this Sunday I was feelin' there wasn't much left to go on livin' for. Fact, for two pins I'd have taken the joint out of the oven and put me 'ead in instead. Well, in comes Alf, with 'is belly full of old and mild as usual, and asks me why do I look as if I'd lost a pound and found thruppence. Well I felt that fed up I told 'im straight out. "Never mind, old cock," 'e says, "we won't 'ave to bother wiv French letters now." Cheered me up somethink marvellous it did.'

''E's a good sort, is Alf,' said Dolly, nodding gravely.

'"Never mind, old cock," 'e says, 'we won't 'ave to bother wiv French letters now."'

'You don't still . . . do you, Gert?'

'What, at our age? It wouldn't be decent, dearie. Besides, Alf can only just about drag hisself to the King's Arms and back once a day, and then e's finished. 'Ow's your Stan?'

'Oh, can't grumble. Still 'as trouble passing 'is water, but the doctor give 'im some new medicine. Comes of drinking too much in the past, I told 'im. But 'e don't listen.'

'What doctor's that?'

'The young one what took over from old Wilkins.'

'Oo, 'e's lovely, i'n 'e? 'E's got such lovely warm 'ands. Old Wilkins used to make me shiver every time 'e touched me.'

Mr Berkley smiled behind his curtain. A couple of genuine characters. Real Cockneys of the old type, once the music-hall's main source of supply, and now, like the music-halls themselves, nearly extinct. The good old songs round the pub piano were dying with them. *Nellie Dean, Daisy, Knees Up Mother Brown.* . . . Humorous, good-natured, industrious, resilient. Vulgar perhaps, but how honest, realistic and uncomplicated Dolly's and Gertrude's attitude to sex appeared in comparison to the modern cult of 'luv', with its tedious machinery of psychology, pop songs, broken-heart columns and cinematic sex-symbols. Once Dolly and Gertrude had been in the back row of the chorus at the Palladium, and Gertrud? had even had a solo spot with a comic song . . . he had seen a photo of her somewhere as Burlington Bertie. . . . Now all they had to show for it were lumpy figures, thin hair, flowered cotton overalls and carpet slippers, as they swept the scene of their former modest triumphs. It seemed rather pathetic, but they never permitted you to feel sorry for them.

'Good morning, ladies,' said Mr Berkley, stepping forward.

'Mornin', Mr Berkley,' they answered. Gertrude rose from her seat with dignity.

'I was just takin' the weight off my feet, Mr Berkley. They're swollen somethink shocking,' she explained.

'I'm so sorry to hear that, Mrs Halibut,' said Mr Berkley sympathetically. 'Have you anything for me this morning?'

'Only this glove,' said Gertrude, drawing a man's black kid glove from some hidden recess in her attire. A few rows down Dolly was hard at work. 'Well!' she exploded indignantly. 'Just look at this, sir. Don't it make you wild.'

He inspected the badly-slashed seat.

'Hmm. Made quite a mess of it, hasn't he. Why d'you think they do it?'

'It's them young Teds, sir, you mark my words. A lot of 'ooligans what's got nothink better to do. Ooh, if I caught them, I wouldn't arf box their ears. They wouldn't do it again in an 'urry.'

Mr Berkley shook his head sadly.

'Well I'd better go and make a note of it. Good morning, ladies.'

'Good morning, Mr Berkley.'

As he climbed the stairs to his office he inspected the glove in his hand. Black was an unusual colour for a man's glove. A clergyman perhaps. A clergyman's gage.

* * *

The front door slammed shut, and cut off abruptly the babble of the family's voices. They were going to Benediction. In the silence that followed their departure the muffled movements of the other occupants of the house became surprisingly audible. Reluctantly Mark opened Klaeber's forbidding edition of *Beowulf,* and propped up Clark Hall's translation in front of him. No work done that day. He would have to grind on till one o'clock. It was an agreeable house to live in, but the atmosphere was not conducive to study. Always you felt the warmth and humanity pulling you downstairs like a magnet.

Another Sunday had almost passed; another pleasant, uneventful Sunday. Uneventful—yet, as he recalled the day's happenings, they stung his memory with tiny, pleasant sensations, tastes, smells: there was the taste of eggs and bacon which really did break a fast, the scent of the first cigarette, and the agreeable weight of the Sunday paper in his hands.

After breakfast he had flattered his ego by assisting Patricia with her homework. Though teaching was so wretchedly paid, he was beginning to think that it was the only possible profession for him—passing on information to

118

others gave him such profound pleasure. Patrick, crouched over his books at the other end of the table, never asked his advice; but then Patrick had always been faintly hostile and jealous of a masculine encroachment on a territory that had been his alone since the departure of the two eldest boys. Not that Mark had minded in the least. In fact he found Patrick's grim determination not to be charmed rather amusing. Though there had been something a little strange about Patrick that day. He had been very quiet. He hadn't, as was his practice, eaten a second breakfast when the rest of the family returned from the nine-'o-clock Mass. He hadn't joined them in their walk that afternoon. He was nursing some secret or other. . . .

Later in the morning he had accepted Mr Mallory's offer to buy him a drink in the plain, four-square, oddly restful pub at the end of the road. They had talked about cars, of which Mr Mallory was a salesman. They discussed very thoroughly the merits of the Bentley Continental, with all the candour and eloquence of two men who would never conceivably own one. Nevertheless Mark wondered why, since he was in the trade, Mr Mallory did not own even a modest vehicle.

'Very simple, Mark. Couldn't afford it. Can't run eight children *and* a car. They've all had good schooling, and there was James's training—you're expected to contribute something. But I've no regrets—I don't really want to own a car. Too much worry and hard work looking after it. Why, I wouldn't have a moment's peace on a Sunday, what with tinkering all morning and driving all the rest of the day.'

On their return Mr Mallory said Grace for a splendid, old-fashioned roast prepared by Mrs Mallory, refulgent and perspiring in the kitchen. Mr Mallory and Patrick habitually washed up after the Sunday dinner, and with a glowing sense of virtue Mark offered to help them. The gesture lit a smile in Clare's face that was well worth his trouble.

Damien had called in the afternoon, and joined Mark, Clare and the rest of the children (except Patrick) in a walk round the park. Neither the latter's damp, dying appearance, nor Damien's similar demeanour, had affected their energetic nonsense with an old tennis ball. They trailed home under a red, smoky sky, to the cosy, fire-lit parlour and high tea.

It was all very different from his life of the past year, when Sunday began at about noon in a room that smelled of bed, crawled sluggishly through an afternoon of too many newspapers, and, in final desperation, sought escape at a film or some theatre club.

It wasn't with such a Sunday that he made the most significant comparison, however, but with the Sundays of his childhood. His memory was indistinct—a few details only stood out in odd clarity: listening to 'Palm Court' on the radio, followed with awful inevitability by 'Variety Bandbox', the last hours of the week-end petering out, wasted, joyless, empty; bed, and school again the next day. His father dozing open-mouthed in his chair, his mother knitting vacantly, neither understanding the misery of their son, who fidgeted by the window, not knowing what to do, but knowing the futility of asking 'What shall I do?' He wasn't able to remember many details, but he could remember that feeling, the sickening slump of the heart that was Sunday in his boyhood, a day his parents kept holy with somnolence, dullness and decorum. For hours he would sit by the window, and look out on the empty, Sunday street, as the church bells tolled dismally from different points in the town. Rain brought a little variety and relief, as he listened to its faint patter on the taut pane, pressing his hot cheek to its cold surface, watching the dull, grey street become a glittering river.

He had wanted for nothing—and for everything. He had been well-clothed, well-fed, carefully guarded against illness. Yet retrospectively he envied the Mallory children their hardships—the shared beds, the shoes that pinched, the heaps of washing, the inconvenience of too many babies in too short a time, the lack of privacy, the meagre pocket-money, the quarrels and tears, because with these things went other things infinitely precious, laughter and love, tenderness and the joy of living, things signally missing from his own childhood.

PART TWO

FATHER KIPLING slowly mounted the shaking wooden steps and placed the monstrance containing the Host above the tabernacle, in the sight of all. As he stepped down and turned to kneel before the altar, he directed a swift, appraising glance at the 'all'. About twelve worshippers dotted the empty, evenly-spaced pews, like lonely beads on a child's abacus.

> *O salutaris hostia*
> *Quae coeli panis hostium,*

they sang, without conviction. O saving victim, opening wide the gates of heaven. . . . A motor-cycle roared past the church, tyres hissing on the wet road, insolently drowning the feeble chant. The Saturday Benediction was slowly dying of indifference. Barely twelve people, and those good pious souls who never went to the cinema anyway.

The crusade against the cinema had never caught the imagination of the parish since he had launched it with such lofty aspirations five—or was it six?—months ago. Nevertheless he had persisted with the Saturday Benediction, and Lent had impelled a respectable number to attend. But now, a week after Easter, his failure stared at him from the empty pews. A pitiful dozen worshippers. Where were the other two thousand souls in his parish? Slumped in their cinema seats no doubt. Failure was embarrassing when one had committed the success of one's mission into God's hands. It was almost as if God had failed. Surely He didn't *want* people to go to the cinema? Yet nothing had gone right for the crusade. There had been that unfortunate controversy in the local Press with the manager of the Palladium, when he had been compelled, under pressure from his bishop, to issue a statement to the effect that all films were not necessarily harmful in the eyes of the Church. The parishioners had required no further encouragement to flock back to the picture-palace. They really didn't seem to see anything harmful in it. Mr Mallory had said to him once, 'With all due respect, Father, I think you've got to be more broadminded these days. What shocks you now—and would have shocked me when I was a lad—it just rolls off these kids like rain off a duck's back.' 'Broadminded' was a popular word, a word he just couldn't understand. The context was always a plea for tolerance of something which he had been taught to regard as sinful.

Mr Mallory had advocated switching Benediction back to Thursday night. He said more people would come to Benediction then. He said everybody liked to go out and amuse themselves on Saturday night. He said everyone had to have some relaxation. He was a good man, but typical of his fellow-parishioners. Like converted pagans, they were reluctant to give up their old gods. But did they not realize that the God of Israel was a jealous God? Apparently his wife did, for she was in the church this evening. But their children were not. The Church of Christ was rapidly becoming the Church of middle-aged women. Soon it would be said in England as it was said on the Continent, that a good Catholic is a man whose wife goes to church.

The *Tantum Ergo* quavered to its conclusion. Emptying his mind of everything except an awareness of the Presence of his Creator, Father Kipling enfolded the stem of the monstrance in the ends of his humeral veil, and held it high, and made with it the Sign of the Cross in the air.

Damien shook the bell as he adored the Sacred Host, with faith, piety and love, saying inwardly, 'My Lord and my

God!' and mentally deposited another seven years in his bank of indulgences.

★   ★   ★

It was 7.15. Dismally Mr Berkley haunted the foyer of the Palladium, confirming, from the overheard remarks of his patrons as they left the cinema, that his experiment had not been a success.

'Queer sort of ending.'

'Well, I thought he would get his bike back after all that performance.'

'Sort of left you in the air. You know.'

'Not bad I s'pose, but it brought you down a bit.'

'All those foreign voices, it got on my nerves.'

'Bloody wops.'

Mr Berkley hovered by the box-office.

'How's business, Miss Gray?'

'Quiet, Mr Berkley,' answered the girl, without interest.

He wandered towards the doors that opened on to the wet street, and stared out at the people hurrying along the pavements, feet splashing in puddles, sodden raincoats, barging umbrellas, gleaming cycle capes. Despite the low rain-clouds, it was still light. The hour had gone forward last Sunday. Soon the long, light evenings would be luring yet more customers away from the stuffy cinema.

Bill, in his faded Ruritanian sergeant's uniform, edged over to him.

'Not so good, is it, Mr Berkley?'

He shook his head.

'If we don't pack 'em in this weather, we never will pack 'em in, that's what I always say.'

'Yes, always, Bill,' replied Mr Berkley unkindly. He was fond of old Bill—one felt affection for anything that was sufficiently old—but really he was too much of a prophet of woe. Mr Berkley turned aside and began to study the stills of *Bicycle Thieves* in the portico.

It seemed particularly appropriate to him that Antonio was sticking up a poster depicting Rita Hayworth when his bicycle was stolen—a subtle juxtaposition of artificiality and realism in the cinema. But it was artificiality the public wanted—swollen busts and happy endings. His idea of introducing foreign film classics had misfired. Receipts had slumped alarmingly that week.

Of course there were plenty of foreign films that peddled sex much more effectively than Hollywood, but it was risky to resort to the Continental X-port market. He had learned to his cost, when the 'Empire' had staged nude reviews in a desperate attempt to keep going, that using sex quite frankly as the basic attraction meant losing the reliable, come-every-week family audience to gain the dubious favours of a fickle, rowdy mob of hooligans. Besides, he didn't want to awaken the wrath of that turbulent priest again. He had won the last contest on points, thank God, but he knew that a series of 'X' films, and the suggestive posters that were essential to their promotion, would give Father Whatsisname just the chance he wanted to point the accusing finger. That would knock the bottom out of his own defence of the cinema as the clean, healthy *family* entertainment.

He had seen Father . . . Kipling, that was it, one day. A Catholic friend had pointed him out as he hurried through the streets with a small boy at his side, clutching a worn black leather bag—probably answering a sick call, his friend had suggested. Grey-haired, stooping, shabbily dressed. Mr Berkley had almost felt pity for him, and genuinely regretted that they should be at war. They were both, after all, in show-business of a kind, both presiding over a declining form of entertainment, both desperately concerned to pull in the customers. They should be allies, not rivals.

With an effort he redirected his thoughts to the problem of what films the Palladium should show in the near future.

128

Something new, something up to date was needed. Something that was associated with youth. Everyone was mad about youth nowadays. Youth set the fashion, and the old followed. Of course that had always been the case, the young always did set the fashion; but never before did it change so rapidly, never before were the older generation so pathetically afraid of being left behind.

★   ★   ★

Mr Mallory was not at all enjoying his Saturday evening at the cinema. An uneasy conscience chafed him like his new, scratchy tweed suit, caused him the same persistent discomfort as the broken spring he was hatching out beneath his buttocks. And it was not the film to soothe and smother a disturbed conscience. A worthy, well-made film in its way, no doubt, but rather depressing. Not his idea of a Saturday night's entertainment. When you went to the pictures you didn't want to be reminded of the problems that dogged you outside the cinema: jobs, children, money and so forth. Particularly if you had just had a row with your wife, and rather suspected that you were in the wrong.

But then, damn it, *was* he so obviously in the wrong? After all, there was no *necessity* to go to Benediction on a Saturday evening. It was making a fetish of religion. Of course Bett was still a superstitious, God-fearing Irishwoman; you couldn't expect her to appreciate that a person could have too much of a good thing—even religion. It was a question of religious capacity. Some had more than others. He knew his own religious capacity. He knew whether or not he would benefit from going to church. And tonight he would not have. Bett was not bound to go. It was not as though she had been slack in her church attendance in the past. In fact, she was so far ahead of the majority on points that she could afford to let up a bit. Her religious capacity might be greater than his. In fact, he was willing to admit that it was. But it was a wife's duty to obey her husband in all that was not sin. That was the teaching of her own Church. It was ridiculous to pretend that there was anything immoral about the cinema. That old fallacy of Father Kipling's had been exploded long ago, and should never have been taken seriously in any case. In fact, he had forced Bett to admit as much, but she had countered by claiming that nevertheless they should set the children a good example. At this transparent piece of blackmail, he had walked out of the house.

He had roved the district in search of cinematic distraction, of some foolish, enjoyable, Hollywood farrago, preferably set in the ancient world, with all-Americans dressed in togas, and luscious drug-store dames in tailored slave-rags. He had rejected a British war-film, *The Sea Shall Not Have Them* (And They Shall Not Have Me Either he had vowed as he passed by), and a jolly double bill comprised of *The Return Of Frankenstein* and *The Monster*, before turning into the Palladium as a last resort. *Bicycle Thieves* did not sound very promising, but he could not return home now. How typically vexing that there should be a rotten crop of films on, just when he really wanted a good one.

His worst fears had been realized. It was a depressing film. Perhaps on another occasion, in another mood, he would have been more sympathetically disposed towards it, but at the moment it seemed merely the repetition, however well-prepared, of a diet he knew only too well. Not that he had ever been as poverty-stricken as the poor fellow in the film. But the dreariness, the frightful struggle of life, the indifference of people, the troublesomeness of children— he did not want to be reminded of them at that moment. He had made up his mind to be morally irresponsible this evening. Where were the luscious slave-girls with swelling breast and buttocks like ripe fruit, on which he could feed his harmless, middle-aged lechery? He felt cheated. He felt only too conscious of being in a cinema, on a seat with

130

a broken spring, inhaling rank, second-hand air, his eyes smarting from cigarette-smoke, and his head throbbing with the heat. An ice-cream girl lurched slowly backwards down the aisle. Stretching out a hand, he purchased a choc-ice. It was thickly covered with milk chocolate, which increased the sickly sweetness of the ice-cream to a nauseous intensity. Why couldn't those concerned realize that plain chocolate combined best with ice-cream? War-time restriction on milk-chocolate seemed to have given confectionery manufacturers a fanatical devotion to the stuff. Plain chocolate was becoming quite absurdly rare. It would soon be necessary to organize a National Society for the Protection of Plain Chocolate. The N.S.P.P.C.

Mr Mallory perceived that his ice was warm and half melted inside its chocolate coating, and that it was dripping on to his new suit. He deposited the sticky, oozing mess under his seat with a nasty feeling of satisfaction at the inconvenience it would cause the cleaners the next morning.

Patricia sensed, with some satisfaction, that she was an object of curiosity to the cinema attendants. A young, unescorted girl in a grubby man's raincoat, taking a 3s. 6d. seat when the last programme was half-over, upset, for them, the natural order of things. As she was shown to her seat, she noted that trailers were being shown, which indicated that the last, and principal film had not yet started. She took advantage with both elbows of the luxury of padded arms, and felt soothed by the warm, impersonal darkness, the bovine torpor of those around her, and her own pleased consciousness of wasting time and money when she should have been studying. Why did she feel so much more a *person* when she was not being virtuous?

A few hours earlier she had been grinding wearily at Latin prose composition, when she had caught a shocked glimpse of her pinched, haggard face in the mirror. The words of *A Grammarian's Funeral* came into her head:

> *Learned we found him.*
> *Yea, but we found him bald too, eyes like lead,*
> *Accents uncertain: . . .*

Snatching an old raincoat from the hallstand she had plunged out into the rain. 'Where are you going at this hour?' Mummy from the kitchen. 'Out.' A pleasingly curt, truthful and enigmatic reply.

They would probably worry like anything. Not that there was any need. After all, she was seventeen, and capable of looking after herself. But they insisted on treating her like a child—or, what was worse, like an adolescent. You could almost hear their good intentions creaking as they made allowances for 'the difficult age'. Even Daddy, wisest and kindest of men, seemed to suffer from the same delusion. 'We've got to treat Patricia carefully,' she had overheard him say to her mother one night. 'After all, she's at a difficult age.' Good heavens, did they think her 'moods' were due to a mere period, or to a growing bust measurement? When she was fourteen perhaps; but now? Didn't they think her capable of adult emotions, of real suffering, genuine worry? The younger you were in a family, it seemed to her, the harder it was to convince your parents that you were growing up. If only people would realize that all she wanted was freedom: freedom to think and act for herself, freedom to let life happen to her, instead of having to shape it to her parent's expectations. If only they realized that she was under strain. Only Mark seemed to have an inkling of this strain; but he (thank heaven) didn't seem to realize that he was part of it.

She ignored the flickering screen, and let her thoughts drift on, because it was one of those rare times when she was thinking well, when striking and truthful ideas seemed to occur to her effortlessly, rising fully articulated into the

132

mind, when it seemed possible that one day she might write poetry.

She had gulped in this exciting sense of heightened perception with the wind and rain, as soon as she found herself on the pavement outside the house. While everybody else hurried to their destinations, she had walked slowly and aimlessly through the streets, lifting her face to the stinging rain, and watching the low rain clouds driven across the sky like waves seen from under the sea.

It grew dark. She took advantage of the last half-hour before the grimy little park closed to wander round it. Fingers touching across her stomach in the pockets of her raincoat, she watched with agreeable melancholy the duck-pond tirelessly forming circles under the ceaseless battery of the rain. Scuffling and tittering emanated from a round shelter sliced into four sections like a cake. It harboured a girl and two boys, about fifteen. They chased each other from one section to another. Their mean, human activity was discordant, and she moved on, until she could hear only the swish of the trees in the wind, and the patter of falling rain.

Idly she unravelled the muddle of paths, wandering past low, stunted railings, and dwarf 'Keep off the grass' signs sprouting from the balding turf; past desolate putting greens; past tightly-shuttered refreshment kiosks; past the narrow lanes marked 'Men' and 'Women' that commenced at a modest distance from each other and wound through dark shrubbery to merge in a single, dripping tomb, divided by a wall. Affection, melancholy, and other emotions that eluded classification, surged and slopped inside her as she noted each detail as if for the first time—or as if for the last. For slowly, half-consciously, but inexorably, there was growing in her mind the conviction that she would have to leave home.

She followed a path into a wide macadam clearing, in the centre of which stood a bandstand, gaunt, skeletel, deserted, like some abandoned pagan temple. In her early childhood, in the war, the puzzling structure had symbolized for her mythical 'pre-war' delights—like talking-dolls, pineapples, and sea-side rock. The disused bandstand had been a useful playground in wet weather—useful, but limited, because there was very little you could do in a bare, empty bandstand once you had played tag in its confined area, and walked round the parapet. Always you felt it was holding something back, waiting.

It still retained its mystery. It had been repainted since the war, but, as far as she knew, it had never given forth music. Despite its new coat of paint it was still something of a relic, something of an enigma, resembling, in its apparently purposeless massiveness, some strange arrangement of stones on the site of a vanished civilization.

Leaving the bandstand, and heading for the gate at the summons of the park-keeper's doleful bell, she decided that like the rest of Brickley, it exuded the odour of decay, hopelessness, regret. Decay had a certain undeniable pathos and character, but it meant death—death to the heart, death to the mind, death to the spirit. The family were kind and well-meaning, but they could not help, they had been too long in Brickley. The Church—she had had more than enough of Brickley parochial Catholicism. Brickley: its very name choked and stifled. Mark had blown in like a fresh breeze, hinting, with wild scents, of other delightful worlds where the air was free, pure, invigorating. Experience that she had once accepted as belonging only to the dream-world of the cinema screen, really existed, was to be grasped at the cost of a little determination. A Bohemian student life in Paris, the beaches of the Mediterranean, travel, talk, people —Life in a word. She thirsted for it.

And then there was Mark himself. It was him above all she would be trying to impress by her break with convention—impress in a quite futile way, because it was obvious that he and Clare were permanently attached. But still, it would be satisfying if he ever experienced in future years a tinge of regret that he had not appreciated the potentialities of the young schoolgirl he had coached with such distressing kindness. Distressing, precisely because it was so genuine, so guileless. As soon as she had realized that he was making no attempt to disguise his liking for her, she had known that there was no hope. She was sentenced for life to be Clare's younger sister in his eyes. If somehow she could have been given a meagre share in their relationship, if one or the other had treated her as a confidante, it might have been more bearable. But Clare was always inscrutable and uninformative, and Mark (it was the only flaw in his sensibility) plainly thought her either blind or indifferent to their relationship. Their love was like a bonfire behind someone else's high fence. You stood in the dark watching the glow and the flare of fireworks, and it never occurred to the other people to invite you in, and you couldn't ask.

As she walked along the High Street, these thoughts had infiltrated her mind like the scouts of an advancing army of depression and self-pity. The hour of acute awareness was running out into the usual hopeless analysis of a hopeless situation, the usual emotional slush. A cinema offered a refuge, and she had clutched at it. She couldn't afford it, but no matter; she would make do with her appallingly riddled stockings for another month. Besides, it was a good film, a continental film, part of the more abundant life she sought.

The impulsive and irresponsible gesture had the effect of recovering her sense of identity, and now she sat waiting expectantly for *Bicycle Thieves* to begin. It was important to concentrate so as to be able to discuss the film intelligently with Mark.

* * *

Patrick held his cigarette in one gloved hand. It was

135

uncomfortably warm, but it kept the nicotine off your fingers. He pushed back a long, greasy spike of hair that kept slipping down and pricking his ear. The hair which his mother said was too long, and the grease which his father said was too much. It seemed that they were probably right.

But at least they restricted themselves to *saying* now. He would wait a few days before having his hair cut, so that they could not think that they had *made* him. That was the main thing.

He could do more or less as he pleased now. Within reason. He could go to the pictures on his own. It so happened that Clare and Mark were here tonight, but that was just chance. They didn't know he was here. Just as well, as he wasn't allowed to smoke. Not that they would tell. Patricia would, though, if she saw him. She would like to get her own back for that row she had got into last October.

This was rather a dull film. He didn't really care whether the man got his bike back or not. He was rather soft, Patrick thought. Him and his little boy.

Patrick professed to scoff at 'soppy love stuff' in films; but he suspected that he was disappointed by its absence from this film. He hesitated over recognizing or dismissing this thought. It was rather important. After all, it was expected that he would become a priest, like James. But a priest must give up all that. It was a difficult problem—were you spoiling your vocation, or didn't you have a real vocation anyway? It was rather worrying.

His attention was captured by the appearance of a young woman on the screen. Not very big. He had slipped into a rather alarming habit lately of looking at every girl or woman he encountered to see how big her bust was. Bust. That was a word he had just discovered. There were several words that meant the same thing. Bust, bosom, breasts. Bust was a funny word. Sometimes they called statues of people's heads busts. It was probably wrong to look at women's busts, but he couldn't bring himself to mention it in confession, not until he had decided about his vocation, one way or the other. It was part of the evidence he was collecting against himself: he looked at *Blighty* furtively in the barber's; he tried drawing women, sometimes in the nude, always with big busts, in a drawing-book he kept hidden at home; he desperately wanted to kiss a girl to find out what it was like.

He inhaled a slight whiff of smouldering wool, and hastily stubbed out his cigarette.

It was funny he should have remembered the row that week-end, when Patricia had left him in the cinema, and the per . . . pervert had touched his leg, because that was when all this had really started. All that Sunday he had brooded on the episode in the cinema. He had wanted to tell his father, but for some inexplicable reason, felt shy and slightly ashamed. In the end, coming home from Benediction, he had blurted it out, rather boastfully, since he had felt that a brush with a real pick-pocket had a certain adventurous quality about it. His father had asked a few questions, and looked grave. He had been frightened, wished he had kept quiet. When they got home, he was told to go to bed, and meekly obeyed. Patricia was rowed for leaving him behind in the cinema. As he slowly undressed in his room, he heard her come snivelling up the stairs. Then his father had come in. 'Son, I want to have a word with you about this man in the pictures, so that you'll know what to do in future. Get into bed now, or you'll catch cold. Never mind about your prayers—you can say them in bed. Now listen, son. You don't know what a pervert is, I suppose. No, not a klepto-maniac. Heavens, what a word! No, this man was no pick-pocket. To explain what he was I'll have to explain a few other things. Now, you've probably heard the lads at school talk of certain things. . . .'

Yes, he had heard them. And it had been easy to ignore them, not to listen, to walk away, when he believed them to be just dirt. But when they were made respectable, vouched for by his own father, when they were associated with his own parents, and with his own existence . . . it was quite different.

Many things had fallen into place as a result of his father's explanation: drawings on lavatory walls, the shape of girl babies, the strange scufflings in Jimmy Thompson's rabbit hutch when they put the black buck Jumbo in with Snow White. . . . He had lain awake for hours that night, as a whole new world of discovery and excitement and evil unrolled before him. Never had he learned and understood so many new things at once. Never had his mind worked so fast or so clearly, leaping on from one conclusion to the next, some exhilarating, some appalling. It changed everything.

He had to know, of course. A priest had to know. But perhaps one day he would want more than just to know. That would not be all right for a priest.

★ ★ ★

Harry brooded, frowning terribly as he toyed with his knife. He was bored, and Harry didn't like to be bored. It was usually necessary for someone to suffer when Harry was bored. Christ, what a film. The only reason he was here was that he had seen every other programme on locally. He didn't like foreign films at the best of times: you couldn't understand what they were saying. It was too much trouble to spell out the sub-titles. But at least you usually saw some hot stuff in foreign films, to make up for it—tarts in bed with blokes and that sort of thing—which you didn't see anywhere else. But this film was dead tame. Not a good-looking tart in the whole picture. And a putrid story. *Bicycle Thieves!* You might have thought from the title that it would be a good gangster. He should have guessed. Who would want to knock off bloody *bicycles*? There was only one good bit in the film—when they showed you the little

138

bastard pissing up a wall. Harry smiled his thin smile as he recollected the scene. But soon he relapsed into his dangerous black mood, fingering the razor-sharp edge of his knife, open in his pocket.

An ice-cream girl sauntered slowly up the aisle with a loaded tray, up to her tits in choc-ices and orange drinks. Sullenly Harry stood up to allow someone to push past into the aisle. Bloody people were always eating. The youth stumbled and trod heavily on Harry's black suède shoes. A flame of pain and anger enveloped him. *A blade glinted, and as if by magic a crescent appeared on the man's cheek, with little beads of blood seeping out like juice from an orange.*

'Sorry, mate,' said the youth.

Harry sat back in his seat without answering. Dwelling on the sentence, memorized from a paper-covered novel he kept at home, he felt revenged. He wanted the youth to go away, for in his mind he saw him fall back with a suppressed scream of terror and pain, holding a handkerchief to his face. He wiped the blade of his knife on the plush cinema seat, as if to clean it.

Loosening his shoulders inside his jacket, and smiling his thin triumphant smile, Harry turned to appraise the bloke's tart, who was now separated from him only by an empty seat. She blushed under his scrutiny, and anxiously looked towards the aisle. Her face seemed familiar, but it was some time before he realized that she was the curly-haired bint who had given him the slip some months back. Lived in Barn Street. Quite a doll—good shape, good teeth, nice skin, and most likely a virgin, to judge from the wet bloke she knocked around with. And here was the bastard back again with his bloody ice-creams. Harry felt physically sick as he pushed past again, the short, flat hair, red, boil-pitted neck, corny blue sports jacket—inches from his face.

'Sorry about treading on your feet.'

The repeated apology only added to Harry's rage and

humiliation. He closed his eyes and went through in detail what he would like to do to the curly-haired tart. And then he began to think, why not do it, why not? It was time.

It was tricky, eating ice-cream with your arms linked, and she didn't want to get a stain on her new frock. That was the worst of the cinema, it was so dark you didn't notice till you got outside. But she had linked arms with Len because she was so glad that he was next to her, between her and that boy who had looked at her as if, well as if she was indecently dressed or something. Some men were like that, as if they had X-ray eyes. There was Raymond at the cafeteria. Like Gladys said, you felt your clothes falling off every time he looked at you. Not that there was any harm in him, it was his nature Gladys said. She had been to Italy on a coach tour, and the Italian men couldn't control themselves she said. She said if you went out alone in a tight skirt you were black and blue before you'd gone a hundred yards. But that boy was different; there was something nasty about the way he looked at you. He wanted to do more than pinch. . . .

She was so glad that Len was back by her side, and yet she dared not tell him why, because he would only be angry and perhaps start a fight and worry afterwards anyway. Like that time she had been followed, last October. After she had told him, they hadn't gone to the pictures for a month, so that he could see her home. And as Old Mother Potts wouldn't allow men visitors, and Len didn't like dancing, it had been pretty dreary just walking about the wintry streets together.

Still, now the lighter evenings were coming on they wouldn't depend on the pictures so much; there would be walks in the park, kissing on the benches in the shadows, lying on the warm, grassy banks. . . . Her train of thought halted with a sickening jolt as she remembered that this summer there wouldn't be many evenings like that. Len was going into the Army next Thursday. She put her ice-cream, half-eaten, on the floor under her seat.

'All right?' he asked.

'Mmm. Lovely.'

Len scraped his cup, licked the spoon, and deposited both on the floor. As he straightened up he seemed to have left his heart on the floor with the empty ice-cream carton. Already he could feel depression and worry creeping over him like a periodic fever. Already he was beginning to steal glances at the clock, comparing it needlessly with his own watch, missing bits of the film while he made rapid calculations as to whether he might conceivably be able to see Bridget home, and, when this had become out of the question, as to how long they would have to say good night at the hated corner.

★ ★ ★

When the film ended with an unexpected *FINE*, Clare stood up and shook the folds of her coat. Then, noticing that Mark was still seated, gazing abstractedly at the screen, she sat down again. Almost at once the National Anthem summoned them both to their feet, but Mark responded sluggishly.

'Brilliant, wasn't it,' he remarked, as he clumsily helped her on with her coat.

'Yes, it was good,' she replied, rather vexed in case she had betrayed a lack of appreciation by standing up too quickly. 'Strange sort of ending though.'

'Ah, but that's just the point, that's just the brilliance of it. No American or English director would have dared to end it there.'

They were wedged in with the patient herd of people who were shuffling slowly and quietly up the stairs to the foyer, but Mark talked in a clear, excited voice, as if oblivious of their presence.

'The point of the film, you see, is in the plural in the title: *Bicycle Thieves*. The man himself becomes a thief out of sheer desperation, and a sense of injustice, and, ironically, accepts the pardon which he is not willing to accord to the person who stole *his* bike. On another level of course, the whole film is an indictment of the society. . . .'

Clare found it difficult to concentrate on what he was saying. They were in the foyer now, and the procession fanned out towards the doors, only to jam there once more, hesitating to plunge into the rain, adjusting macs and umbrellas.

'Oh drat!' said Clare. 'I left my umbrella under the seat.'

'O.K. I'll fetch it,' said Mark. 'Wait here.'

Tired of being buffeted by the eddying crowd, she moved over to the wall, where a sofa seemed to dare her to sit on it. She sat down defiantly, and rummaged in her handbag. Opening her compact, she checked her appearance, and dabbed at her hair. Did Mark like the new style? It was difficult to tell. He seemed uninterested rather than disapproving. The crowd had almost disappeared, and the attendants were giving her 'looks'. At last Mark appeared with the umbrella.

'Thanks, darling,' she said, as she took it from him.

'Couldn't find the seat for some time,' he explained. 'You know, I think you may be partly right about that ending.'

She paused at the brink of the wet, shiny pavement.

'Which way?' she asked, hoisting her umbrella.

He peered into the rain.

'Well, there's a hell of a queue at the bus stop. We might as well walk. We'll get just as wet standing there. D'you mind?'

'No, of course not. I know how you love to walk about in the rain.'

'Yes, I always get a kick out of it. Especially when there's some wind. I feel I'm battling against the elements. Defying them anyway.'

142

'I know.'

She listened with a kind of exultation to the rain battering the taut umbrella, trying to get in, trying to squeeze between their tightly welded bodies, as they forced their way on.

'About that ending,' Mark continued. 'It's something I've always had doubts about. I mean, whether the cruelly realistic medium of the cinema is *entitled* to tragic endings like that.'

'Well, things happen like that. I remember when I lost a fountain-pen Mummy and Daddy gave me for Christmas: I prayed and prayed, and I never found it.'

'Yes, but because a thing could happen in life, that doesn't make it good art. You see what I mean.'

'Yes,' she lied.

'What I mean is, that whereas poetry—Shakespeare, for example—can have tragic themes without merely upsetting the audience—because it *is* poetry, a higher plane of existence than normal life. . . . And it follows the action to its logical conclusion, death, so that you don't worry about the characters any more. But one does feel sometimes—is a film entitled to sweep you so compellingly into someone else's life so completely that for an hour and a half you *are* them —is it then entitled to drop you just when this character is in a perfectly hopeless situation?'

'I know,' she replied, 'I shall be thinking of that poor man and his little boy all night.' Liar!

'Yes, there you are. I feel the same way. I keep reminding myself that this was a film, a work of art, a dramatic illusion, but it's not easy to detach yourself from a film, as you can from a play.'

For a time they trudged on in a silence punctuated by occasional reminiscences of the film.

'I liked the way he composed his pictures, like those continual shots of long, depressing concrete vistas.'

'It was good when they were on the bridge in the rain, and bicycles kept criss-crossing behind them.'

'Yes, that was good,' he replied in answer to this, and she glowed with pleasure at having said the right thing. She always felt rather uneasy when he became absorbed in anything like this. Pretending to be deeply interested was rather a strain. When she was first going out with Mark—and it wasn't so long ago, she was really moved by films, even bad films. But now nothing seemed to matter except Mark. There was nothing of interest to her in the present conversation except as a means of promoting their intimacy and retaining his arm around her waist.

Now they left the main road for the quieter, dimmer back streets. They turned into the bottom of High Hill, and began to ascend it, leaning forward against the incline, and against the rain that drove down upon the umbrella. Clare began to feel a foolish kind of affection for the umbrella that was doing them both such sterling service.

At the top of the hill they paused. It was always a slight, pleasant shock to realize how high you were. It was impossible to walk across the top and ignore the great panorama of London, even if its lights were obscured by the rain, even if the downpour was steadily soaking you. By common consent they sat down on the wet seat of 'Traveller's Rest', huddled under the umbrella, and stared out across the city.

'We always seem to end up here, somehow or other,' said Mark.

'Yes. D'you remember the first time?'

'When was that?'

'Don't you remember?' She was disappointed. That evening, its precious intimacies, belonged to her most treasured memories.

'You remember. I think it was the first time you really spoke to me. Told me your real feeling about . . . oh, about life and writing and things.'

'Oh, yes. I talked a lot of nonsense, I remember.'

'Well, I'll never forget it anyway.'

'You've got a fearsomely retentive memory, haven't you, darling?'

Darling. It always kindled a glow of security and peace when he called her that, however casually. It had marked a crucial phase in their love—it had in fact signalled his recognition that they were in love. That was how he had greeted her at Euston on her return from Ireland after the New Year. 'Hallo, darling, good to see you.' Now she listened eagerly for the word, and felt a twinge of disappointment whenever she heard 'dear' or 'Clare' instead, fearing that he had fallen out of love since the last 'darling'.

'Well, perhaps it wasn't all nonsense. But I get a different feeling now when I look out over London. Not completely different perhaps. It's still the sense of multiplicity that's oppressive. But not in the same way.'

'What way, then, darling?'

'Well . . . religion, I suppose. The enormous indifference. The millions and millions of people in London and beyond who don't know about God, and don't want to know. Or who know about a different God to mine. It's like looking at those maps that colour in the World's Religions. It's demoralizing to see what a small area the Universal Church commands. You begin to wonder whether you're right after all.'

'But, Mark, that's all beside the point. The Church would still be the True Church, even if there was only one Catholic in the world.' The answer came out pat, like a bar of chocolate from an automatic machine, stale and predictable. It wasn't easy to lose the mental habits of the convent. Sometimes she hankered after the luxury of doubt; often she envied Mark the bouyancy of his new-found faith.

'I acknowledge that intellectually, of course,' he replied, 'but statistics are horribly insidious. Don't worry though, it doesn't seriously disturb me.'

'And this multiplicity business?'

'Well that's interesting really. I don't get the same feeling of despair and helplessness any more. . . .'

Now he was scarcely talking to her, but more to himself, analysing and defining as always. A woman with a dog stared at them curiously as she passed. Indeed, they must have looked pretty mad, sitting on the sodden bench in the pouring rain. Mark talked on.

'I think it was because I had nothing, no idea or concept which would contain the appalling multiplicity. But now I see that, quite simply, God contains the multiplicity. You see, what troubled me most I think, was the apparently vast, shapeless extent of it. It's reassuring to get things into some kind of cosmic perspective, to realize that the total of man's activity is no more than a faint line on the infinite creativity of God's hand.'

Guiltily, Clare became conscious of a feeling of boredom. Six months ago it had been her dearest wish that one day he would discuss the great truths of their shared religion with her. By some miracle this had happened. But she felt none of the joy she had anticipated. To be honest, she almost regretted his conversion. This was no credit to her own piety—but what was the use of pretending that she had any piety left? She felt towards her religion as she imagined some women felt towards their dreary, loveless marriages: something trying, but inescapable; cluttered with apparently futile chores, yet from which there was no question of escaping. Would her own marriage be like that? No, it was too hellish a prospect even to consider. Marriage had now come to occupy the same central position in her mind as religion had formerly: on it all her hopes were based. She looked back on the transformation in herself with a kind of helpless resignation. She couldn't help thinking that it was Mark himself who was largely responsible for the change. But it hadn't brought him any closer to her. Like a see-saw, her drop had sent him soaring into religiosity.

Once they must have been dead level, but not for long. It was Student Cross that had really swept him out of her reach.

Even now it seemed incredible that Mark—cynical, idle, sophisticated Mark, had actually joined that file of Catholic students who, during Holy Week, carried a heavy wooden Cross through the public streets and along the open road between London and Our Lady's shrine at Walsingham. He had not completed the pilgrimage. After three days he had limped home, crippled by blisters. To her he had seemed a hero: all she wanted was to kneel at his feet, kiss them and bandage them. But he had blocked all her attempts to anoint him with love and sympathy. He wouldn't talk about the pilgrimage, except to say that he was disappointed at having had to abandon it. He seemed far from exalted. Rather, it was as if he was having an affair with another girl, and had quarrelled with her. Absurdly, she felt jealous of Student Cross as of some unknown quantity, some hidden source of fascination, whose attraction she could neither understand nor compete with. Oh, Lord! Now he was talking about eternity.

'. . . eternal life doesn't put earthly life in the shade simply because it's *longer*. That's the point where we go wrong—I mean in the way we think about eternity. Tell me, Clare, how did you give an idea of eternity to your kids at the convent?'

'Oh, I used the old illustration: a ball of steel as large as the world, a fly alighting on it once every million years. When the ball of steel is rubbed away by the friction, eternity will not even have begun.'

'Precisely. You build up a frightening picture of an immensely long, empty passage of time, only to cancel it out with your last breath, leaving your audience thoroughly confused, but clinging to the idea that eternity is "like" a great length of time.'

'Well, what else can you do?'

'Say simply and honestly that eternity is as much like an instant as like a million years, because it's equally unlike either. It's not like a length of time, it's just different. Eternity should be visualized as a blessed state of being without past or future. Instead the word always has an unpleasant connotation when used colloquially—"I waited an eternity for a bus".'

'I'd like to see you explain all that to a first form,' said Clare, exasperated.

'Well they take far more difficult things without turning a hair: transubstantiation for instance.'

She sighed.

'Darling, my bottom's getting awfully cold and damp. Could we go?'

'All right,' he replied flatly, unresponsive to her invitation to some facetious joking about bottoms, which might have jolted him out of his philosophical mood. Clare felt chastened and annoyed. What was the matter with him? They plodded through the rain in an unhappy silence. He offered her his arm, instead of putting it round her waist. Then he said suddenly:

'Clare, you never told me why you left the convent.'

'No.'

'Why?'

'I didn't particularly want to think about it.'

'No, I mean, why *did* you leave the convent. What made you decide that you didn't have a vocation?'

Clare hesitated. Of course she *had* thought of it. It was with her always, like some unforgettable sight or sound, like the cry of a drowning man, always echoing in the back of the mind. But she had never discussed it with anyone, and the idea of doing so now, with Mark, made her tremble. But perhaps, by telling him of it she might break through the shell of quiet self-sufficiency and recollection that had kept her at bay since his return from Student Cross. Still she hesitated, wanting him to appreciate the gravity of such a revelation and the trust it revealed in her if she chose to make it.

'Why do you want to know? Some more fodder for your stories I suppose,' she grumbled.

'You know I haven't written anything for months, darling. No, I'm interested to know, that's all.'

Darling again. So everything was all right. Perhaps she could seal their reconciliation by divulging her secret. Love was like childhood friendship. The development of the relationship depended on shared secrets, on entrusting the other person with more and more important parts of yourself. She had found it so with Mark. He had been, particularly in the early days, insatiable in probing after facts about her private, secret life, her thoughts and feelings in childhood and adolescence. At first she had been shy and reluctant—until she discovered the power over him this could give her—that she could always command his interest and attention by resurrecting some memory long buried by forgetfulness and, sometimes, shame. She came to know instinctively the kind of candid, vivid anecdote that found favour with him, the sort of thing that made him chuckle with delight, and sometimes scribble it down in a note-book. But now she was beginning to regret her prodigal outpourings: he had almost sucked her dry, and she was afraid, afraid that when there was no more mystery about her, he would cast her aside like an empty container.

She thrust this thought away, despising her own lack of confidence. She looked at him. He was walking outside the shelter of the umbrella now, braced against the driving wind and rain, his head thrown back, and lips slightly parted. His hair was a damp, matted tangle. His raincoat was turned up at the collar, but not to protect him against the rain, for he always wore it that way. He had a boyish, slightly abstracted look, that was his most endearing expression. He glanced at her, and must have recognized the feelings that were laid out frankly on her own face, for he

149

slipped his arm round her and kissed her. She clung to him, and they stopped in the middle of the pavement, with the rain falling all round, its liquid percussion in drains, in gutters, on trees, on the umbrella, the only sounds. Then the noise of a car grinding up the other side of the hill broke in upon the blessed peace of their embrace, and separated them.

'What's the matter, Clare?' Mark asked gently, noticing her tears.

'Nothing,' she replied, leaning heavily against him as they moved on.

'If I've done anything. . . .'

'No, honestly, darling, I'm not upset. It just does things to me when we kiss. I don't think you realize.'

'Perhaps I don't,' he said quietly.

After a little while Clare said:

'I didn't leave the convent of my own accord. I was asked to leave.'

It seemed to shake him more than she had anticipated.

'I—I'm sorry, Clare,' he said awkwardly. 'I shouldn't have been so inquisitive. If you'd rather not tell me——'

'No, I want you to know, Mark. I'd have told you one day. There mustn't be any secrets between us, must there?'

'No, I suppose not.'

She drew breath to begin.

'Well——'

She exhaled suddenly with a strained laugh.

'Well, after making such a song and dance about it, there's very little to tell. I've never really understood it. In fact, at the time, I thought I was a real martyr. One of the girls at the convent was called Hilda Syms. . . .'

She paused, surprised by the wave of pain and nostalgia that passed through her at the mention of the name, leaving her weak and trembling; as if the sights, sounds, smells, tastes, feelings, sufferings of years could be experienced again in a single spasm of sickening intensity: the cold

150

cubicle, the rustle of habits and the squeaking of boots as the nuns filed into the chapel, the stink of stew in the refectory; her first lesson, the children shaking their up-stretched hands, eager to please the new sister; Hilda, dew-fresh in her white blouse and neatly-pressed gym-slip, shy and ardent in the back row; Hilda and herself together in the copse, in the chapel, in the cloisters, praying, talking, joking, sharing secrets, confidences. . . .

'Yes?' prompted Mark.

'Well, as you know, when I was a novice I used to do quite a lot of teaching, because the nuns were short-handed, and it was useful practice. One of the girls I taught was this girl Hilda Syms, and she got a crush on me. Well, there's nothing unusual in that. You know what girls' schools are like.'

'No—but go on,' said Mark, smiling.

'Well, they're like that, believe me. Lots of girls had crushes on me—it was inevitable. I was young, you see, and——'

'Beautiful,' interposed Mark.

Clare smiled.

'Well, the other nuns were rather grim and ancient. Anyway, most of these girls grew out of these crushes—soon the great problem was to keep them away from the Grammar School boys at the other end of the road. But Hilda was different. Hilda didn't grow out of it.'

She paused again, struggling for words to convey the innocence and intimacy of that friendship, words that had to be like a spider's web, strong yet delicate, if she was to communicate to Mark's coarse masculine intelligence some inkling of what that friendship had meant to her and Hilda.

'Hilda wasn't interested in the Grammar School boys?' he prompted.

'No, she wasn't. But you mustn't misunderstand. Look, you know that queer book you lent me, about a girls' college in France?'

'I remember it.'

'Well, there was nothing like that between—— Our relationship was quite different.'

'What was your relationship exactly?'

'Well, it's difficult to explain to a boy. You'll probably laugh, but, well, we thought we could help each other to be good—in a spiritual way I mean. When I realized that Hilda's was more than a normal crush, I should have stopped it I suppose. But I hadn't the heart. It would have been like stamping on a little bird you watch learning to fly. And besides, I liked Hilda. I suppose that was where I went wrong—I was selfish. The other sisters were very severe; I liked Hilda's admiration. She was gay and trusting. I thought I could help her spiritually, perhaps show her that she had a vocation too. You see, she was a convert. Her parents had sent her to the convent, and she begged them to let her become a Catholic after she'd been there only a year. They agreed, but they weren't very keen, and she didn't get much encouragement in her religious life at home. I thought that she deserved a little special attention.

'Then gradually it began to get out of control. I kissed her once when she came out of the chapel on a First Friday. She had just received Holy Communion, of course, and her face was radiant and pure—I can't explain why I did it, but I couldn't help kissing her. After that she came to expect a kiss whenever we met or parted—if we were alone, of course. However, I think we must have been observed, for I sensed an undercurrent of resentment among the other girls, and Hilda was persecuted by some of them. This threw her more passionately on to me for solace and support, but I was losing patience—I didn't know how to cope. We had quarrels, reconciliations—it was a love affair really. These storms usually blew over quickly, but they got more frequent. Then one day——'

She faltered at the memory of that day. A blistering July day, her thick woollen underwear sodden with perspiration under the hot black habit, a throbbing headache, Hilda more insistent than ever; a scene in the playground, only a few words exchanged because other girls were watching, but a few words that shrieked under the stress of the emotion that they bore; an impatient phrase, more cutting than she had intended; Hilda turning away with a passionate sob, running, running. . . .

'There was a scene. Hilda got hysterical and tried to kill herself with aspirins. She wasn't in any real danger, but it was very serious of course. It all came out. I was asked to leave. No recriminations, no sermons. But there was no appeal. I was simply told that I had no vocation. I left.'

She noticed for the first time that they had stopped, and looking round, discovered that they were outside the house.

'Goodness! I didn't realize that we were home.'

The rain was still streaming down, swept into folds by occasional gusts of wind. Wearily they climbed the steps to the porch. Mark collapsed the umbrella.

'We're both sopping wet. We'd better go straight in,' said Mark.

'Can we wait just a minute?'

She felt limp and exhausted, but there might be someone in the kitchen, and she couldn't face anyone else at the moment. More than anything in the world she longed for Mark to take her into his arms and comfort her like a baby. As though humouring her, he put out his arms and held her loosely round the waist, smiling at her in a sympathetic way, as one does to an invalid.

'Well, now you know my awful secret,' she said. 'I didn't leap over the wall. I was shown to the door.'

'Poor Clare.'

'Poor Mark, to have a neurotic ex-nun for a girl-friend.'

'I'm not complaining,' he said, drawing her into his embrace.

Without warning, something gave inside her, like some part of a dam long under unsuspected strain. Emotion seemed to gush out of her eyes, nose, mouth, as she sighed, wept, mumbled between kisses, covering his face with spit, tears, lipstick and rain, clinging to him with the frantic strength of a drowning swimmer. But even in this tumult she felt that Mark was the sane, controlled life-guard, trying to calm her. She wanted to pull him down with her. She was seized with a desire to feel his hand on her breast again, as she had felt it for a fleeting second months ago. Seizing his hand, she kissed it, and thrust it under her raincoat and pressed it to her bosom. For a moment she felt his fingers cup her breast, then he snatched his hand away.

'No, Clàre.'

She was stunned by the rebuff. It wasn't until they were inside the dark hall, and Mark had taken off her coat and carefully hung it up, that shame and humiliation began to return to her numbed consciousness like the blood to her face. Then she ran soundlessly to her room. She heard his low, troubled call, 'Clare', as she turned at the top of the stairs. But there was hesitation and doubt in his voice, and she did not turn back.

★ ★ ★

Damien writhed in anger as he stood penned in the bus shelter like an animal, with this herd of obnoxious Cockneys. The meeting at the Presbytery after Benediction had dragged on far too long, but he had caught his bus, and was congratulating himself on being out of the rain, when the conductor had bawled 'All change!' and he had been ejected, despite his protests, on to the streaming pavements, with less than half his journey completed. The 'shelter' was a ridiculously inadequate affair, consisting only of a tubular metal frame with a narrow roof, thus allowing one to be squashed by the crowd packed into its small area, and soaked by the rain that swept in through its open sides. Moreover, he was so near to the kerb that heavy vehicles passing close by spattered his shoes and trousers with filth.

He had apparently had the misfortune to be dumped at the end of this bus-queue at the very moment when cinemas, dance-halls and public-houses were spewing forth their patrons on to the pavements. The indignity of the situation infuriated him: that he, straight from church, should be swamped by this ribald, vulgar, beer-reeking mob reeling out from their godless pleasures. Swearing, grumbling, joking in loud voices, they heaved in a damp, excited mass, struggling for a place on each bus, as it drew up, already full. A fat, smelly old harridan with a stick became quite offensive when Damien attempted to thrust his way to his rightful position at the front of the queue.

''Ere! Where d'you think you're goin'? You orter be ashamed of yourself. Sum people can't wait patient. There's others was 'ere before you, yer know.'

She continued to mutter threateningly to herself and to anyone who might listen. 'Sauce! Some people got no manners at all. . . .'

Damien, sickened, and a little frightened, turned his back on the crowd, and stared sulkily across the street.

Suddenly he caught sight of Clare and Underwood walking arm in arm along the opposite pavement. They were half-hidden beneath an umbrella, and had evidently not seen him. A sudden rush of emotions—jealousy and envy, mingled with satisfaction at observing them unbeknown— made him forget his uncomfortable situation for a moment. Then, acting on an impulse, he drove his hip viciously into the side of the old woman, and taking advantage of the space momentarily gained by this manœuvre, ducked under the rail, and crossed the road. A stream of foul language issued from the old woman's lips, but Damien ignored her.

In fact, he scarcely heard her. His thoughts were with the two figures ahead, so tightly linked beneath the sheltering dome of the umbrella. Too tightly. It was quite unnecessary that Underwood should clasp her waist like that. For all his much-vaunted 'conversion', it seemed that he still lusted after the pleasures of the flesh, still itched to finger the curve of Clare's side, to feel her thigh brush against his. Conversion! One had to admire his cunning. Clare was a gullible girl, and a show of religious fervour had been all that was needed to make her quite infatuated with Underwood. She probably believed that *she* had converted him. He had bewitched her. Not nine months out of the convent, and she was behaving like a trollop, encouraging him to hold her tightly round the waist, tossing back her head to laugh, looking into his face with a silly, fatuous smile. Yet when he himself had offered to kiss her. . . .

He stiffened suddenly as if in sudden pain, as he recollected the incident. It was the dark hall of the Mallorys' house on Christmas afternoon. Clare was in the bathroom, and he waited for her at the bottom of the stairs. He tried to suggest it was a casual encounter as he stepped from the shadows, but realized at once that his subterfuge was painfully obvious. Doggedly, however, he went through with his rehearsed speech: 'Ah, well met, Clare! Won't you salute your cousin in the spirit of the season?' He was conscious that his words creaked and grated like machinery in the wrong hands, and that his smiling glance upwards at the bunch of mistletoe was more of a leer, a leer that stayed, unnaturally fixed by confusion and rage, as he observed Clare's hesitation. Then she forced a smile, and said, 'Of course, Damien,' and proffered a cheek, averted as though she was expecting a blow. It was so insultingly different from the embrace he had seen her allow Underwood earlier in the day, that on a mad impulse he made a clumsy grab at her, and pulled her towards him, with a hollow imitation of a roguish laugh. And she had broken free with a scandalized exclamation: 'Damien!' And he had stood for several minutes in the passage, paralysed with embarrassment, and shame and chagrin. For the first time he had been unable to recover his self-possession, to escape from his humiliation.

He suddenly realized that the impact of this too-vivid

memory had slowed him down and finally arrested him in the middle of the wet pavement. Two girls in a shop-doorway were staring at him and giggling. They could not have been more than fifteen, but their faces were heavily coated with cosmetics, and they were dressed with a tawdry precociousness which allowed no illusions as to their innocence. He glared at them, incensed by the immorality they carried so lightly, their ignorance of sin, and his own too exact awareness of it. He hurried on, sighting Clare and Underwood in the distance just turning off the main road up the hill.

They stopped at the top of the hill and sat down. Quite extraordinary behaviour—the rain was pouring down. It was awkward too, as he could hardly walk past them without being recognized. So he hung back for what seemed an interminable length of time, in the shadow of a dripping tree, waiting for them to move on. He thought about the two girls in the shop doorway, surprised by the detailed impression they had left on his memory. Immorality in a man was, regrettably, normal. Immorality, or even immodesty, in a woman, was far more disturbing. It was as if a woman who thus lowered herself disowned her right to be considered a person, a soul; as if it would be no sin to take advantage of her lust because one could not possibly soil her any further.

Another spectre of his too-vivid memory rose up to tempt him. One day he had taken a walk in the country, and had surprised two lovers in a wood. He had caught a glimpse of two bare legs, an exposed breast, a man with his trousers about his knees, before they had seen him, and he had run off, blundering panic-stricken through the undergrowth. Even now the recollection seized him in the abdomen, and a kind of sick longing made him tremble. Curiosity. That was the terrible thing about concupiscence. The Devil and the World were easily dealt with: one could appraise coolly what they offered, balance it against eternal damnation, and draw the obvious conclusion. But the temptations of the Flesh were different: they could not be dealt with in cold blood. You could not hear the voice of reason, only the terrible curiosity, insisting that it be satisfied.

Underwood had satisfied it of course. There was no doubt about that. Clare, if she had any sense (which seemed questionable), must realize that a person of his background and way of life would scarcely have remained pure. Yet there had never been any reserve in her bearing towards him on that account. There was a kind of bias in Christianity in favour of the loose-liver who was converted. One accepted the parable of the Prodigal Son of course; salvation was possible for all. But the libertine who turned to religion in maturity seemed to get undue credit. There was nothing particularly creditable in giving up an immoral life when you had fully satisfied that nagging curiosity. Yet Augustine was more honoured than St Aloysius Gonzaga. The really heroic man was the one who practised chastity as a young man. But what was his reward? If the grace of repentance was so easily obtained, why worry about holy purity? He was not a fool; he knew what went on in the fields about his home in summer; he was not himself without desires, desires and curiosity. Yet he had kept himself apart, uncontaminated. To what end? Rejected by the priesthood, he found himself unfitted in some way for normal life. For whatever it was in Underwood that attracted Clare, and that he himself lacked, seemed to derive from what she would call Underwood's 'experience', his 'maturity'—which meant quite simply, his sin. In Ireland he was called 'a shpiled priesht'. Was he not also a spoiled man?

At last Clare and Underwood moved on, but he was compelled to halt again, as they kissed, passionately, in the middle of the pavement.

For Damien it was the final condemnation of Clare. She had soiled herself to the point of revulsion by submitting to his pawing in the public street—as shameless as the casual coupling of two dogs. He would never be able to wipe out completely the pain of his hurt pride, but henceforward he would never be able to think of Clare in any honourable way. He looked back contemptuously at his dream of an ideal Christian marriage with this . . . this renegade nun on heat.

It afforded him a measure of satisfaction to insult her, and to document her improper behaviour with Underwood. He followed them home with something of the elation of a successful spy, and when he eagerly observed Clare's final self-abandonment in the porch it seemed to him that he had obtained some immensely pleasurable secret. He hurried up to his room, and warmed himself with it. That night he prayed devoutly that he might be upheld in the purity which he had so far maintained, in spite of the temptations and evil example which encompassed him on all sides. And with great generosity, he prayed that Clare would not be led into mortal sin—if indeed she had not already fallen.

Harry shivered slightly in the shadow of the sagging wooden hut that had once been somebody's garden shed—some poor bugger that was blown to bits by a buzz-bomb most likely. Beyond him was the blank, windowless side of the house, smooth and flat, as if the row of houses had been sliced with a cheese-cutter. He had played here as a kid just after the war, when it *was* a bomb-site, with tottering, gutted houses, uncovered cellars, bits of furniture, twisted pipes, water tanks. They'd had a good time. And tonight he was going to have a good time. A bloody good time.

The rubble had been cleared away long ago, and a line drawn between houses that were lived in, and blank space. Soon they would be filling in the space with houses again.

And the curly-haired bint would not be walking across it on her way home from the pictures. But tonight she was walking towards the bomb-site, towards one hell of a surprise. She was going to find out shortly that she couldn't get on the wrong side of Harry without paying for it. It was a long time since he had decided to have her. But he would have her, in the end. There was no escaping from Harry. In the end.

He had it all worked out: the hand over her mouth, the knife under her eyes, and drag her into the dark shed. Probably she would lap it up. They usually did. Underneath all the skirts and the modesty and the 'Who me? The idea!' was the same dirty pleasure.

He shivered again, and began to tremble violently. Cursing under his breath, he struggled to control his body. Then he heard the tip-tap of her high heels approaching, and something gripped him hard, and squeezed out all the shivers. Breathing in quick, noiseless gasps, he eased the knife from his pocket, and thumbed the press-button that released the blade.

* * *

The tip-tap of her own heels on the pavement was Bridget's only company during the long walk through the bleak backdoubles. The vile weather had emptied the streets, and made them particularly frightening. She tried to forget her fears of the unknown in hearty cursing of the rain. There was a girl at work who said she loved the rain—she would dress up in a mac and goloshes and tramp around in the rain just for pleasure. She must be mad. Personally she hated the rain—spoiling shoes, spattering stockings, making her clothes look like rags, and her hair go frizzy. She would really *have* to get an umbrella, she decided, not for the first time. Her headscarf was already soaked through. She shivered as a gust of wind dashed the rain rudely in her face. How she longed to be indoors, snuggled up in bed, driving out of her system the damp cold, and the misery of parting from Len, with a hot-water bottle and impossible dreams of their future life together.

It hadn't been much of a picture for dreaming on. She didn't see how she could fit Len and herself in anywhere. Or rather, they would fit in just too well. . . . It was just the wretched sort of life that might so easily be theirs: the cramped lodgings, the worry, the sense of wearing yourself out against life. . . . But it was fatal to think on those lines. Almost desperately she sought solace in her own private 'pictures', the programme she never tired of, which she had projected on to her drowsy mind countless times as she lay in bed before dropping off to sleep, or half-awake on Sunday mornings. Just a normal day of married life, nothing that thousands of other people didn't take for granted—but what heaven if ever that was normality for herself and Len!

The basic pattern of her dream did not vary. It began with the morning sun shining through the curtains of their bedroom, dappling the wall over Len's still, sleeping form. She thought she would probably always wake before him, and lie quiet for a while, just being happy. The rest of the day followed predictably—Len's breakfast, seeing him off to work, cleaning the small, semi-detached house they were steadily paying for, looking after the baby, making Len's evening meal, sitting by the fire in the evening watching the telly, before they went to bed. . . . The basic pattern was always the same, but Bridget liked to make minute adjustments each time she reviewed it. She would change the furnishings of the bedroom, for instance. Tonight the sun shone through elegant Regency stripes of red and cream instead of through the chintz which had hung at the window for the past month. She was tiring of the steak and chips which she regularly served up for Len's evening meal. Although he doted on steak, she decided she would study continental cooking, and produce something to surprise him. 'What's this queer stuff?' he would say, as he sat down at the table; then: 'Hmm. Not bad, I must admit.'

She clutched the warm, glowing vision to herself like a hot-water bottle to keep out the cold and loneliness of the night. But it was easier to believe in the impossible when you were tucked up in bed and half-asleep, than when you were walking the wet, comfortless streets, and the bloke you loved was on a bus going in the opposite direction, staring hopelessly out of the window, and wondering how on earth he was ever going to marry you, with no savings and going into the Army next week and a widowed mother who imagined herself an invalid and hated you for taking away her son. She wished she hadn't started to dream so early. Now each absurdly impossible picture returned to her with a sardonic caption attached: *Oh, yeah? You'll be lucky! You don't say?* wrecking one cherished wish after another, until she was reduced to longing desperately for just an end to the regular death of the street-corner parting, the fear and loneliness of the long walk home.

Tonight she was particularly nervous, after the encounter with that boy at the pictures. She hated the way boys looked at you, as if they were giving marks at a cattle show. Not only boys either, men too, married men, old enough to know better. Len was different; she had never seen him look at another girl like that. He wasn't abnormal, just good. One evening in the park the previous summer he had made a frank gesture that was like a question, and one side of her had wanted to say 'Yes', but she had said 'No, Len,' and he had taken his hand away, and kissed her, and quietly accepted her decision. And that was ever so good of him really, because he didn't believe in religion or anything, and if ever two people were entitled to belong to each other before they were married, she and Len were those people. But they mustn't. She wasn't what you might call strict either, but she knew it wouldn't be right, that their last chance was to hold on until they were married, so that,

162

however mean and poor it was, their marriage would have that at least to make it special.

She hesitated before the dark, muddy bomb-site, particularly reluctant that evening to cross it. But to avoid it meant a long detour to get into Barn Street, and she was shivering with wet and cold. She stepped on to the bomb-site, and began to pick her way along the slippery path worn between the piles of overgrown rubble. Soon she was in the shadows.

★ ★ ★

Having checked that all the doors were secure, Mr Berkley toiled wearily up the stairs to his office. Doreen had pulled out the studio couch, and was briskly undressing. She did not look up when he came in. Already their affair was like marriage, with its own dispiriting routine, this shabby coming together for a few hours in the shabby office. There was still pleasure in it somewhere, but it was choked by exasperating routine: waiting for the staff to go, getting undressed, making up the bed, before the fleeting moment of physical relief was attained. And then to lie there, the flesh warm and satisfied, but the mind calculating that soon one would have to get up, dress again, and drive Doreen home; worry and responsibility rapidly replacing the excitement of pursuit and conquest.

Doreen stepped out of her slip, and draped it over a chair. He stared.

'Good God!'

Doreen glanced down, and blushed for the first time in a long while.

'I know. Aren't they awful.'

'But they've got finger-prints all over them!'

'Yes, they're Laurie Landsdowne's. I was crazy about him once. They were all I had clean.'

She peeled off the pants, and tossed them on to the chair.

Then she got into the bed and waited for him. A few crumbs from the biscuits they had eaten the night before, pricked her skin. Her eyes fell upon the finger-printed pants again. They were an oddly disturbing relic of her youth and innocence. It was only a few months ago, but it seemed like years, since the young girl, who kept herself to herself, and thought she knew what she wanted from life, unpacked them with secret glee. God, but she had grown up a lot since then.

'Come on, Maurice,' she said. 'I want it tonight.'

Her coarseness almost shocked him. Not I want you, but I want it. Love had already become an impersonal sport, an itch to be satisfied. It wasn't long before the butterfly dust of innocence and romance brushed off a girl nowadays. Then he caught sight of Doreen's pale, tired face, the tiny, delicate Cockney features set in a characteristic expression of grave determination, and he regretted the unkind thought. By her coarseness she sought to make things easier for him—she committed herself to the relationship, to this way of life, which, God knew, wasn't much fun for her.

Doreen fidgeted between the sheets. The vision of the vain, silly girl she had been seemed to accuse her in some obscure way. But she hadn't known anything about life in those days. This was life: going to bed with a man twice as old as yourself who was married to someone who wouldn't divorce him. The sort of thing you read about for a cheap thrill in the advice column of a woman's magazine—it really happens, it happens to you. And when it does, you're proud of it, because it's life.

'Damn!'

'What's the matter, Maurice?'

He was staring into the drawer where he kept the doings.

★ ★ ★

164

Mary shut the front door, and leaned back on it, closing his eyes. His mouth ached, and his heart thudded painfully from exertion and fear. He lurched forward and groped his way up the staircase, gasping and retching in the stale air. In his room he fell on his bed, and buried his head in the pillow. But her screams still echoed in his ears, ringing out into the night, summoning all his enemies, the whole world, who only wanted this opportunity to hound him, to tear him. Again and again the nightmare rose into his mind like bile into the mouth; he threshed about in a desperate attempt to shut it out, but again and again he suffered the humiliation, the panic, the pain. Again he tore his bleeding fingers from her mouth, and gaped in horror as she screamed, and went on screaming. He heard again the noise of doors opening, voices, saw a light streaming across the street, and he was scrambling frantically over the bomb-site, tripping over a pile of rubble, tearing his coat on a fence, and running down the shockingly open street, running for his life.

Gradually rage began to absorb fear. Jesus Christ! Had he allowed her to make a fool of him again? He sucked at his hand. The bitch had teeth like knives. Right to the bone. And all for nothing. Her virginity still taunted him. If he'd had his hands on her for one minute, he could have given her something to remember him by; if only he'd spat a single obscenity into her ear before running off, it would have been something. But he had been utterly routed.

He put a hand down to his groin, and began to mouth into the pillow all the obscenities he knew, repeating them in a kind of chant. In his imagination he subjected her body to every abomination he could think of, until the blankets twisted round his legs were damp and sticky. But it gave him no comfort. Finally he lay prone, still, exhausted; and bitter tears oozed out between his eyelids. He buckled under the final, inescapable realization that he had failed, and would always fail; that the jeering kids, the mocking men, the

165

scornful tarts, were right; that he was nothing but a turd in the gutter.

*   *   *

Frowning, Mark went into the kitchen for his customary cup of cocoa. It was late, but Mrs Mallory was still ironing, the line of her mouth grim and purposeful in a face that was unusually tired and unhappy. Mr Mallory was smoking behind a newspaper, sunk in the depths of his arm-chair. Patricia was at the table in her dressing-gown, eating corn-flakes—her favourite food. The creaking of the ironing board, the crackle of corn-flakes and the occasional rustle of the newspaper were the only sounds. Mark sensed a tension that was like static electricity in the air.

'Hallo, Pat,' he said. 'Been working late?'

Patricia pulled a face behind her mother's back.

'No she hasn't, the more's the pity,' rapped out Mrs Mallory. 'She's been roaming the streets, worrying the life out of her father and mother.'

'I told you I went to the pictures,' said Patricia into her corn-flakes.

'I suppose you think that your father and I have scrimped and saved to give you children a good education so that you can waste your time and money at the pictures,' said Mrs Mallory, pressing down fiercely on a handkerchief.

Patricia's spoon dropped into her bowl with a clang, and she left the room.

Mr Mallory flipped down the top half of his newspaper:

'You shouldn't have said that.'

His wife put down her iron with a thump.

'Now don't you start. I've had quite enough.' She stopped abruptly, remembering Mark's presence. He shuffled awkwardly towards the door.

'Well it's getting late. I'll be pushing off to bed I think,' he said, glancing at the clock and his watch. 'Clare's gone already. She was feeling tired I think. Good night, Mrs Mallory. Good night, Mr Mallory.'

'Wait till I get you a cup of cocoa, Mark,' said Mrs Mallory.

'No thank you, really.'

'But you always have a cup of cocoa.'

'Thanks, but I don't really feel like one tonight. Thanks very much.' And he managed to make good his escape.

He climbed the dark, tortuous stairs heavily. A roar of falling water as a door opened and closed indicated that someone had just emerged from the lavatory. He hung back in case it was Clare. But it was one of the twins, in fluffy pyjamas, who flitted across the landing like a moth, eyes half-shut under the electric light.

He had scarcely closed the door of his room when there was a tap on it.

'Come in,' he called in a low voice, expecting Clare, and steeling himself for a long and exhausting reconciliation. But to his surprise Patricia slipped into the room.

'I hope you don't mind me coming in like this, Mark. It's an awful cheek I know.'

'S'alright, Pat. Er, sit down, won't you?'

He gestured to the divan bed, and turned his chair to face her.

'I want some advice, Mark,' said Patricia, fiddling with her dressing-gown cord.

'Well, anything I can do to help. . . . By the way, I'm sorry if I dropped you in the soup just now.'

'Oh, it's all right. Mummy only wanted an excuse to get at me anyway.'

He did not take up the point.

'Well—shoot!'

It was a sweet sensation to give sympathetic audience to Patricia. There was no offering more gratifying to him than the trust of adolescents. For one thing it was not as easily won as the trust of adults, or children or animals. For another—well, there was something peculiarly touching about adolescent suffering; and their sins and neuroses, like babies' excrement, gave no offence. As decisions became for oneself increasingly final and far-reaching in their implications, it was refreshing to deal with problems that would be solved by the mere passage of time. It was with a certain self-indulgence that he adopted a pose of relaxed attentiveness, and put Patricia at her ease by casually offering her a cigarette. She accepted, and the picture of precocious, and faintly absurd depravity she presented, in her old, handed-down dressing-gown, with her feet tucked up under her, her lank auburn hair about her face, and the cigarette cocked flamboyantly between the fingers of her left hand, gave him the keenest pleasure. However, he was somewhat startled by the sober determination with which she spoke of leaving home.

'You see, I want to do something worth while. I mean, there wouldn't be much point in my leaving home unless I did. You've travelled, Mark, and done lots of odd jobs and things. But it's so much easier for a boy. So what can I do?'

'Why exactly do you want to leave home so badly?'

'Don't you see? Didn't you see tonight? Mummy and I— we love each other of course, but we just can't go on living like this any longer. I'm making everybody miserable. I heard Daddy and Mummy after I left the room just now. I don't mind being miserable, but I'm not going to let Daddy and Mummy quarrel because of me."

Mark leaned forward and took her hand. To his surprise she was trembling.

'You're a good girl Pat,' he said.

'Better for everyone if I went 'way,' she mumbled, hanging her head.

'The first thing you must get out of your head is that you're the predestined black sheep of the family, that you and they are necessarily opposed.'

'It's true.'

168

'It's not a bit true.'

'You don't know.'

'Yes I do. Look, you trust me, don't you, Pat?'

She looked at him with tears brimming in her eyes. The whole thing had suddenly become disconcertingly serious.

'Well, listen then. I've travelled a bit, done things as you put it, but that doesn't mean a thing. Believe me it doesn't. There are too many people nowadays who think they are achieving something by changing the scenery as often as possible: hitch-hiking through Europe, peddling across Asia, rowing across the Atlantic and so forth. But so what? When you've done it you're still left with the same vacuum inside you waiting to be filled. Your memory is a confusion of too many faces and places encountered too rapidly. Much better to dig your roots in somewhere—anywhere—and dig deep. Mark out some small area and cultivate it really well. I've knocked about a bit in the last few years I suppose, but I was always restless until I came to a very ordinary house in a rather dingy London suburb, where there was a large and interesting family who had been in the same place for a long time. It was good to feel I belonged somewhere—if only by adoption. It's difficult for you to appreciate that feeling. But don't throw it away lightly.'

Patricia wasn't going to cry after all. She stood up, pulling the lapels of her dressing-gown together across her neck. Beneath the faded material was a figure full of promise.

'Thank you, Mark, you've been very kind.'

'But no help?'

'I didn't mean that. But I don't think you could ever quite understand.'

'Why?'

'About a large family I mean. How it sort of suffocates and devours you. Sometimes I think I was intended to be an only child, and got born into a large family by a mistake. Perhaps with you it was the other way round. I don't know. But I like being lonely.'

She paused, as the noises of going to bed reached them from downstairs—the snick of the light switch, the clang of the damper on the boiler, the sharp reports of bolts being shot home.

'I must go. It was lovely of you to listen.'

The door closed silently behind her.

Mark sat on the edge of his bed, one palm in the warm depression left by Patricia, troubled by a sense of failure, almost of humiliation. Was it true, what he had said to her about the value of this family life? Or did his advice derive from the crooked workings of a twisted kind of covetousness —perhaps the kind prohibited by the Ninth Commandment, Thou shalt not covet thy neighbour's wife, which had always seemed superfluous after the Sixth. True, Patricia was no one's wife—yet. But she would make some man happy some day. Did he subconsciously wish to deprive that man? Had Patricia, with her flattering attention, touching gratitude, and diverting problems, become a necessary part of the furniture in his mind? It was true. It was terrible. He really wished to prevent her from discovering life. He was trying, insanely, to preserve everyone in this family in just the state in which he had first encountered them, when they had given him that delightful sense of secure, harmonious, integrated living. As if he could arrest their development at that stage, and set them working like articulated models in a shop window, mechanically repeating the same gestures— Mrs Mallory always pouring out a cup of tea with a warm, motherly smile; Mr Mallory always easing himself blissfully into his chair; Patricia always reaching for the aspirins with womanly resignation, Clare always shyly yielding to the one good-night embrace. . . .

Shy wasn't exactly the *mot juste* now. It wasn't many months ago that she had been offended by his exploring fingers, but tonight she had given her breast to his hand as if to a baby. It had been an unsettling evening. People were not behaving as he had ordained they

170

should behave. First Clare, then Mr and Mrs Mallory, then Patricia. . . .

Restlessly he moved to his desk and focused the reading lamp on a book, some potted critical work on Marlowe. He only had time to read potted critical works now, with Finals a few weeks off.

Marlowe was a puzzling character. A notorious atheist, yet capable of dramatizing the interpenetration of the natural and the supernatural more effectively than any other playwright. *Why this is hell nor am I out of it.* It is the man who will not submit to God who is most compulsively aware of his reality. The more violently you abuse God, the more completely you affirm his existence. You can't win in the end, whichever way you play it.

That the angel Gabriel was bawd to the Holy Ghost, because he brought the salutation to Mary.

The sort of thing that would have delighted him a few months ago—he would have chuckled over its witty irreverence, and imagined with pleasure Clare's shock and embarrassment had she come across it. It was difficult not to be ashamed of his behaviour at that time. Shocking and embarrassing Clare had been a kind of sexual indulgence. To lend her, under the pretence of 'educating' her, a book which contained frank or scurrilous passages, was a kind of vicarious rape. And perhaps, indeed, he had succeeded in corrupting her. Perhaps this explained her behaviour tonight, and the gradual change that had come over her lately. There was a change, though it was difficult to define it, except by reference to a few trivial details of behaviour. She was longer in the bath and quicker out of church than when he had first known her. She didn't blush any more at jokes about somebody's bust—but this was his fault for teasing her about being narrow-minded. Now she wasn't narrow-minded any more, he didn't feel inclined to make the jokes. She had learned all about dress and make-up. She looked desirable all right. But did he desire the well-groomed young woman in high-heels and with figure held firmly in place by a good foundation garment, as much as the callow, untidy girl, so soft to touch and hold, he had first known?

Tonight, as she spoke of the convent, that frightened, insecure schoolgirl-woman had broken through the shell of sophistication and touched him again, moved him to be tender. But not tenderness she wanted now. Passion now.

If dishonoured her, must then make an honest woman of her? Marriage with Clare. Nothing said, but it was expected. Suppose could do worse. Logical really, after what he had said to Pat. Merge with the Mallorys; marry a Mallory. Name the day, bride in white, radiant, nuptial Mass. Our Lady of Perpetual Sucker, till death do us, special graces, Mendelsohn, the happy couple, pause for photo, confetti, into the car, what to say, what the hell does one say—roll on bed? The reception, a buffet, so glad you could come, yes didn't she, yes I am, O ha ha Uncle Tom's sozzled ha ha good old Uncle Tom, accustomed as I am to public speaking, a glass of champagne cider each, I give you the Bride's parents! My own parents looking a bit sick of all the tipsy Irish. Thank God we're going, kippers in the car, confetti, small hotel, double bed, a baby started, could do worse. . . .

Mark sagged forward on to his desk, straightened up, and dragged himself from the brink of sleep. No good; must get some work done tonight.

He lit a cigarette and gazed at the page of his book until the printed words ceased to dance about. Where was he? Oh yes.

That the angel Gabriel was bawd to the Holy Ghost, because he brought the salutation to Mary.

Strictly speaking, it was quite true. The irreverence was verbal, not conceptual. Annunciation—assignation: only the associations differed. Marlowe had been tricked into vividly illuminating the miracle of the Incarnation.

172

That if there be any God or any true religion, then it is in the Papists, because the service of God is performed with more ceremonies, as elevation of the Mass, organs, singing men, shaven crowns, etc. That all Protestants are hypocritical asses.

The common mistake of outsiders, that Catholicism was a beautiful, solemn, dignified, aesthetic religion. But when you got inside you found it was ugly, crude, bourgeois. Typical Catholicism wasn't to be found in St Peter's, or Chartres, but in some mean, low-roofed parish church, where hideous plaster saints simpered along the wall, and the bored congregation, pressed perspiration tight into the pews, rested their fat arses on the seats, rattled their beads, fumbled for their smallest change, and scolded their children. Yet in their presence God was made and eaten all day long, and for that reason those people could never be quite like other people, and that was Catholicism.

Again his mind had wandered from the text before him. It was hopeless. For effective study one required emotional calm, self-satisfaction, routine, the minimum of distractions and discomforts, mental or physical. The troubled conscience, the tortured mind, compelling one to come to terms with life, made one impatient of the mere accummulation of facts.

But after all, he had come far in the last few months. Should he not have acquired a deep mental calm and certainty? But there was the rub. One could never say 'I have reached the limit of my religious development; it is time to return to the secular plane and develop there correspondingly.' One was never finished. Just when one had decided to go no farther, one caught a glimpse of something ahead, challenging, enigmatic, and one wearily set off again.

The Christian life, as exemplified by Christ and the saints, offered countless possibilities for self-perfection; but you couldn't do everything. Or could you? It occurred to you that you might say the Rosary every day. There seemed to be no reason why you shouldn't, and to decide not to, after having had the thought, seemed to indicate a lack of real *caritas*. So you did, and used up a little more time. What about one Mass on a weekday? Well all right. Well then, why not every day? Well that's a bit much, it means getting up every morning at—— But what about the Passion, the sufferings of the saints? O.K. So you flogged yourself a little more. But there seemed to be no valid reason for not devoting one's whole life to religion. Excuses, but no reasons. Yet there must be a reason somewhere, if life was to go on: life, that is, work and play, eating and drinking, copulation and birth. The whole structure seemed to be based on the indifference of the majority. It was Original Sin and not love that made the world go round. Perhaps nothing would embarrass God more than if every one of His creatures took His Word literally and to heart. But for those who tried to do so, there seemed to be only a progressive involvement in guilt. Take Student Cross for example. If he had never seen that leaflet pinned up on the Catholic Society notice-board at college, he would never have dreamt of participating in the pilgrimage. But God had made bloody sure he did see it—and He had safely left the rest to the inevitable reflex of challenge-acceptance. For why, having seen the leaflet, had he been unable to dismiss the idea? It was preposterous enough, a medieval demonstration grotesquely out of place in modern England. Its purpose Augean—no less than to perform an act of reparation for the sins of students everywhere. It had immediately struck him, of course, that the latter, had they been aware of it, would have strongly resented the interference of spiritual sanitary workers. Yes, you could mock at the idea, but that wasn't enough to rid yourself of its insidious appeal, politely, persistently tugging at your soul. No doubt his motives for going on the pilgrimage were varied. No decision of his was unmixed with

174

egotism, and an agreeable consciousness of impressing Clare and the rest of the family had made his decision easier. Again, he always savoured the bizarre, eccentric experience —it would be useful material. But these motives would not have been sufficient in themselves. After all, he detested physical pain and discomfort — and this excursion had promised both. So what was it that had made him go, but a furtive, half-acknowledged sense that not to have done so would have been like turning one's back on the Crucifixion, that here perhaps at last was the litmus which might determine the validity of his readopted faith?

At that time he had been a practising Catholic for two or three months. The experience had been undramatic. He was, in the eyes of the Church, already a Catholic, since he had been baptized into the Church, and had received the sacraments of Penance, Communion and Confirmation before leaving the convent. To the Church he was not a convert at all, but merely a lapsed Catholic who had returned to the practice of his Faith. Not for him was the formal ceremony of admission, with its conditional baptism and its awesome recital of categorical promises. He had undergone a course of instruction with Father Kipling: the evidences for the truth of the Catholic Faith were acceptable if one was disposed to accept them, and he was so disposed. He could have raised objections to Father Kipling's arguments —but then he could have raised objections to his objections. Catholicism was a reasonable Faith, but like any other, it could not be justified by reason alone. He had returned to the sacraments, become a dutiful practising Catholic. But he had felt that he was still the same Mark Underwood, drearily going through the motions of belief instead of drearily going through the motions of disbelief; that the searing, galvanic experience men called conversion was like an unexploded bomb ticking away inside him. Perhaps Student Cross would provide the detonator. In a sense it had. He flipped back the pages of his note-book, and found the scrappy diary of those few days.

Saturday: evening
Today we started, from the University Church in the City. First there was Mass in the crypt, with the Cross standing before the altar. A plain wooden cross, about twelve feet tall, and six feet from arm to arm. It weighs, I believe, about 120 pounds. It is grubby from the sweat and dirt of several pilgrimages. We walk in a column, line of three. The Cross leads, carried horizontally on the shoulders of three students, one to each arm, and the other at the foot. You carry it for the duration of five decades of the Rosary (about ten minutes), recited by the trio immediately behind. Then they move up to take the Cross, and you drop back to the end of the file. The body of the column sing hymns now and again, led by the Dominican chaplain Fr Courtney. Otherwise, we talk quite freely.

The students are a curious lot. A good proportion of hearties, well-equipped with rucksacks, sleeping bags, and studded boots: for them the pilgrimage is a kind of spiritual hike. They probably do the same thing for pleasure in the Lake District every summer. There are a few like myself, who look as if they wished they weren't there, and would like to get the whole thing over as quickly as possible. Then there are some pathetic, weedy-looking swots, inadequately equipped and unsuitably dressed, in gaberdine raincoats and Oxford shoes, unwieldy packs all done up with string, who look as if they have never walked farther than a hundred yards at any time in their lives. But appearances are deceiving. You can't categorize in this neat fashion. You find that some of the hearties are doing the pilgrimage for the first time, and begin to limp quite early on; that some of the weeds have been on the pilgrimage once or even twice before—and finished. There is a lot of humorous reminiscing by the veterans about previous pilgrimages, about blisters, about the student who was cautioned for cooling his feet in a public reservoir, about the crippling last mile of the pilgrimage which, apparently (who says we're not living in the Middle Ages?), we walk barefoot.

All this chaff makes me feel uneasy and isolated—or rather, *did* make me. For I am writing this on Saturday evening, and already I have been blooded. I have pricked my first blister, squeezed out the fluid, and dabbed it with surgical spirit. Already I feel I belong. On the whole I have enjoyed the day. It certainly was a curious experience to flaunt one's religion in the face of London. First, through the City with a policeman holding up the traffic with an impassive countenance which implied that he would do the same for the Seventh Day Adventists, the Anti-Vivisection Society or the Paddington Communist Party. The City streets were fairly quiet of course, but as we passed into the suburbs we found ourselves in the midst of the Saturday morning shopping rush. It is such a bizarre situation, that it is difficult to believe that one is really there, really carrying a wooden cross through bustling, irreligious, unreflective suburbia. The reaction of spectators was less marked than I had expected. Plenty of curious stares of course, but quite as many people would look hastily away, more embarrassed than we were. There were no jeers or cat-calls. Children seemed to find us particularly intriguing, and would gaze unselfconsciously, with the characteristically grave, uncommitted regard of the young, before being yanked away from the kerb by their mothers.

At Enfield, the destination of our first day's march, we were met and accompanied for the last mile by a procession of Catholic parishioners. This part of Enfield has those yellow sodium lamps that have that delicate rosy glow for the first few minutes after they are switched on. It was a beautiful evening. Even when the sun had disappeared, the night sky was like a dark blue glass globe, lit by a faint glow from within. Against this background the rosy-tipped lamp standards seemed like fabulous lantern plants in a land of faerie. This transformation of a suburban arterial road was assisted by the historic chant of the *Credo* which rose impressively from the throats of the pilgrims and parishioners.

Altogether, I have enjoyed the first day more than I anticipated.

Palm Sunday: evening

This, then, is the real thing. The pain, the exhaustion, the monotony of one's own thoughts (I was too tired to talk for most of the day): how many miles to go? how many miles have we covered? can I keep going? When is the next break? when will we get to the top of this hill? Will there be more hills like this one? Is it my turn with the Cross already? How many more minutes must I carry it? What mystery are they saying? only the third sorrowful mystery? When is the next break? How many miles to go? Can I keep going?

Yesterday was a deceiving dream. I encountered the reality of a penitential pilgrimage the moment I woke and levered my stiff limbs off the hard school-room floor where we slept last night, and winced as my blister contacted the floor. Blister? That one blister I was rather proud of, is now lost in a rich crop of blisters, bloated, white, obscene—a big blister on each heel and sole, and small blisters disposed neatly on the underside of each toe. Tonight we are staying at St Peter's seminary, and mercifully there are baths, and mattresses spread upon the floors, and nursing sisters in grey habits with gentle fingers and sympathetic cluckings and sterilized needles and soothing ointments and bandages. Even so, it was agony to shuffle in slippers into the chapel for Compline. And this is only the *second day*! Five days and God knows how many miles to go. Eighteen miles today, and tomorrow, the worst leg of all, twenty-six miles to Cambridge that can't be broken because there is nowhere to stop overnight. How can I go on tomorrow? For that matter, how did I keep going today?

Again and again you tell yourself, as you place each throbbing foot before the other on the hard tarmac, that the whole thing is monstrous, insane, self-inflicted torture.

178

If only you could believe that! But you can't. Something forces you to stumble on, and that is the conviction that what you are doing has a meaning. That meaning is in front of you—the Cross, like a magnet, dragging you up hill and down dale, a magnet that attracts not iron and steel, but suffering flesh and bone. I think. . . .

I was interrupted, and am too tired to remember what I thought. A seminarist has brought me a blanket off his own bed. Absurdly, my eyes almost filled with tears of gratitude. One of the things this experience does is to make one appreciate small mercies and small acts of kindness. While the sisters were tending my blisters, I felt an inexpressible love choking me, I regretted all the uncharitable things I had thought or said about nuns, I felt as if I were the Magdalene, and Christ were anointing my feet.

Monday: evening

Well, it's all over already. I have given up. I am writing this on the train to London, carrying me on smooth, oiled wheels away from the pain, the exhaustion, and, above all, the one worth-while thing I ever did—or tried to do—in my life. This morning was hell. I decided early in the morning that I would struggle somehow to Cambridge, and then go back home. In the end I didn't even walk to Cambridge, but went ignominiously by bus from Royston, where we stopped for lunch. As soon as you set a limit to your endurance, you are lost. As soon as I decided not to go farther than Cambridge, I wanted to stop dead in the middle of the road. Somehow I got to Royston—somehow? I know how. There was one tremendous hill before Royston. My heart sank as I looked at it. On top of everything else, my line had to take over the Cross at the foot of the hill.

We took that hill at a cracking pace, and as we handed over at the crest, and dropped back to the end of the column, Fr Courtney called out 'Well done!' to us. I know it was only the *extra* weight of the Cross that got me up that hill. Walking alone I would never have made it. It was an extraordinary experience. But as we stumbled down the other side of the hill, and into the dark, dingy pub where we ate our sandwich lunch, the exaltation of that moment passed. I sat silently in a chair by the fire, not moving, getting stiffer and stiffer, and yet not moving. I couldn't go on. I knew that several of the others were in as bad shape as myself—probably worse. I knew that the Cross would drag me to Cambridge if I allowed myself to be dragged, but I refused.

I feel the onus of that refusal now. To shake off my depression I thought I would get myself something light to read on the train. I addressed myself thus: 'All right, you have given up; but you tried, you did your best (*hollow laughter*), you are in a mood of religious melancholia. Shake it off. You've absorbed too much religion too rapidly. Try an antidote.' So I bought a glossy, frivolous 'man's magazine'. But something has happened to me. These breasty pin-ups, these laboured mutations of suggestive posture, these roguish captions, fail to arouse even a flicker of my usual amused interest. My thoughts are with that pitiful, struggling file, stumbling through the dusk into Cambridge, bowed under their packs and the Cross.

Yes, something has happened to me.

Something had happened to him all right. The detonator had worked, his 'conversion' had gone off bang, and all the king's horses and all the king's men could never put the old Mark Underwood together again. But the task of rebuilding was a daunting one. The foundations might have been securely laid if he had got to Walsingham. But he had brought back with him from the pilgrimage no feeling of achievement or merit, only a sense of failure with which he was already too familiar. It was no use comparing yourself with those who never started; you had to compare yourself to those who went on.

He was beginning to understand the appeal of the religious life, particularly of the life governed by a religious

Rule, with its vows of Poverty, Chastity and Obedience. First, it brought the body into subjection. One wasted so much time arguing with the body, urging it through the laborious and uncomfortable routine of physical existence— getting up, washing, shaving, even moving. Little acts of kindness which required the body's co-operation, such as helping with the washing-up after a good meal, demanded a prodigious amount of persuasion; while a really big thing, like finishing Student Cross, just met with stubborn resistance. The body was like the surly, recalcitrant electorate of a democratic state, with the mind a nervous, impatient, and ultimately helpless executive. The body required autocratic government. It had been his mind, not his feet, that had given up at Royston—the mind which foolishly recognized the right of the feet to protest.

He was tired of his body, tired of dragging it after him everywhere like a petulant child. Part of his admiration for the Mallorys derived from the cheerful, uncomplaining way in which they put up with discomforts and performed small acts of self-denial. Or was this part of the Mallory myth he had been constructing? In any case, self-denial was a habit with them. His own lazy, selfish body might require a more drastic discipline. Then, with the body subdued, one might at last grapple with the real problems.

He began to reread his account of the pilgrimage, and became suddenly impatient of its posturing, self-dramatizing artificiality. He ripped the pages from the note-book, screwed them up, and hurled them at the waste-paper basket. The ball of paper hit the lip of the basket and fell to the floor. He picked it up and smoothed it out. Then he clipped the pages together and slipped them into a file. There was still enough of the egotistical writer in him to protest at its destruction.

★ ★ ★

Mr Berkley hurried through the early Sunday-morning

streets, empty but for Catholics, car-cleaners and cats, wincing under the glare of the sun which shone with a brutal cheerfulness into his eyes. It would have been more in keeping with his mood if yesterday's rain had persisted. Mr Berkley was worried. Last night he had forgotten the necessary, but Doreen had insisted on going through with it. For the first time no thin rubber insulation had kept them ultimately apart, and Mr Berkley had found the experience oddly moving and disturbing. Physically he had been just one millimetre closer to Doreen than ever before, but emotionally he had crossed a frontier. Afterwards he had felt absurdly near to tears. Doreen, loyal to her role of concubine, had tried to cheer him up by saying that it had never been so good. But, for once, he had not been concerned with his own pleasure. Instead he had been overwhelmed by a sense of gratitude and a sense of responsibility. Gratitude because of the unhesitating generosity with which Doreen gave him the hospitality of her body; responsibility because he had ceased to be a passing visitor to that body, taking what he could get, and had become a guest, leaving behind something as a token of their intimacy. That was what was worrying Mr Berkley this morning. The tender emotions of the night had evaporated, to leave only a bitter sediment of anxiety as to whether he had fathered a bastard on Doreen.

Mr Berkley slipped into the Palladium by a side-exit, and burrowed gratefully into the darkness. The thought that Doreen might be pregnant, that the processes of gestation might be irretrievably in motion at that very moment, returned at regular intervals with more and more force, pumping worry into his heart as if it were a balloon. His chest felt intolerably tight, and he leant against the passage wall to allow the tension to subside. Half-consciously he listened to the murmur of Dolly and Gertrude talking in the auditorium, their voices carrying through the curtain which screened him.

182

'Just look at this—i'n it disgusting?'

'What?'

'Why somebody's left an 'ole choc-ice on the floor, and it's run all over the place. What did 'e buy it for if 'e didn't want it? That's what I'd like to know.'

'St! Terrible i'n it?'

'One of them young teds, I 'spect.'

There was silence for a moment, punctuated only by the grunts and wheezes of the two ancient dames, until Gertrude said:

''Ow's the family, Doll?'

'Oh, mustn't grumble, y'know. My Stan's been very bad with 'is bladder again.'

'St!'

''E's overworked it. That's what I tell 'im: three or four pints every weekday, and Gawd knows 'ow many on Saturday night. Now 'e's payin' for it. 'Ow're all yours, Gert?'

'Well Alf's much better. They bin' givin' 'im 'lectrical treatment at the 'ospital. Done 'im a world of good it 'as. Says 'e feels like a young man again.' She cackled. 'I told 'im not to be so silly, or e'd strain 'imself, and oo'd 'ave to look after 'im then, I'd like to know? . . . No, Alf's all right, but our Else is drivin' us all barmy.'

'Oh?' said Dolly with sympathetic interest.

'Would you believe it, she's gone and got religious.'

'No!'

'Yerse. I never thought it would 'appen to one of me own children, the youngest too, what I was always most fond of."

'Well I never. It just goes to show, don't it?'

'You're right there, Dolly. I was never so upset in me life as when me own daughter called me a sinner.'

'Well!'

'If she was younger I'd 'ave smacked 'er arse. But you can't if she's twenty-five and a married woman, can you?'

''Ow did it 'appen then?'

'Well, she went up with 'er friend from work, Mabel, to this Billy Graham at 'Arringay—you know, where they 'ave the circus.'

'Yerse.'

'Well, she went just for a lark, y'know, but this Mabel, she's very serious, never got married, y'know—not surprisin' either when you see 'er in a strong light. If you ask me she 'as a kind of influence over Else.'

'I know the type. In the old days she would 'ave joined the Salvation Army.'

'That's right the 'ole thing sounds just like the Salvation Army, only posher. Y'know, at 'Arringay they 'ave choirs and a blooming great organ and flowers—masses of white lillies, Else said.' A note of involuntary admiration crept into Gertrude's voice for a moment. 'Well, as I said, Else went along more for a night out than anything. So she sat there for about 'arf an 'our, listenin' to the singin' and so forth, and then, just as she was beginnin' to get a bit bored, this Billy Graham comes on to the platform. 'E just looked at all the people for a minute without saying anythink. Else says a shiver went up 'er spine, and she knew she 'ad been called.'

'Called?'

'Called to testify 'er faith in Jesus Christ or somethink. Anyway, 'e spoke for about an 'our and at the end of it 'e asked for people to come forward and testify that they were saved. Well, for a little while there wasn't a movement, until a man in the third row from the front stepped forward. Alf says 'e was planted, but Else says it was genuine, because she went up and she wasn't planted.'

'Else went up?'

'Yerse, would you believe it? In front of all them people. Makes me go 'ot and cold just to think of it. Says she couldn't stop 'erself, she was so sure she'd been saved.'

'It don' arf sound like the Salvation Army.'

'Salvation Army plus sex, if you ask me. You seen this

184

Billy Graham? 'Andsome ain't the word. Soon as I saw 'is picture I knew what 'ad "saved" Else. Now Sidney, 'er 'usband, 'e's a decent bloke, but 'e's no oil paintin'.'

''Ow's 'e takin' it—Sidney?'

'Badly. Well, it ain't surprisin', with 'is own wife callin' 'im a sinner, and tellin' 'im 'e ought to wash more. . . . I ask you.'

'What's washin' got to do with it?'

'Well Else read out this bit from a book by Billy Graham, *The Secret of 'Appinness* it's called, where 'e says that a man told 'im 'e only took a bath once a week, and Billy Graham told 'im there was something wrong with 'is purity of heart.'

'Once a week! Why, I don't think Stan 'as a bath once a year, unless 'e goes into 'ospital.'

'Well, y'know, Else always was one for washing, she gets it from me, but Sidney, 'e don't go in for baths much, well men don't, do they? So when Else read this out 'e said that some of the 'oly men in the olden days never washed at all, and were crawling with lice. Else told 'im not to be disgustin', and now every night there's a terrible row before they go to bed—our bedroom's right underneath theirs— and Else says she won't sleep in the same bed with 'im until 'e washes 'imself.'

'Poor Sidney.'

'That ain't all. The other night. . . .' Gertrude lowered her voice as she yielded up the spiciest morsel of her story.

As for Mr Berkley, the conversation seemed to him like the macabre chorus of some drama in which he was eventually to appear, by some unexpected twist of the plot, as the despicable villain. Images of sin, of unwashed bodies locked together in obscene attitudes, apocalyptic denunciations of lust, visions of Else scrubbing herself fiercely in a tin bath, disconnected Bible phrases from his chapel-going youth, coursed through his distracted mind. With a tremendous effort of will, he straightened up and stood against the wall. Adjusting his tie and smoothing down his hair, he tottered into the auditorium, greeted Dolly and Gertrude, and proceeded slowly towards his office.

* * *

It was a strange pilgrimage she was making this Sunday afternoon. Hilda's home was near the convent, and the tube train seemed to be boring a hole into the past, bearing her inexorably back to the source of her purest happiness and pain. Weary of staring at the advertisements opposite her, Clare took Mrs Syms's letter from her handbag, and read it once more.

Dear Miss Mallory,
    I hope that is your surname, if I have made a mistake, you will probably understand why I'm sure. It is probably a surprise to you to receive a letter from me. At the convent a year ago I think I probably said many things which I wish now I had kept silent. But you will understand that I was very upset.
    Now I am writing to you to ask for your help, and I can't blame you if you don't come. At the time it seemed to us that Hilda was not the happy, carefree girl her father and I wished her to be. But since we took her away from the convent she has worried us both to death. She's not like other girls of her age, I just don't understand her. In fact, looking back, I can't think of anyone who ever understood her, except you, and I wish you would come and see her and take her out of herself. She hasn't any friends, except one who is bad for her, and she won't mix with other young people. The doctor says there is nothing he can do. Mr Syms and I would be most grateful if you could come and visit us, perhaps on a Sunday.
                                          Yours sincerely,
                                          Margaret Syms

By a coincidence the letter had been waiting for her on her dressing-table when she had got in from the pictures the previous night, just after she had been thinking and talking

186

of Hilda. The reticence which had surrounded the subject for so long had suddenly collapsed on all sides. It was undeniably a relief. A few weeks before it would have seemed inconceivable that she should ever see Hilda again, but now she almost looked forward to the meeting. She had to admit, however, that the main reason that she had phoned the Symses and answered their appeal so promptly was that it took her out of the house, and away from the strain of being with Mark in public while the incident of the night before still divided them.

Now the rattle and roar of the tube faded abruptly as it surfaced into bright sunlight. They passed some sidings full of tube trains, looking lost and blind above ground, like worms. The train pulled into Woodburn, and Clare stepped up out of the carriage. Before leaving the station she went to the Ladies' to check up on her appearance. She wanted to make an impression, to show Hilda quite clearly from the start how much she herself had changed, what their relationship must be now. Looking in the long mirror, she was satisfied with the tailored, dark-grey worsted suit and simple white blouse, the black suède courts, white gloves, and sleek, long black umbrella. After some reflection she removed the brooch, but retained the small, black stud ear-rings.

She walked out of the station into the spotless, tree-lined, Sunday-afternoon streets of Woodburn. But somehow it was always Sunday afternoon in Woodburn, as she remembered it. The people on the pavements were always sprucely dressed, they pushed their prams or followed their dogs at a leisurely, unhurried pace; the cars purred quietly on the smooth roads; there was always somebody playing at the Tennis Club. It would be nice to live here, to leave smoky, dirty Brickley, and come and live here, with Mark, in one of these elegant, attractive houses.

Her heart thumped a little as she approached Hilda's house. But she pushed open the low, wrought-iron gate without hesitating, and walked carefully up the narrow path to the door. She pushed the bell-button, and two chimes politely intimated her arrival.

Mrs Syms's astonishment at her appearance was almost comical. She could see the older woman's eyes darting incredulously over her, swiftly assessing style, quality, cost, as she stumbled through vague expressions of welcome and gratitude.

'Would you like to wash your hands? No? Well, I'll take you straight up to Hilda's room, and then I'll make you a nice cup of tea. Did you have a reasonable journey?'

Before Clare had finished her reply, Mrs Syms had continued in an undertone: 'I told Hilda to change into something nice for your visit, but she wouldn't. She won't wear any of her pretty clothes nowadays.'

She led her upstairs, and opened the door of Hilda's room; the sound of music from a gramophone flooded the landing.

'Get up, Hilda. Here's someone to see you,' said Mrs Syms brightly. Hilda was lying on the floor. She opened her eyes and said, 'Wait till the record's finished.'

Her mother's patience was brittle.

'Get up at once, Hilda! and don't be so rude.'

Hilda closed her eyes.

'It's all right, Mrs Syms,' said Clare, sitting down.

'I'll get you some tea,' said Mrs Syms, as she withdrew, angry and impotent.

The record seemed to be of some unremarkable string music. While it spun away, Clare had time to take in the appearance of the room. Cheerfully and expensively furnished, it was littered with photographs of men—no, of one man. They were large and glossy. On one she deciphered the signature 'James Dreme', and recognized it as the name of a film star. Pinned to one wall was a large poster advertising one of his films: *The Young Can Suffer*.

The record came to an end; but Hilda stayed prone with her eyes closed for two long minutes. Then she opened her eyes, and rose to her feet. She was wearing a black shirt out-side black jeans, with black ballet shoes. Her hair was scraped back into a bun. She wore no make-up.

'Hallo,' she said. "What should I call you?'

'Hallo, Hilda,' replied Clare, smiling. 'It's nice to see you again. Clare.'

'Clare. Sounds funny after "Sister Agnes".'

'Yes. What was that music you were playing?'

'Theme from *This Side of Paradise*. Didn't you see it?'

'What was it—a film? No, I don't think I've seen that.'

'Of course, you wouldn't have. . . .'

'Oh, I often go to the cinema now. But I must have missed that film. Was it good?'

Hilda leaned against the window frame, and stared out.

'It was the greatest movie ever made.'

'Oh? I must try and see it then,' said Clare politely. But Hilda seemed scarcely to hear her.

'Yet in a way I still prefer *The Young Can Suffer*. Because it was the first I saw, I suppose. *Mammoth*'s not half so good as either.'

She turned, and Clare looked into the eyes of a fanatic.

'I know it's a terrible thing to say, but I wish sometimes Jimmie had died before he made *Mammoth*. It would have been more poetic. Just the two masterpieces.'

Clare felt her grip on the situation slipping.

'Er, I'm sorry, but who is it that has died? Not some-one . . . ?'

Hilda stared.

'You mean you don't know. Surely even you must have read about it somewhere? About James Dreme. The greatest actor in the history of the cinema. Killed last year in an auto-mobile accident. He loved driving fast automobiles. It was a white Porsch. . . .'

'You liked him very much?'

Hilda's reply was flat and quiet.

'I love him.'

189

The door opened, and Mrs Syms steered a tray into the room.

'How about a nice cup of tea?'

'How lovely,' said Clare, rising from her chair. 'Can I help you with the tray?'

'Thank you, dear, I can manage, if you'd just clear that table. Hilda, will you take your books off the table?'

Her daughter, who had turned back to the window on her mother's entry, sulkily moved a pile of film magazines and dropped them on the floor. When she had spread out the tea-things, Mrs Syms said:

'Well, I won't interrupt your chat any longer. I expect you've got a lot to talk about.'

Hilda maintained a sullen silence. Clare decided that normal, polite behaviour would get her nowhere.

'Why are you so rude to your mother?' she asked bluntly, as Mrs Sym's footsteps receded down the stairs. For the first time the girl seemd to lose her self-possession.

'I don't see that it's any of your business. You're not my teacher now, you know.'

'Nor your friend apparently,' said Clare, rising. 'So I might as well leave.'

'No, don't go,' said Hilda anxiously. 'It's because she doesn't understand me. She won't let me lead my own life.'

Clare sat down.

'Well, after all she *is* your mother. She's entitled to some say in what you do. And she's very kind to you. This lovely room. . . .'

Hilda shrugged her shoulders.

'You don't understand. Go and see *The Young Can Suffer*. Then you might understand that nice rooms aren't enough.'

Clare thought of telling her what it would have meant to her as a young girl to have a nicely furnished room to herself—what it would mean to her now for that matter—but sensed that such remarks would serve no useful purpose.

'You seem to think of nothing but this James Dreme.'

'I told you—I love him.'

'You mean you loved him when he was alive.'

'I didn't know anything about him when he was alive. I didn't see *The Young Can Suffer* until three weeks after he was killed.'

'I just don't understand, Hilda. If he was alive, yes. But it's so hopeless, pointless!'

'If he was alive it would be just as hopeless. More, probably, as some flashy film-star would have grabbed him before long. As it is there are thousands of girls like me, and at least we have the comfort of knowing that he belonged to no one, and can belong to no one. It's enough for us to be able to mourn him.'

The significance of Hilda's black clothes struck Clare suddenly with a little spasm of horror.

'But this is terrible! You mean to say that you sit in this room all day, brooding on the memory of a dead film-star? It's not natural.'

Hilda's eyes flashed.

'Nuns aren't natural then. They sit in their cells, brooding over Jesus, don't they? He's dead, isn't he? And they love Him, don't they?'

'Hilda! How can you say such things?'

Hilda collapsed slackly on to the divan bed.

'Anyway, I don't stay here all day. I have to go to secretarial school, worse luck. But there's another girl the same there. We go to see Jimmie's pictures together. I've seen *The Young Can Suffer* forty-one times and *This Side of Paradise* thirty. Sometimes we travel miles to see them. Then we play the theme music of his films here, and meditate. We don't talk for hours.'

'D'you still practise your religion, Hilda?'

'No.'

Clare passed a hand over her face. She had a bad headache. Realizing that her tea was getting cold, she gulped down half of it.

191

'Why, Hilda?'

'I don't believe in it.'

'You did once.'

'I thought I did. It's easy enough to make a little girl believe in religion when she's in a convent. When you grow up you realize that it's like the icing on a cake. Religion is a kids' party for adults.'

'You didn't think that up for yourself.'

'I did, so there! Well, what if I didn't? It's true.'

'Do you call this James Dreme business adult?'

'Oh, you wouldn't understand. Why won't people understand? We just want to be left alone.'

Clare was silent. Then she asked hesitantly:

'Hilda, was it anything to do with me—with us?'

'What d'you mean?'

'This cult of James Dreme. . . . I'd hate to think it was because of what happened at the convent. I know you suffered a lot. So did I. I'm sorry, because it was mainly my fault for letting things go that far. But if that was unhealthy, this is . . . diseased. You must see that it isn't natural. Your parents are desperately worried, and no wonder. You've got to shake yourself out of this dream.'

'Dream? You seem to think that it's all a game, a make-believe. D'you know that I cry myself to sleep every night? Veronica and I don't have much fun, you know. We don't dress up and go out dancing. We've vowed never to get married. But it's our life, to do what we like with it, what we feel is right. We have a duty to Jimmie's memory which comes before everything else.'

Clare shook her head dumbly. Hilda seemed to be getting more animated as her own bafflement and distress increased.

'You must do what you feel must be done. That's Jimmie's great message. No matter how people misunderstand you—and they usually do, you've got to act as you feel is right.'

There was a flush of excitement discernible in the pale, slightly puffy face.

'I'll show you something,' she said, 'if you'll promise not to tell Mummy.'

From a drawer she took out a cardboard box, and laid it on the table. She began to untie the string around it.

'I got it from America. You can't get them in England.'

She opened the box, and reverently extracted a white plastic object.

'His death-mask,' she explained, and kissed it.

PART THREE

IT was hot in the park. Almost too hot. Mark was carrying his jacket, and Clare regretted that she had not taken off her stockings and belt before coming out. But there was no question of turning back. Both of them, she felt, had simultaneously decided that they must be alone to talk—something that was impossible at home without arousing unwelcome curiosity. For some reason people did not seem to be able to accept the possibility of two people who were 'going steady' being in a state of temporary misunderstanding—the common condition of love; it had to be make or break, 'very fond of each other' or 'broken it off'. So you had studiously to act out a charade of affection and natural ease until, like politicians, you had settled the issue in private, one way or the other. But the elaborate public pretence could cripple private honesty. Nearly two months had passed since the last crisis in their relationship—the night they had seen *Bicycle Thieves*—and still neither of them had had the courage to face its implications. Now they would have to.

A sudden sickness and fatigue swamped her, and she felt incapable of facing the long, painful inquest that would start in a few minutes—incapable of sustaining any longer the intolerable labour of love.

It was a dazzling Saturday afternoon, and the park was full of contented people: children stood knicker-deep in bliss, stroking the paddling-pool as if it were some great tame animal; attendant mothers soaked in the sun; lovers were prone and entranced on the grass. But to her the heat was oppressive, stifling.

197

'Let's sit down. I'm hot,' said Mark.

They sat down on hard, knobbly ground, sparsely covered with grass, in the grudging shade of a withered tree. Mark took out a cigarette, and began to smoke. Clare stretched out flat, but he remained sitting upright, one arm locked behind him. It was not a position anyone could maintain comfortably for long, and it seemed to Clare that he was deliberately refraining from lying down beside her.

'Pretty hot," he said.

'Mm,' she grunted, closing her eyes against the glare. After a pause he said:

'I dropped in on Father Courtney this morning.'

'Courtney?' How long was this fencing going to continue. She was impatient for the heavy swing of blunt, simple statements: 'I'm sorry'—'I was a bitch'—'It was my fault'—'I love you.'

'You remember the Dominican. Student Cross.'

'Oh yes.'

'I told him I wanted to join the Order.'

Clare remained supine, her eyes closed, paralysed by an utter confusion, a sense of the inadequacy of any reaction. Not for a second did she doubt the truth of what he was saying, but to gain time she licked her dry lips and croaked:

'You *what?*'

'I want to try my vocation, Clare.'

Suddenly, like thunder following lightning after a breathless pause, it hit her; she turned over on to her stomach and wept bitterly.

'Clare,' said Mark. 'Don't.'

He laid a hand on her shoulder, and she felt already in his touch the conscious, prudent reserve of the religious; remembering the sensitive fingers that had once tuned her body like a fine instrument, her soul howled with the sense of loss.

'Clare! Clare, what's the matter?'

She felt she had been tactically outwitted, and she hated

198

him for it. How answer his question? He had never asked her to marry him, he had never even said directly and seriously 'I love you', he was not bound to her in any way explicitly. But he knew—surely he must know?

'Nothing. Nothing's the matter with me.'

'I know that we've become very attached to each other since I came to live with your family. But I don't think things have gone so far between us that——'

'Oh, you don't, don't you. *You* don't think. That's just the trouble—you *don't* think—about other people's feelings.'

'I do, Clare. Of course I didn't go and see Father Courtney without thinking hard about our relationship. And I mentioned it to him.'

'What did he say?'

'Well, it sounds rather callous. . . .'

'He said I must cheerfully accept the sacrifice?'

'I suppose it boils down to that. . . . Look, I'm terribly sorry, Clare. I had no idea . . . I didn't realize you cared so. . . .'

She twisted over on to her side, and glared fiercely at him, knowing that this was what she shouldn't do, that she was humiliating herself, that her face was red and puffy and ugly.

'Then it must have been two other people that have been kissing on our front porch for the last nine months. It obviously wasn't you and me.'

Mark avoided her eyes. It was the first time she had seen him really abashed.

'I'm sorry, Clare. I am really.'

There was a hot silence. The sounds of summer—crickets, bees, the distant shouts of children—were like heavy objects being moved around in her head. She tossed restlessly under the heat, as if under too many blankets. 'Hell is other people' Mark had once quoted to her. No, Hell was things, when people fell out. She remembered another hot day, a baking play-ground, and the chafing of a rough wool habit. Things waited till your defences were down, and then turned on you, all together. If she had taken her stockings off, she felt she might have managed the situation with dignity, but as it was, racked by physical as well as emotional misery, she felt she might become insane at any moment.

Mark sat stolid and silent. She was torn between a desire to hurt him, by releasing the hate and resentment which had been steadily accumulating inside her ever since he had casually annexed her mind and body, and a craven reluctance to precipitate their separation. Reason told her that it would be less painful to remove the bandage with a sharp tug, even if it broke the skin, than to peel it off slowly. But she cherished even the pain that Mark caused her.

'Tell me, Mark, did you ever love me?'

'I don't know how to answer that, Clare. I know that sometimes I used to say "I love you" in a light-hearted way. . . . But I think you realized that I was never using the words seriously.'

'Yes; you were always very careful.'

'But I felt less affection and respect for you when I said it then, than I do at this minute, when I can't honestly say it. It was just part of the routine. Pretty despicable I know.'

'Yes.'

'But I can't be true to the old evil in me, and be false to— whatever may be potentially good in me now!' he cried. 'Don't you see that, Clare?'

The pain in his voice gave her a measure of satisfaction, but she didn't answer. She knew the part for which she was cast was that of the self-sacrificing heroine, encouraging the man she loved in his spiritual aspirations; but she withheld the words of sympathy and understanding. There was a point where self-sacrifice became dishonesty and dishonour.

'I realize now that I've hopelessly misunderstood you, Clare. I'd say I'd marry you tomorrow, but I know that it would be an insult, now you know the kind of worm I am.'

'All right, say it. Marry me tomorrow.'

'Now, Clare, you don't want——'

'How would you know what I want? I want you, and I don't care how humiliated I am in the process. D'you understand that? I despise you, and I despise myself for needing you, but I do *need*.'

She sagged back on to the ground again.

'Clare, you frighten me. What have I done to make you feel like this? I just don't understand. I'm not worth it.'

'I, I, I. What have *I* done? D'you know, I think you're the most selfish person I've ever met.'

'You're probably right, Clare.'

'Oh God,' she groaned. 'You've got one foot in the seminary already. When do you go? Next week? I don't suppose Father Courtney will want to expose you to the temptations of the World and the Flesh a day longer than necessary.'

'On the contrary, he turned me down.'

In spite of herself, hope leapt within her.

'Why?'

'He said I wasn't ready. He said a lot of rather hard things, like you. Such as that I was trying to use the priesthood as an escape from my personal frustration, that I was dramatizing my own situation, that I was proud and vain, that my idea of Catholicism was up the creek. And so on. He said to go away and come back and see him in a year's time.'

'What are you going to do?'

'Just as he said. Wait for a year.'

'And in between?'

'I'm going back home.'

'To Blatcham?'

'Yes.'

'I thought you detested it.'

'I did. Probably still do. But it's no use running away from it. Must try and change it. No real hope of doing that, of course. But I must make a gesture. . . .'

'Don't you like living with us any more?'

'Of course I do, Clare. That's just the trouble. I like it too much. It's too easy to be a good Catholic in your home. It's no real test. But my own home. . . .'

'So you're going back to "save" Blatcham?'

'Not Blatcham, of course. That's a kind of bourgeois Sodom and Gomorrah. But my parents perhaps. After all, Mother was a Catholic once . . . I don't know.' After a pause he continued : 'I haven't much real hope. But I feel a certain obligation to make amends. For just running away from what I didn't like, instead of trying to change it. It's a kind of disloyalty. I mean, I've often spoken to you about how I hated the loneliness of my childhood—how warm and rich I found your family life. Well, that's true, of course, but after all, I would be a different person if I hadn't had that sort of childhood. I am what I am, and I wouldn't want to change my identity—nobody does when it comes down to it.'

'When are you leaving?'

'I want to go tonight. I think it would be best.'

Was that all then? Well good-bye, it's been nice knowing you, I've enjoyed running my hands up and down your spine, it was so nice of you to give me my faith back, we must keep in touch, I do hope you have a nice life, cheerio.

'Clare. Say something.'

'What do you want me to say? Go in peace?'

'I suppose I do.'

'Well I'm not going to. You don't seem to realize that you have certain obligations to me, a certain loyalty owing to me. From the very first time you took me to the pictures, you started to change me, shape me in your own image, make me like you. Now I'm like you, you're like I used to be. It's like a see-saw : one side goes up, one side goes down. That's me gone down I suppose. I suppose we were once dead level, but I don't especially remember it. There must have been a time when we didn't quarrel, when we were just content to be together. Wasn't there?'

'I don't know, Clare.'

'Oh go away! Go on; what are you waiting for? You want to go, don't you?'

'Do try and be reasonable, Clare. Let me take you home.'

'Oh sure—go home looking like this.'

'Well, I can't leave you here in this state.'

'What's stopping you?'

They glared at each other, hot and miserable.

* * *

Damien mopped his brow, but decided not to remove his jacket, as he was wearing braces. He had been watching Clare and Underwood for some time, but without much of interest developing. When she threw herself down on the grass, he had expected Underwood to take advantage of the situation, but he sat upright and apart. There must be something wrong. They both looked very glum. Was she in trouble, like the Higgins girl? It wouldn't surprise him.

The thought of this possibility gave him some pleasure, as he visualized the consternation of the Mallory household, their rude awakening to the snake in their bosom. He would enjoy taking charge of the situation, compelling Underwood to marry Clare, showing her that he could still be charitable in spite of the past.

But perhaps she was already as hardened as the little trollop in his own house. He smiled to think how accurate his suspicions had been in that direction. As he fingered the black, transparent things hung up to dry in the bathroom, he had scented sin. He had thought of Doreen's absences every night, the front-door banging in the early hours of the morning, the whine of a car drawing away from beneath his window. And there was something about the girl, with her contemptuous mouth and lolling posture, something strong and indefinable, like a smell, the smell of a bitch on heat. He had begun to keep track of her movements, to eavesdrop and observe. Last night he had been rewarded by overhearing a quarrel between Doreen and her mother. Doreen was pregnant by her employer. His heart beat faster now, as he recalled the conversation. He heard again Doreen's rapid, flat speech.

'What d'you mean, you didn't know? What d'you think we do till two in the morning—play tiddly-winks?'

And Mrs Higgins's defensive whine:

'I don't know what your father would have done if he was alive. I've tried to be a good mother to you. . . . What does he say?'

'I haven't told him yet.'

'He'll have to marry you now.'

'I've told you, Mum, his wife won't divorce him. The old cow. We would have been married long before otherwise.'

'Well, he'll have to pay for its upkeep. You can have him up in court.'

'Mum, are you mad? I went into this with my eyes open. And it was mostly my fault that this happened. If he wants to help—well and good. But I'm not going to turn against him just because of an accident. I'll go away somewhere and have the baby. There are places you can go.'

Doreen had walked out into the dark hall suddenly, and seen him walking back up the passage away from the kitchen door. She had called up the hall:

'Your ears are flapping, Mr O'Brien!'

Damien flushed at the memory, and shook himself out of his reverie. Mark and Clare were still in the same position. Something was definitely wrong. But there was no point in staying, as he couldn't get near enough to overhear their conversation. The paint on the seat was hot to his palms as he pushed himself up. He began to stroll round the park, observing the lewd behaviour of the couples lying on the grass. It was a shocking sight to see innocent little children chasing a ball among their hot desires, burning like dangerous flowers in the grass, each couple shameless and oblivious, weaving around themselves a tight cocoon of lust and indifference to others. Damien donned his dark glasses. He deliberately left the path and picked his way through the sprawling limbs, his head erect, and eyes slanting in all directions. He felt himself to be a kind of recording angel; it seemed necessary that someone should see all this who was aware of its sinfulness, of its stench in the nostrils of God. With a thrill of triumph he spotted a youth's hand under a girl's skirt; but her low, appallingly pleased giggle hollowed out his solar plexus. He would never be unmoved by a woman's lust.

* * *

'Well, what a surprise to meet you here, Clare!'

Turning over, she looked up at Damien's dog-face, and then sat up quickly, trying to repair or disguise the ravages to her appearance caused by the emotional racking she had just endured. She was rarely pleased to see Damien, but at that moment she could cheerfully have driven red-hot nails into his ugly wedge of a face.

'Where is your usual escort?' asked Damien, smiling and showing his crowded, carious teeth.

'He—Mark you mean?—he had to go back. I like it here. I thought I'd stay for a while.'

He stood over her, his black suit and ugly, smiling face contributing to a vague impression of evil. But she had to sit there fighting to regain her composure.

'You look flushed. Are you sure it's wise to lie in this sun without a hat?'

'I'm quite all right, thank you, Damien.'

'It seems a long time since we had a chance to talk alone.' His pale, piggy eyes scrutinized her.

'Is it?'

'Yes. I think so. You have been very much in Mark Underwood's company, have you not? You will be thinking of a more permanent relationship soon, no doubt.'

His impertinence infuriated her. All the hell of the afternoon, and now this odious cousin of hers had to come poking his sharp nose into her private affairs.

'If you don't mind, Damien, I think that's my business, and I wish you'd leave me alone.'

'Very well, Clare. I only thought I might be able to help.'

Help? What the hell does he mean, help? She watched his black, angular figure move at a sedate, clerical pace, across the grass. But her thoughts seemed to get lost in the heat. She was beginning to feel dizzy. Time to go home. Home? O God, no, not while Mark was there, and the others. Where then? The pictures? Yes, the pictures. It seemed, as her mother would have said, 'a crime' to waste a beautiful afternoon in a stuffy cinema, but she might be able to shed her troubles there for a few hours. And it might worry Mark if she didn't come back till late. Perhaps he wouldn't leave. That was unkind of course, but so what?

She sat up, and, taking out her compact, powdered her face lightly and combed her hair. She stood up, a little unsteadily, and smoothed her frock. Then she set off across the shimmering grass, towards the dank, smelly, but mercifully cool 'Ladies'.

Emerging once more into the glare, she put a hand to her throbbing head, and decided that she must have a cup of tea. She found herself hurrying unnecessarily, weaving her way through the groups of people that drifted along the narrow paths, side-stepping the large and opulent prams that were moored to benches where smug mothers sat knitting and staring, dodging the children who chased each other in and out of the grown-ups' legs. She forced herself to dawdle. She paused outside the wire cage of a tennis court. The sweaty exertions of the players, the movement of their pale, hairy legs, their breathless staccato shouts of 'Oh, well played!' and 'Just out!' occupied her for a few minutes. Then she moved on. Across the bumpy, threadbare putting-green, clots of people moved slowly from hole to hole, children eager and competitive, adults bored and tolerant. A group of Teddy-boys in full uniform emerged from the keeper's hut, incongruously equipped with golf sticks and little white balls. A monumental granite drinking-fountain towered up, with battered, insanitary metal cups hanging from it by chains. A little boy stretched up, struggling to work the plunger. Clare stopped and held him up while he drank. When she thought he had had enough, she put him down, and he ran off without a word.

She had never done this before. She had never really been out alone. Before she met Mark she had very rarely gone out except to the school or church.

Mark. It wasn't long before the pain of loss began to penetrate the anaesthetic of crowds, of other people's activity. What was to happen, what would happen tomorrow, and the day after, and the day after that—what on earth could fill the vacuum that yawned in front of her?

She had come to the refreshment hut, a crowded, sticky bee-hive. She stood in the queue for some minutes, till she was served by a sweating, grimy woman, who sprayed from a height a tray full of cups, and slapped the change down on a counter awash with various fluids. Clare levered the coins off the counter, and carried her cup out into the small enclosure, where she balanced it on an unsteady iron table, her feet cushioned by a carpet of litter. An unwholesome little boy, his face smeared by jam and snot, stared up at her, writhing slightly, with one hand between his legs, and one finger poked up his nose. Clare looked away. When she looked back, he had mercifully disappeared. She took three aspirins from her handbag and swallowed them, grimacing, with the last tepid mouthful of tea. Then she rose, and walked towards the park gates.

Yes, already the numbness of shock was fading, and she felt the first spasm of the enormous pain that awaited her, and she was frightened. Self-pity welled up in her. I'll never be nice to anyone again, she vowed, like a child in a tearful rage. It's trying to be nice to people that gets me into trouble—and it doesn't help the people either. First Hilda, then Damien, then Mark. Hilda's life was ruined—she was a complete neurotic. Damien was all queer and twisted because he had thought she liked him when she didn't. And Mark—he would never make a priest. He would end up as another frustrated religious failure like herself and Damien. Religion had ruined him. Religion had ruined them all. Making them think there was nothing they couldn't do with their own lives, and other people's. Love thy neighbour as thyself. It was dangerous advice. Love was like a bus driven by a child: the more passengers, the more fatalities. Mark wouldn't suffer too much though. He was lucky, he couldn't really love. He came from a loveless home, where the emotions were sterilized to avoid infection. But her own home was a hot-bed for the emotions. The strain of living there in the weeks to come would be intolerable. You couldn't be alone with your tragedy, you were expected to bring it into the living-room with you, as the others brought their newspapers, knitting, homework.

She increased her pace, anxious to get to the cinema quickly, to distract her mind from too clearly visualizing life without Mark. She stepped off the pavement, and a car with squealing brakes drove her back again, frightened and flustered. The driver yelled something at her as he passed, and the bystanders regarded her disapprovingly. She crossed the road, and continued walking a little unsteadily. Thank God the Palladium was just round the corner. It was a pity perhaps that the car had not knocked her down. She saw herself, wan and bravely smiling in the hospital bed, with Mark grave and repentant at the bedside. . . . Oh, don't be so stupid. Forget him.

She turned the corner and glanced up at the hoarding above the cinema's portico, to see what was to be her fate for the next three hours. Just about the last thing she wanted to see—a noisy film all about Rock 'n Roll. Oh well, she couldn't drag herself as far as the Rex. As she made for the doors she was suddenly halted by the realization that she had no money with her. She had spent her last sixpence on the tea. She had a cheque-book, but the banks were shut. Oh fool! What could she do? She couldn't go home for money.

A noisy group of young people passed her as they turned into the cinema. They were singing, and one couple executed some jive steps on the pavement. The girl was wearing a tight, white sweater with 'ROCK' embroidered across her bosom. Clare moved on purposefully, as if it was necessary to disguise the fact that she had no money. But she had no purpose either. She was tired, hot, upset. She felt foul. She wanted to die. Or sit down, anyway. But where? To sit down in a café you had to buy a cup of tea. The park was too far away. She experienced for the first time the frightening inhospitality of city streets. You couldn't just sit down in a street. There was only one place left to her.

★ ★ ★

Mrs Mallory stepped out of the doctor's into the sunlight and bounded down the hill, scarcely able to contain her glee. For the first time in her life London—Brickley—semed beautiful. The tall Victorian houses, propped against the side of the hill, the railway lines shimmering in the heat, even the pungent odour of the Marmite factory, seemed transformed by her happiness. She beamed at two scruffy little girls who were pushing a doll's pram, grotesquely shod in their mother's high-heeled shoes. Lovingly, as if repeating one of the poems she had learnt as a girl, and never forgotten, she crooned to herself the doctor's words, 'Nothing to worry about, Mrs Mallory. Just a lump of surplus tissue.'

'But the pain, Doctor?'

'Probably a touch of heartburn which you associated with the lump because you were worried about it. Or may have been completely imaginary. How long has it been there?'

'Oh, years, Doctor.'

'There you are. You've been worrying about it for years. Why didn't you come and see me before?'

Why indeed? How glad she was that Tom had finally badgered her into going. And how glad he would be when she told him. It would be about seven o'clock when he got back from the cricket match with Patrick.

It would do Patrick good to get a bit of fresh air. He had been off form lately. He had probably been worrying about his vocation. But it was too soon to worry about that. He had asked if he could go to the seminary school at once, but he had seemed relieved when Tom advised against it. As Tom said, both Clare and Damien had tried their vocations too early in life. As he said, you ought to know what you were giving up before you gave it up.

She crossed Maple Road to get into the shade. It was very hot. Perhaps they would have a good summer this year. It was time they all had a holiday. The whole family together. Perhaps Mark would come with them. He was looking washed out after his exams, and Clare would like it.

She let herself into the house, and made herself a cup of tea. Everyone was out, and she was impatient for them all to come in. She was so happy she wanted to be especially nice to everybody. They would have salmon for tea, she decided. She went to the larder and opened two tins. She laid the table, but it was no use preparing the salad yet. She would go and clean Mark's room.

It was a shambles as usual. Boys' rooms always were. The desk was a chaos of open books—she never understood how he could read so many at once. She had difficulty in dusting the desk. An exercise book slithered towards the edge of the desk and she just managed to grasp one cover. The book flopped open, and a loose page fluttered to the floor. She recovered it and was about to slip it back into the book, when she realized that if she put it back in the wrong place, Mark might think she had been snooping. As she hesitated, she glanced at the loose page to see if it offered any clue to its rightful position in the book. What she saw made her read the whole page carefully. As she read her right hand strayed up to her left breast.

★ ★ ★

Mark wearily climbed the steps of number 89, and let himself in. The hall was deliciously cool and dark. He decided to go upstairs and pack. How on earth was he to explain his abrupt departure to the family?

'Is that you, Mark?'

'Yes, Mrs Mallory.'

She came out of the kitchen, looking oddly grave. Perhaps this would be the ideal opportunity; but he didn't feel prepared.

'Could I have a word with you, Mark?'

'Of course.'

They didn't go into the kitchen, but into the front parlour which was rarely used on weekdays. It was the room that Mark liked least. Cheap, ugly furniture acquired a certain character when it was battered and well-used. Here it was in an artificial state of preservation. But what was all this about anyway? He began to feel rather uneasy as he sat down on one of the hard, rexine-covered arm-chairs. Mrs Mallory sat down on an upright, wooden chair.

'Mark,' she began, 'you've been with us for some time.'

'Yes, Mrs Mallory. It must be at least nine months.'

'You've become one of the family. You eat with us, go to church with us, though how you can. . . . You take my daughter out. . . .'

'Yes, Mrs Mallory?' This could only be leading up to one thing: when are you going to marry my daughter? He was surprised and annoyed by Mrs Mallory's lack of tact. And what was that bit about church, anyway? She looked away from him, and went over to straighten a picture on the wall.

'What I mean is, that what I have to say to you, I wouldn't say if you hadn't been one of the family. If you were just a lodger, coming and going in your own way, I'd say it was none of my business.'

He took out a cigarette and lit it.

'What are you trying to say, Mrs Mallory?'

She pulled a piece of folded paper from her overall pocket, and handed it to him.

'I found this in your room, Mark. You must take my word for it that I saw it by accident. But I'm not ashamed of having read it. I call it filth, and I want an explanation.'

He unfolded the paper, and recognized it as a page from his note-book. It must have come loose after he had torn out his diary of Student Cross. He glanced at it. It comprised a number of jottings, recording odd thoughts about Clare early in their relationship:

'Clare is still a respectable girl. You can always tell a respectable girl. Their bodies can be mapped out like butchers' charts. . . . Touch one of the forbidden areas— breast, rump or loin, and you encounter resistance. . . .'

He turned over the page.

'In the cold light of day it seems incredible that I toppled to my knees in so abject a manner. But it was the frustrated libido seeking spiritual orgasm . . . if I could have copulated with Clare, or merely stroked her breasts a bit. . . .'

There were several other pieces, including the first stanza of the unfinished *Ode On His Beloved's Urination*, but he didn't bother to read it all. He folded the paper, and put it in his pocket.

'Well?' said Mrs Mallory.

212

'I don't know what to say, Mrs Mallory.'

He really didn't. He could probably clear himself with Mrs Mallory if he really applied himself to it. She was a reasonable woman, and he knew that she liked him. He could explain that this had been written a long time ago, when he was quite a different person. He could even show her the diary of Student Cross, which had once, ironically, been attached to the offending page, to demonstrate the sincerity of his change of heart. But would this solve any problems? Any such explanation must inevitably end with a declaration of his honourable intentions towards Clare. God, what a situation!

Then suddenly, he came to a decision, and plunged on before he had time to reconsider it.

'Mrs Mallory, I haven't got any excuses.'

She looked troubled.

'I'm very disappointed in you, Mark.'

'You have every reason to be. I'm sorry. Obviously I can't stay here any longer. I'll leave tonight.'

'Leave? Tonight?' She seemed frightened and bewildered.

'Yes. I'll go and pack now. I don't think it would do any good to go on talking.' He rose, and moved towards the door.

'Mark.'

He stopped.

'I shouldn't have looked at the paper——'

He looked into her troubled eyes, and saw that the consequences of her act were beginning to dawn on her.

'You said it was an accident,' he said gently.

'It was—but——'

'Don't worry about Clare, Mrs Mallory. We broke it off this afternoon.'

'Oh.' Her evident relief pained him, and it was an effort to continue:

'And, Mrs Mallory. You'd better not tell Clare why I'm leaving.'

She looked at him sadly.

'I shan't tell anyone, Mark.'

* * *

When Clare got to the church, Father Kipling was standing in the forecourt, looking about rather anxiously. His face registered relief when he saw her.

'Clare! You're the answer to my prayer. Would you mind very much witnessing a marriage? It won't take long.'

'All right, Father.'

She felt mildly perplexed, but too punch-drunk to care. Jilted, nearly run over, penniless, witness to a marriage of strangers—so what? All in a day's hell. Mallory can take it.

'I feel sorry for the couple,' said Father Kipling confidentially, as he ushered her into the church. 'She's a foundling, and his people are opposed to the marriage, so there aren't any guests. His aunt and uncle promised to be witnesses, but were dissuaded by his mother at the last moment. But they're determined to go through with it. As he's a non-Catholic it's worse. They haven't much money, and he's in the Army. I hope they're doing the right thing. I can't remember having seen them in church before. Still, there's nothing I can do. They're both over twenty-one, and he's signed all the papers.'

Clare muttered vague replies to these remarks.

Our Lady of Perpetual Succour was a church that contrived to be acutely uncomfortable under all climatic conditions. Thus it was both dark and hot that afternoon: the tall buildings on either side causing the one, and the low ceiling and tightly shut windows the other.

Clare helped herself liberally to holy water at the entrance, but it was warm on her forehead. At the back of the church knelt Mrs Duffy, the school caretaker, saying her beads. In the front pew the couple sat waiting to be married. Father Kipling stooped and said a few words to them as he

214

passed into the sacristy to vest, and they turned round and looked at Clare. She smiled, and the girl smiled back. The man looked grave and worried. How absolutely awful to be married in this way. The girl—it seemed sarcastic to call her the bride—was wearing a cheap costume in lilac that looked stiff and new. The man wore a rough, uncomfortable-looking uniform. His hair had been cropped cruelly short, and a piece of plaster covered a boil on his red, raw neck. She was kneeling; he sat stolidly, hands on knees.

Father Kipling emerged from the sacristy with a small, intrigued acolyte. He motioned them all up to the altar rails. With a twinge of horror, Clare realized that Mrs Duffy was her fellow-witness. She scuffed up to the altar in her carpet slippers, and stood next to Clare, with the ill-tempered, tight-lipped expression she always adopted when in church or in the presence of the clergy.

The service was curt and joyless. Clare had planned so often the details of her own wedding, so often pictured herself, radiant in a long, white dress with train, leaning on her father's arm, advancing with a slow, fragile step down the aisle towards Mark, handsome and smiling in morning dress, while the organ pealed and the candles and flowers blazed, and the guests beamed and whispered in the crowded pews—that she felt a surge of pity for the girl who would have nothing to remember but this sordid little ceremony. The sentiment backfired at once with a sharp reminder of the hopelessness of her own dreams. However, it was true that there were other people as unfortunate as herself.

But were they, this pair? At least they would lie in each other's arms that night. . . . She grabbed her train of thought just in time and hauled it back. She forced herself to listen to the service, the man's responses firm and gruff, the girl's scarcely audible. Almost imperceptibly, they were married. Clare and Mrs Duffy followed them into the sacristy and signed their names as witnesses. As the couple left, Clare smiled and mumbled something about 'Good luck'. The girl smiled back and murmured a reply; her husband didn't smile, but he shook hands with Clare and Mrs Duffy, and gravely thanked them. They walked out into their new life, and Clare didn't know whether to envy or pity them. It was strange that their paths had crossed at this crisis in all their lives. Would they ever cross again?

Mrs Duffy left at once, but Clare felt it would be more polite to linger for a while, rather than rush out after the couple, as if the wedding had been an annoying chore. Father Kipling seemed anxious to chat also.

'It was lucky that you happened to drop by,' he said, as he tugged off his surplice.

'Yes it was, Father. I nearly went to the pictures.'

Father Kipling looked momentarily disconcerted, and a second later Clare remembered his sermon.

'I—I didn't feel very well—the heat I suppose—and I just wanted somewhere to sit down,' she explained hurriedly, trying to smooth over her *faux pas*. 'But I found that I hadn't any money with me, so I came along here instead.' That sounded worse than ever. She just couldn't cope this afternoon.

'Well, it was the good Lord who directed you to supply my need, no doubt,' said Father Kipling, a trifle mechanically. He was in his shirt-sleeves now, and went over to the sink to wash his hands, rolling up his sleeves over thin, white clerical forearms, covered with black hairs. She had never seen him engaged in such mundane activity, and yet he did not seem to find her presence an embarrassment.

'Do you go often to the cinema, Clare?' he asked. 'You can be quite candid,' he added with a wry smile, as he perceived her hesitation. 'I shan't preach at you—my last sermon on the subject was pretty disastrous.'

'I think there was a lot of truth in what you said, Father. It needed saying.'

'It's very kind of you to say so. The bishop didn't share

216

your view. I wonder—I've wondered for a long time—was I right, or was I wrong? I must have been wrong I suppose. The crusade was certainly a failure.'

He stooped over the sink, leaning heavily on locked arms, and staring at his hands, flattened against the bottom of the bowl. The sense of failure that haloed his bowed head made Clare conscious for the first time of his identity as a person. He had never been an impressive priest—dispensing sacraments, sermons and whist-drive announcements with the same patient ennui, like a weary shopkeeper who has forgotten why he ever started to sell. But now, at this moment, she understood his inadequacy in personal terms, realized what it meant to him not to be able to move people, not to be able to find the encouraging word, the inspiring slogan.

'I had a very enlightening conversation about the whole subject with the young man who's staying with you at the moment.'

'Mark, Father?' What malicious devil had turned the conversation in this direction?

'Yes, young Underwood. He came to see me the other evening. I think he may have a vocation—that's confidential, of course.'

'Of course, Father.'

'I thought I'd tell you, because you could probably help him. I know what an important part your family has played in his return to the Faith.'

'Yes, Father.'

'He's got some rather unorthodox ideas mind you, but that's all to the good when you're young. It's his university education you know—it tells, it tells. Now I went into a seminary straight from school. I don't regret it, of course— I might never have been a priest otherwise—but I often think that that's why I just don't seem able to come to grips with the modern world.' He reached for a towel. 'It was just at the end of the First World War when I went into the seminary. I came out seven years later, and the whole world had changed. I don't think I ever caught up with it. Do you know,' he said, with a rather pathetic, confiding tone, like a patient describing embarrassing symptoms to a doctor, 'I sometimes think that either I'm mad, or everyone else is. I switch on the radio, open a newspaper or a magazine, glance at an advertisement—it all seems like madness to me. Madness. Now Father Dalby over at All Souls, Bayditch—he organizes dances with this—what d'you call it—Rock and Roll?—for the young people of his parish on Sunday evenings. He says attendance at evening service has doubled as a result. I just couldn't bring myself to do it. But he was a late vocation you see. He understands all these things. I can see Mark Underwood turning out like that. Remarkable young man you know. Remarkable.'

This was to be her special torture then: just when she had discovered what a selfish, callous, calculating person Mark was, everybody was going to try and sell him to her.

'He told me some extraordinary facts. For instance, we were talking about the cinema, and he told me that the average Hollywood film reaches a larger public than the Holy Scriptures. Did you know that?'

'I think I've heard Mark say it before, Father,' she replied. Eleven times to be exact, she added savagely, under her breath.

'*His* criticism of my sermon was that I had not gone far enough,' continued Father Kipling. (Oh, Mark had cheek all right, criticizing the parish priest's sermons to his face. Perhaps he would make a successful priest after all—he had the glibness, the assurance that this old man lacked—but not a holy priest.)

'In his opinion. . . .'

One by one the words and phrases with which Mark had bored her, were regurgitated by the credulous old priest . . . 'exchange of values . . . living by proxy . . . the superlife . . . ultimately through television . . . substitute for living. . . .' She felt an irresistible urge to object, to protest.

218

'I sometimes wonder whether Mark really knows as much about ordinary people as he likes to think. After all, there are lots of people for whom the cinema is just a place to go, to get away from the children for a few hours, to be together perhaps, for a courting couple. For an old-age pensioner, a warm place on a winter's afternoon. They all know what *real* life is—only too well. They don't confuse it with what they see on the screen. Take those two you just married, Father. It's quite probable that they did most of their courting in the cinema. But they're not turning their backs on life, are they?'

'No, they're not. Quite the contrary. They're really brave I suppose. I wish I could help them somehow.'

His face twitched slightly with helpless regret.

'Well, I must go now, Father,' said Clare, suddenly anxious to get away.

'Yes, you've been most kind. I hope I haven't delayed you unduly.'

'Oh no, Father, not at all.'

She was surprised to find the newly-weds still in the church forecourt, until she saw a photographer packing up his equipment. She visualized the photo in its cheap frame, enshrined on the mantelpiece, the pathetic couple smiling determinedly out into the dingy bed-sitter, where nappies steamed in front of the fire, and the smell of fried food lay heavy on the air.

They seemed anxious and hesitant about leaving, as if uncertain of which direction to take. Clare had a nose for worry and unhappiness, and she scented it now. But this sense was always leading her into trouble—why get involved again?

'Can I help at all?' she asked.

The girl smiled gratefully.

'We were just wondering where's a good place to eat round here.'

'Well, there's a Lyons not far from here.'

'That'll do,' said her husband.

'I'll show you where it is,' said Clare.

'Won't you come and have tea with us?' said the girl.

Clare was about to decline, when she looked into the girl's timid, pleading eyes, and realized with surprise that the invitation was genuine—that she was to represent, however inadequately, their 'reception'.

'Well, I *would* like a cup of tea. Are you sure you don't want to be alone with your husband?'

'No, you come along,' said the man. He didn't seem quite a *man*, standing stiff and awkward in his ill-fitting uniform. Neither did he seem quite a boy. He was obviously making a great effort to cope with a load of premature responsibility.

'You see, I work in a cafeteria,' confided the girl, as they moved off. 'And I don't really know any other places round here. Naturally I don't want to go *there*.' She clung to her husband's arm, but seemed grateful for Clare's company.

'Of course not,' Clare agreed.

It was almost certainly the first wedding breakfast that particular Lyons' teashop had provided. Recollecting that she had no money with her, Clare asked only for a cup of tea; but Len made her and Bridget sit down while he queued, and returned with a loaded tray. They had beans and bacon on toast, sugar-coated buns, ice-cream and tea. Clare ate bravely, anxious not to disappoint them.

'Bridget tells me you've just began your National Service, Len,' said Clare.

'Yes, worse luck.'

'Are you far from London?'

'Only about three hundred miles,' he said wryly. 'Catterick.'

'It takes him about seven hours to get home,' said Bridget.

'That's if Sergeant Towser lets us go in time to catch the 4.15 from Richmond. Then I can get the 4.47 from Darlington. Gets into King's Cross at two minutes past eleven. If I miss that, it's the 5 o'clock from Richmond, and the 6.30 from Darlington, which doesn't get into London till twenty past twelve. You can get the 4.29 from Richmond to York, which is supposed to connect with the 4.47, but it's always late. . . .'

He discussed the railway time-table earnestly for some minutes. It obviously dominated his life at the moment. A slender column of arrival and departure times was the only link between him and Bridget, and he counted his happiness in hours.

They talked about Len's life in the Army for a while. Bridget was indignant and rebellious.

'It's disgusting, the huts they have to live in. Windows missing and doors off the hinges. It doesn't sound fit for pigs.'

'Fit for sheep though,' said Len, laconically. 'The hut we moved into last week, we had to sweep the sheep-dirt out first. They had been living in it for years. Condemned, the huts were, in 1941.'

'And once he woke up in the early morning, and saw a rat in the middle of the floor, looking at him. Ugh!' Bridget shuddered.

'It's not the conditions I mind so much though,' said Len, 'it's the officers and N.C.Os. The way they treat you. Like bits of dirt. "Go here, go there, do this, do that. Double!" And their stupid wisecracks. "Did you shave this morning? Well put a blade in the razor next time." Blimey, the times I've heard that! And you can't do a thing. Not a thing.'

'Oh, don't let's talk about it, Len,' said Bridget miserably. 'It just reminds me that you're going back on Tuesday.'

A glum silence descended on them. A limp, faded woman in a blue overall cleared away their dirty plates, and passed a damp rag over the table, which left small particles of food in its wake. Clare tried to start a new and more cheerful topic of conversation.

'Where are you going to live?' she said.

221

But she only seemed to uncover more and more misery and misfortune whichever way she turned. Gradually the appalling insecurity of their position was revealed to her, item by item: how Len had a widowed mother. How he had intended that they should live with her for a while, and how his mother had a grudge against Bridget, and the terrible row they had had the previous night, and how they didn't know where they were going to live.

'It was too late to postpone the wedding, I suppose?' said Clare, thinking that in reason this was all they could have done.

'I wasn't going to,' said Len emphatically. 'I made up my mind that we were going to get married, and nothing was going to make me change my mind. I'm not sorry either.'

Bridget clasped his hand and smiled at him. 'You see, we hadn't intended to get married for a long time yet—there being so many drawbacks,' she began.

'I always meant that we should have a real start—a place of our own. And that Bridget shouldn't have to go on working. But it didn't work out that way. You see—I could never see Bridget home when we went out.' He stopped, as though this explained everything.

'He lives so far away you see,' explained Bridget.

'And one night she was attacked,' said Len thickly.

'How terrible!' exclaimed Clare.

'Oh, nothing happened to me. I got away. He was only a rotten little Teddy-boy.'

'I'll break his neck if ever I get hold of him,' said Len, looking fiercely round the teashop. 'Are you sure you've never seen him since, Bridget?'

'I told you I haven't. Don't think about it, dear. It's all over now. It can't happen again, now we're married. We've him to thank for being married I suppose.'

'That's why we got married see. As quick as we could. And that wasn't quick enough for my liking.'

'That was Father Kipling. He would insist that Len had

Instructions. But he was very nice. He arranged for Len to have them at the camp.'

Clare admired their resolution, but could not understand the logic of their action. If Len was away in the Army for most of the time, Bridget would scarcely be any safer than before. But she kept her thoughts to herself.

'I don't seem to remember seeing you in church, Bridget,' said Clare.

'No, I never go now. But I was brought up in a Catholic Home you see. I was an orphan. Len wanted us to get married in a Registry Office, but somehow, I wouldn't have felt properly married. You know.'

'Yes,' said Clare.

'I got nothing against religion—any religion,' said Len. 'I just wanted us to be married as soon as possible. He was very long-winded, that padre.'

'Why did you stop going to church, Bridget? If you don't mind me asking.'

Bridget looked slightly embarrassed.

'I don't know really. We were never out of church at the Home. It was one long church. And Sunday's such a short day—I'm always so worn out.'

'You've got somewhere to go now I suppose?'

The couple looked glum. They hadn't.

'We'll have to spend the night at our own places. Till we get something worked out,' said Bridget.

'But that's awful. It's bad enough not to have a honeymoon.'

'Blast it, we'll have a honeymoon,' exclaimed Len.

'You know we can't afford it, Len.'

'Will you let me lend you five pounds, Len, and take a couple of days at Southend, or somewhere?' asked Clare. 'I could give you more, but you might worry about paying me back.'

Len hesitated. Clare took out her cheque-book.

'You can repay me at any time, of course.'

'No, Len, we can't take it.'

'Honestly, it's the best thing, Bridget,' said Clare. 'After all, you're only married once. You must get away, even if it's only for a couple of days. While you're away, I'll make some inquiries. I think I may be able to help you. You see, the parish owns some property which is rented very cheaply to deserving people. Old Miss Mahoney had a little house in Tanner Road, but she had to go into hospital last week, and if she ever comes out, she'll have to go into a home for old people. So the house might become vacant. And Father Kipling mentioned that he'd like to help you. So I'll hold him to his word.'

'Would you really? Oh, that would be wonderful!' exclaimed Bridget.

'It's nothing wonderful, I assure you. It's old and dirty, and I think it's due to be condemned in ten years' time.'

'That doesn't matter—it would be somewhere to live, on our own.'

'Well, I'm not promising anything. But I'll do my best.' She paused. 'There's one snag.'

'What?' said Bridget anxiously.

'Well . . . you realize that it doesn't matter to me whether you go to church or not. But it would probably matter to Father Kipling.'

'Oh *that's* all right,' said Bridget with relief. 'I don't mind going to church again if it means we get a house. I'd quite like to go, really.'

Len hadn't spoken for some time. Now he said:

'Why are you doing all this?'

She shrugged and smiled.

'There aren't any reasons, Len. Here, take the cheque.' She sensed that he didn't know what to do with it, and didn't want to admit his ignorance. She explained.

When they parted outside the Lyons, Bridget reached up and kissed Clare lightly on the cheek. It reminded her of Hilda, and she felt a wave of panic, but fought it down.

'See you on Monday evening then,' she said, smiling. 'Have a lovely week-end.'

As she walked back towards the Presbytery to interview Father Kipling, she did not feel unhappy any more. She didn't feel happy either. What was the name of her feeling she did not know, but she was prepared to go on.

She passed the cinema again. There were queues outside now—a young and noisy crowd. They were singing and clapping to the rhythm. She couldn't remember seeing such a cheerful crowd queuing for the cinema, and she took pleasure in their high spirits; but she was glad that she hadn't gone to the pictures.

★ ★ ★

It was the climax to a stupendous week.

'Just like the old days, sir,' said Bill, as he staggered out on to the pavement with the long-disused queue signs—so long, in fact, that he had had to alter the prices.

'Yes, Bill,' replied Mr Berkley, surveying the crowd benevolently. 'Just like the old days.'

It wasn't really like the old days, but he was too pleased to quibble. All the week the receipts had been unusually high, but this evening he expected to break all records. And in the summer too. This Rock and Roll film had been a brain-wave. The audiences were noisy but not, so far, violent. They enjoyed themselves immensely. That was the most refreshing thing about it.

Bill unleashed from the two-and-nine queue a score of eager young people. Mr Berkley beamed on their youth and vitality, their preposterous clothes and hair-cuts, as they surged past him. The audiences were mainly young, but the older people seemed to find the high spirits around them infectious, for they were grinning and smiling, amused, but not contemptuous. Cinema-goers took their pleasure so glumly as a rule, it was good to see smiling, eager faces, to hear a continual murmur of excitement and enjoyment in the auditorium. Audience participation: that was the really interesting aspect of the thing. The way they clapped their hands to the music, sang the words, and applauded rapturously after each number. It seemed to create that relationship, that tension between the audience and the performers which you got in a theatre, in a music-hall, but not usually in a cinema. He heard a muffled cheer from the auditorium, and glanced at his watch.

'You'd better tell them that the last showing has just started, Bill,' said Mr Brickley. 'I don't think there's much chance of any more getting in now. I'm going inside.'

'Right-o, sir,' replied Bill, giving his jaunty Ruritanian salute.

Mr Berkley's good spirits almost made him forget the Doreen affair. But the face of the new usherette he had just engaged to replace her rapped his conscience like a dentist's probe on a decayed tooth. He thought of her on the night train to Newcastle (where he knew of a kindly, broad-minded landlady who would see her through her trouble), and shuddered sympathetically. She had been a little brick, Doreen. When she told him calmly about the baby, he had genuinely wished that his wife would divorce him. She wouldn't, of course, but the realization that he really wished she would, made him feel a little less guilty. Not so guiltless, however, that he did not plunge into the warm, lively auditorium with a fervent desire to avoid introspection for a while.

He stood at the back of the packed auditorium. There were people standing all along the back, and down the sides. He watched with interest a young girl in front of him in tight trousers. Her buttocks were twitching rhythmically to the music. On each alternate beat a hollow appeared in her left flank.

The mystery remained. It was, judged by normal standards, a poor film of 'B' feature quality, cheaply produced, unimaginatively directed, in most cases poorly acted by musicians playing themselves, in black and white, on a square screen. The plot was minimal and artificial. What was left? The music. This was what the audience wanted. Ideally, a series of filmed band-numbers would have suited them best. The pseudo-dramatic build-up for the band was an irritating formality: each switch from the stage or dance-hall to a love-scene was greeted with groans. And they resented the cliché of representing the success of the band by a series of brief musical sequences alternating with shots of trains, because their clapping accompaniment was interrupted as soon as it began. He remembered vividly one particularly interesting example from the previous evening: at one point in the film the love interest was sorted out in the control-room of a broadcasting studio. Through the glass came faintly the sound of *Rock Around The Clock*. At once the audience had taken up the song, and drowned the dialogue. Now they were at it again:

> *Four o'clock, five o'clock, six o'clock rock,*
> *Seven o'clock, eight o'clock, nine o'clock rock,*
> *Ten o'clock, eleven o'clock, twelve o'clock rock!*
> *We're gonna rock*
> *Around*
> *The clock*
> *Tonight!*

Mr Berkley found himself responding to the insistent beat. The beat was the only genuinely musical element in it, of course. Otherwise it was largely a stunt—the saxophonist acting like a contortionist while continuing to play, the bass-player straddling his instrument on the floor, as if he were raping it; and it was *de rigueur* for the pianist to *stand* at his instrument, and play with one hand, thus giving himself freedom for muscular improvisation.

The saxophonist began a solo. Mr Berkley glanced at the young man beside him. His eyes were closed; he had passed into the body of the instrumentalist; he swayed back, with knees slightly bent, and on his face seemed to flicker an expression of anxiety as to whether his frame could bear the strain of ecstasy. The saxophone was undoubtedly the true *vox humana* of instruments. The organ could not approach this strangled cry that came welling up from the bowels, from the primitive consciousness of life, of pain, of joy; the long, tortured note that slowly unwound your intestines to be twanged by the electric guitarist.

It was the constant enigma of modern civilization: how the cheap, the shoddy, the manufactured, still held an indestructible seed of truth and vitality, could still be a source of salvation. The way a Tin Pan Alley ballad, with its false sentiment and facile melody, could still seem piercingly lovely, and could still evoke genuine emotions; the way a Woolworth's calendar could make someone see beauty; the way a plastic crucifix could inspire the rarest worship. This Rock and Roll was a manufactured music, with scarcely a shred of genuine folk content. In a year it would be dead, forgotten. The men who now promoted it would have found something new to replace it. In itself it was valueless. Yet in this cinema this evening it had awakened how many deadened souls to some kind of life?

As this last thought passed through his mind, Mr Berkley noticed a disturbance at the other side of the cinema. The band on the screen were playing *See You Later Alligator*, and some couples were jiving in the aisles. This is going a bit too far, he thought, as he hurried to the scene.

In the space Mr Berkley vacated, another couple started to jive.

Harry's legs ached. It didn't look as though he was going to

228

get a seat. He had walked a long way that day. He did a lot of walking now—walking and going to the pictures.

He took a packet of chewing gum out of his pocket, and peeled off the wrapping; it slipped out of his fingers, and fell over the barrier on to the seats below. A man looked up in annoyance.

'Sorry,' said Harry.

He tapped his feet to the music. It's got something, this Rock 'n Roll, he decided. He wanted to clap his hands to the music, but didn't. There was a little blonde piece beside him; she couldn't keep still, kept bouncing about every time the band played a number.

'Oh dig that crazy sax!' she shrilled. There was a ripple of laughter around them. Harry smiled. The place was getting noisy. People were getting up out of their seats and were jiving in the aisles. Harry wanted to take the little blonde piece and jive with her. But he didn't.

His arm was grabbed, and he turned to look into the blonde's entranced eyes.

'C'mon, let's go, alligator,' she gasped.

He shrank back.

'No, I can't. I don't know how to do it,' he stammered. But she wasn't listening.

It didn't really matter. He just swivelled around in the middle, while she danced. He champed on his gum in time to the music, and kept a poker-faced expression. She pushed him into the right positions. She jerked up his arm, and spun round under it. Her skirt rose to her thighs. She had good legs. The whole cinema seemed to be dancing now. There was a terrific din, everybody was singing and dancing. It was great. The lights went on, but the music and dancing continued. The blonde was good-looking in a cheeky sort of way. Her hard little breasts poked out under her sweater; they didn't wobble, they clung to her twisting body. It was surprising how strong she was. She pulled him past her, and as he went he let his hand float out casually behind him, as he had seen it done, and was overjoyed to feel her small, damp hand fall solidly into his palm. He turned, and they laughed.

They broke and separated. The space between them seemed to be almost solid, you could see it had edges. They played around it for a while, keeping the rhythm of the music all the time, postponing the pleasure of contact. Together they swooped back. Harry grabbed her hand and jerked her back into his arms. Holding her small, hard waist, he spun her round. Harry laughed out loud.

★ ★ ★

Doreen hunched miserably over her film magazine in the corner of the compartment, as the train rumbled through the night towards the north. It was the longest journey she had ever made in her life, and she had never been farther north than Harringay Arena. She was being carried into strange, alien territory, grim and bleak, in and out of stations with unfamiliar names, where the porters shouted to each other in uncouth accents. It's all your fault, you little bastard, she thought without malice, as she stroked her stomach under her new coat—bought that morning to cheer herself up. She didn't particularly like the tent style, but there was the future to think of. Not that she had much of a future to look forward to. Ah well, no use moping. Things could be worse. Maurice had been quite decent, seemed quite upset to see her go, swore he would try and get a divorce, but the old cow would sooner die, you could tell from her photograph. Anyway, he had given her enough money to have the baby comfortably; and she had already made up her mind that she wasn't going to have it adopted. She turned back to the magazine.

Hottest gossip-point round the Hollywood niteries is Amber Lush's latest escort, beefcake boy Murl Crater.

Murl (remember him in *Sandstorm*?) was the second husband of Barbara Baines, formerly married to Amber's husband Bill Brix. Amber and Bill are separated at the moment. Asked if she was contemplating a divorce, Amber said: 'Murl and I are just good friends. He's so sincere, he helps me to work out my personal problems. Murl is a very rare person, but I'm not rushing into marriage again. I want to concentrate on being a good actress.' Amber is said to have her eyes on the plum part of Beatrice in the screen version of Dante's *Divine Comedy*.

Doreen felt suddenly depressed again. She closed the magazine in disgust. These film-stars were worse than anybody. The man opposite her threw down his *Reveille* at the same moment, and their eyes met. He smiled at her.

'Long ride, i'n it?'

Gratefully she responded to the familiar London accent.

'You've said it.'

'Going far?'

'Newcastle.'

'Newcassle you mean,' he said with a grin. 'They won't understand you up there if you say "Newcastle".'

She pulled a face.

'Nothing like the dear old Smoke, is there?'

'Don't,' she said.

'I know what y'mean,' he said sympathetically. 'Now my job's up north, or I wouldn't be on this train now. I'd be drinkin' a pint of mild an' bitter in the "Elephant and Castle". Bloomin' shame, they're gerna knock it dahn.'

'Are they?'

'Yer. . . . What's yer job?'

'Usherette.'

'What, in the flicks?'

'Yes.'

'Outer work?'

'Sort of.'

231

'Wanner job in Newcastle?'

'Newcassle.' They both laughed.

'Well?'

'I might.'

'Pal-a-mine knows the man'ger of the Regal in Newcastle. 'E'll fix you up. . . .'

'Thanks very much.'

·'Yer. . . . 'Ere, let me sit on your side. All right?'

'Please yourself.'

She wasn't going to encourage him. He might be a real friend, or he might not. In any case she could always find out his real intentions by telling him she was pregnant. That was the quickest way of getting rid of wolves. She smiled secretly as she thought of it. The little bastard inside her was a kind of protection. She could look after herself. But there was no reason why she shouldn't enjoy a bit of company for the rest of the journey.

★ ★ ★

'You mean you never had no girl-friends at all?'

'No.'

'Go on!'

'Straight.'

It seemed to Harry that he had never been so tired. Or so happy.

'I never danced before neither,' he volunteered.

'You're not bad.'

He glowed.

'You ought to go to the Empress Monday nights. They have Rock ev'ry Monday.'

'You go often?'

'Ev'ry Monday.'

'You go with someone?'

'With my friend Mabel. She couldn't come tonight.'

'Maybe I'll see you there on Monday.'

'All right. I'll look out for you.'

She stopped.

'This is our house.'

'Is it? Number sixty-one. I'll remember.'

She sat down on the low wall. There were little spots of cement all along the top, where the railings had been torn out in the war.

'Ooh, my feet!' She slipped off her right shoe, and wriggled her toes. It was a small, neat foot. Everything about her was small and neat.

'Ache?'

'*Do* they!'

There was a pause.

'When d'you have to be in?' she asked.

'Any time I like.'

'Cor, you're lucky. Ar'past eleven me.'

Another pause.

'I enjoyed it tonight, didn't you?' Harry said.

'Mm.'

'I never enjoyed myself so much before.' He laughed. 'That old geyser rushing about all over the place, trying to stop people dancing.'

She laughed too.

'And when they stopped the film, and everybody made such a row they had to start it again.'

They both laughed.

'Well, I'll have to go in,' she said, standing up and slipping on her shoe. 'G'night, Harry.'

'G'night, Jean.'

Again the space between them seemed solid. But it was smaller. Harry bent over it and kissed her, nearly over-balancing.

'I don't usually let a bloke kiss me the first time,' she said.

'Don't you?' he said. He couldn't think of anything else to say.

233

'G'night, Harry,' she said, and moved away.

'G'night, Jean. See you Monday.'

At the door she turned and smiled. 'Yeah, see you Monday.'

For half an hour they had lain in each other's arms in the creaking guest-house bed, too scared with happiness to move. Then Len began gently to stroke her tender body with his rough fingers. Now he was ready, and he covered her body with his own, and breached her body with his own. As they clung together in that unutterable pleasure, he felt that they were defying everything that had persecuted them. He disapproved of the casual obscenity of barrack-room conversation, but as he groped for words to express his triumphant passion, he found to his surprise that he could not say them to Bridget. They would sound to her like a string of incoherent obscenities: — the Army and — second stag on East Wing Guard and — Sergeant Towser who cancelled his last leave pass and — the troop train back to Catterick on Sunday night and — the cold walk from the station to the camp and — the platform where he kissed Bridget good-bye at the end of leave and — the street corner where he had to run for his bus and — the Teddy-boy who had attacked her and — all the people and all the regulations and all the time-tables and all the clocks that had tried for so long to stop them from having this.

* * *

Blatcham station never exuded sweetness and light at the best of times, but the last train from London pulled into an atmosphere of peculiarly depressing gloom and resentment: gloom of the fatigued and silent travellers, and resentment of the station staff, who evidently considered it a gross

234

imposition that they were compelled to keep open the station until 11.20 for a handful of passengers returning from some nocturnal debauch in the metropolis. Most of the lights were already extinguished, and the doors of the station bolted, except for one small aperture through which the passengers stumbled into the street. Buses, of course, had ceased running hours ago, so Mark was forced to carry his bags to his home, a mile away. He had intended to leave them at the station, but the Left Luggage Office, he had just been reminded, closed at 9.30.

His bags were heavy, as he had brought everything away with him from Brickley. He didn't want to have to go back there again—not until he was protected by the Dominican habit, anyway.

In the main street he paused for a rest. The lighted shop windows threw a bleak illumination on to the empty pavements. The arrangements of tins of soup, women's hats and men's shoes seemed exactly the same as a year ago. He sensed already the chill, deadly, bourgeois miasma that seemed to rise, choking and suffocating, from the streets of Blatcham. A sensitive soul walked into this town like a white missionary into a malarial swamp. But he was keenly aware that his own missionary life had begun inauspiciously, not to say unheroically.

It had not been pleasant to leave the Mallorys under a cloud. For, although Clare would never reveal the details of their relationship, and although Mrs Mallory would never tell anyone about their conversation of that afternoon, some hint of his disgrace would inevitably filter through to the other members of the family whom he loved: Mr Mallory, the twins, Patrick, Patricia. . . .

But he was already a fallen idol in Patricia's eyes, all because he had not been able to deny himself a sentimental gesture before leaving. When he had finished packing, he had tapped on her door, and she had looked up from her books, grateful for the interruption.

235

'Hallo, Pat. How's the work going?'

'Rotten. D'you know the principal parts of *insuesco*?'

'No.'

'Neither do I.'

'Pat, I'm going away. I can't explain why, but it will probably be for good. I thought I'd like to give you a little memento.' He handed to her a copy of *A Portrait of The Artist As a Young Man*.

'Going away?' She seemed unable to understand him.

'Yes. I've written in it.'

She did not open the book.

'Leaving Clare?'

For some reason this had been totally unexpected. Patricia had never once mentioned his relationship with Clare, and, absurdly, he had come to assume that it was a matter of indifference to her.

'But you can't.'

He writhed with embarrassment as he remembered the conversation, and cursed his lack of perception. He had smugly recognized in Patricia symptoms of what he was pleased to term an adolescent crush on himself. Because his own emotional life was selfish, he had assumed that Patricia's was also, that she was too involved with her own feelings to trouble about Clare's. And he had confided in Patricia with the subconscious desire of winning from her sympathy and condolence. Instead an unpredictable loyalty to Clare had arisen where he least expected it, to condemn him. Now he had the measure of Patricia's disillusionment. How contemptible his flight must have appeared to her whom, not long before, he himself had urged not to try and solve her difficulties by running away.

He had found it difficult to resist the temptation to tell Patricia, at least, of his intention to become a Dominican, to go out with a bang instead of a whimper. But he had determined not to exonerate himself in the course of his conversation with Mrs Mallory, and he had held grimly to

236

that resolution. It seemed the least he could do—to deny himself the dramatic gesture, to humiliate himself. It was a kind of expiation, the only kind that really hurt him.

He picked up his bags, and walked slowly down the High Street. As he walked he pondered dully on the crime he was trying to expiate, the murder of Clare's happiness. But murder was not the right term. Call it euthanasia: for when love is not reciprocated, it festers. Though she did not know it, for Clare there had been no choice except between a swift or a lingering death.

But he felt keenly the odium of his position. No murder is as cold-blooded as euthanasia, which lacks even the passion of hate. The surgeon is isolated by his deed, his unnatural callousness lit by a cold clinical glare.

But these analogies—murder, euthanasia—were summoned up in order to generate a remorse he did not instinctively feel. One could not ignore the existence of situations in which it was necessary to act the part of the cad. That he himself happened to be a congenital cad only made the whole thing more difficult, not easier.

His mother was watching the weather forecast on television when he let himself into the house. She came out into the hall, surprised by the sound.

'Mark! What a surprise! Why didn't you phone?' Your bed isn't aired or anything. . . .'

'It's all right, Mother. Don't flap.'

He followed her into the living-room. The Union Jack was fluttering on the television screen, and the National Anthem was booming out.

'D'you like the new carpet?'

'Very nice. What was the matter with the old one?'

'Oh, I never did like the colour.'

'Where's Dad?'

'He went to bed early. He's not been too well today. He went to a Masonic dinner last night, and it gave him indigestion.'

'Uhuh.'

'I stayed up to watch TV. Mark, there was a man who won three thousand pounds answering questions on Shakespeare. I wonder you don't go in for it.'

He laughed.

'I'd be hopeless at anything like that.'

His mother seemed slightly affronted.

'But you're doing English Literature at University.'

'Precisely,' replied Mark, with a smile.

It wasn't going to be easy. He could see that already. It wasn't going to be easy.